"You're an amazing father. I can tell how much you love them."

Could she tell that he loved her, too? That he was falling hard and fast? He pulled away and raked back his hair.

"No amount of experience can dampen the need to protect your children and those you... care about."

"I'm not known for keeping quiet," Pippa said. "I'd tell you if I thought you were too buried in work." The corners of her lips lifted into a soft smile and he desperately wanted to kiss her again. But he couldn't. It would make leaving that much harder, not just for him, but for her.

"I'm not known for listening."

"I'd show you. Remind you."

She reached up and wrapped her arms loosely around his neck. Her scent teased him. He slipped his fingers through her curls and held her face close to his, battling the need to either bridge the gap or break free and save them both.

Dear Reader,

When I wrote *The Promise of Rain*, my debut and first book in the From Kenya, with Love series, I knew that I'd end up watching spunky little four-year-old Pippa Harper grow up through the series. I was so moved when readers let me know that she had latched onto their hearts the way she had mine. In *Every Serengeti Sunrise*, Pippa had grown up and was now in her twenties...and experiencing devastating heartbreak. I had my doubts about Pippa ever being able to trust and love again.

But in this book, widower Dax Calder, an earthquake expert working off the grid in Kenya, shows up at the lodge with his impossibly difficult twin girls. Dax has suffered more than his share of loss and has buried himself so deeply in work, he's forgotten how to love life or embrace parenthood. Talk about setting both Pippa and Dax up for more heartbreak! Two people who can't risk falling in love again, yet who each hold the key to healing the other's heart...and two twin girls who turn their worlds upside down.

My door is always open at rulasinara.com. Sign up for my newsletter, get information on all of my books and find links to my social media hangouts.

Wishing you love, peace and courage in life,

Rula Sinara

HEARTWARMING

The Twin Test

—

Rula Sinara

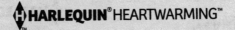

Recycling programs
for this product may
not exist in your area.

ISBN-13: 978-1-335-63361-3

The Twin Test

Copyright © 2018 by Rula Sinara

All rights reserved. Except for use in any review, the reproduction or utilization of this work in whole or in part in any form by any electronic, mechanical or other means, now known or hereafter invented, including xerography, photocopying and recording, or in any information storage or retrieval system, is forbidden without the written permission of the publisher, Harlequin Enterprises Limited, 22 Adelaide St. West, 40th Floor, Toronto, Ontario M5H 4E3, Canada.

This is a work of fiction. Names, characters, places and incidents are either the product of the author's imagination or are used fictitiously, and any resemblance to actual persons, living or dead, business establishments, events or locales is entirely coincidental.

This edition published by arrangement with Harlequin Books S.A.

For questions and comments about the quality of this book, please contact us at CustomerService@Harlequin.com.

® and TM are trademarks of Harlequin Enterprises Limited or its corporate affiliates. Trademarks indicated with ® are registered in the United States Patent and Trademark Office, the Canadian Intellectual Property Office and in other countries.

Printed in U.S.A.

Award-winning and *USA TODAY* bestselling author **Rula Sinara** lives in rural Virginia with her family and crazy but endearing pets. She loves organic gardening, attracting wildlife to her yard, planting trees, raising backyard chickens and drinking more coffee than she'll ever admit to. Rula's writing has earned her a National Readers' Choice Award and a Holt Medallion Award of Merit, among other honors. Her door is always open at rulasinara.com, where you can sign up for her newsletter, learn about her latest books and find links to her social media hangouts.

Books by Rula Sinara

Harlequin Heartwarming

From Kenya, with Love

The Promise of Rain
After the Silence
Through the Storm
Every Serengeti Sunrise

Visit the Author Profile page
at Harlequin.com for more titles.

To parents and teachers around the world—and often far off the grid—for loving and putting children first, no matter what unique challenges must be overcome. Your patience, strength and dedication to their emotional well-being and education paves the way for brighter futures for each of them and, hence, a better tomorrow for all.

CHAPTER ONE

THEY WERE MISSING.

Dax Calder muttered a curse and tossed his laptop, satellite phone and several rock samples, on the hand-carved poster bed that occupied the bungalow's main living space. He double-checked the adjoining bedroom, where his identical twin daughters were supposed to be waiting for him.

The room was in perfect order, down to their suitcases—one purple and one green—sitting uncharacteristically neat and aligned at the ends of their timber-pole framed beds. Two binders of math practice assigned from their virtual classes lay on a small writing table tucked in the far corner. He had a feeling the twins hadn't touched a math problem since he'd left them three hours ago. Sheer white curtains danced over a colorful, handwoven tapestry rug in front of the sliding doors which led to a private, lava stone patio.

Escaped. Not kidnapped. Or killed. Or— God help him—eaten alive.

He raked back his hair and started for the open door. His flash of panic dulled to a smoldering irritation the second he spotted a piece of paper with a pair of cheeky smiley faces drawn on it taped to the glass behind the billowing sheers. *Not again.*

Their modus operandi. Cryptic notes. Nothing but the sketched faces and "bored x 2" written under them. How many times had he told them that they needed to stay put until he returned? Three hours was all he'd asked for out of desperation. Their nanny hadn't arrived in Kenya yet, and the chief engineer overseeing the oil field extension Dax had been contracted to survey had set up a meeting this morning.

Dax ripped the paper down and crumpled it. It wasn't the first time he'd dealt with their escapades. Using their twin factor to play pranks with hotel staff whenever he traveled was probably half the reason the hotels he frequented knew him so well. He wouldn't be surprised if his name was tagged with a warning note: *Beware of the twins.*

Only he'd never stayed here at the Tabara Lodge before. Heck. They'd never stayed anywhere this exotic. He wasn't worried about them sneaking into a hotel kitchen and switching the salt and sugar, or dressing up as the Grady twins from *The Shining* and knocking on random hotel room doors at night. No, at the Tabara Lodge he was more worried about what *they'd* run into. This was Africa...as in safari land.

As stunning as Kenya was, there was dangerous wildlife out there, and the girls' idea of survival and self-preservation was limited to some pact they had never to rat on each other.

Dax tugged at the collar of his polo shirt, where it chafed the back of his neck. He paused only for a second to secure the door they'd left open.

He'd told them a million times to keep the bungalow locked up so that nothing would get stolen. He'd expected them to stay locked *in* because it made him feel more secure about leaving them alone for a few hours. Sure, he'd chosen Tabara because it was family friendly and had flushing toilets. But the guests and staff were still strangers. He had also been warned that wildlife here could be unpredictable and that vervet monkeys considered open doors an open invitation. He made a mental note to check his bags and equipment for anything missing—once he found his missing kids.

An area of flowering shrubs and fruit trees that shaded benches fashioned from thick, twisted branches, extended beyond the rustic stone patio. Twelve thatched-roof bungalows, joined by stone-lined dirt paths, sat in a semicircle around the main lodge, complete with reception area, restaurant and pool. Considering the view of the golden savanna in the distance, this upscale safari lodge watered its gardens well. It seemed a wasteful luxury for a region that suffered severe drought seasons, but then again, for what he was paying for an extended stay, the lodge could afford the extra water.

Water. He knew exactly where to look for them first—the one place he'd forbidden the twins to go alone.

He headed for the main lodge, rounding a small cove where urns of flaming red hibiscus surrounded a metal sculpture of a giraffe and its baby. The scent of pool water and earsplitting squeals hit him before he cleared the garden.

"Out. Now."

"Dad! Jump in!"

Ivy disappeared under the water and shot across the pool so quickly that all he could make out was a blur of purple. Fern popped her head out of the water and pulled one of her green swimsuit straps higher on her shoulder.

Sandy had chosen the two colors when she was planning their nursery and outfits before they were born. The purple-and-green color coding had stuck as a way of telling the identical twins apart and, even now, the girls considered them each their favorite colors because their mother had chosen them. As for Dax, it made life a lot easier when he wasn't wearing his contacts or when he was too tired to pay attention to their subtle differences, like the fact that Fern had always weighed a pound or two less than Ivy.

"Not happening. Now, both of you, out."

He grabbed a complimentary towel from a stack and tossed it to Fern as she hoisted herself onto the edge of the pool. Ivy hedged her bets and flipped around for one more lap before obeying.

"You're not really mad, Dad," Fern said, wrapping her wet arms around him. "Are you? Because I'd feel guilty, and you know how that knots up my stomach and makes it so I can't eat."

Guilt trip, huh? He loved them to death, but these two were going to age him twice as fast. Make that four times as fast if they'd inherited their ability to guilt him into doing what they wanted from his mother.

"I totally am, and I would never make you eat if you weren't up to it." Dax tossed another towel at Ivy as she dripped on over to them. "So glad you could finally join us."

"Oh, come on, Dad. Didn't you have 'physical education' written on the schedule you made up for our nanny? Since she's not here yet, we figured we should get it done anyway, like the responsible individuals you're raising us to be," Ivy said.

"Yep, we're on time and everything. In fact, isn't math up next, Ivy?"

Fern smiled at her sister, and something unspoken passed between them. He couldn't put his finger on it, but his parental instincts screamed conspiracy. Was *math* a code word or something? Man, he wished he could tap into their telepathic twin phone line. He narrowed his eyes and put a hand on each of their shoulders when they tried slipping past him.

"Math and reading were the *only* things you were supposed to do the past three hours. That and staying put."

"But the power went out again," Fern said.

That would make it twice since they'd arrived yesterday—if she was telling the truth. Being at the mercy of generators was something they'd have to get used to during their stay here.

"You don't need power. Your math was printed out and there's plenty of sunlight for reading."

They started to argue and he cut them off.

"I'm not kidding, you two. I set your ground rules to keep you safe. Swimming without supervision isn't okay—"

"But we're good swim—"

"Don't interrupt me, Ivy. I don't care if you're Olympic gold medalists. Things can happen. You could hit your head jumping and get knocked unconscious in the water. Or something even worse. And everyone here is a stranger—staff and guests. What if there was a creep hanging out here? Or a wild animal?"

There wasn't even a lifeguard on duty, for crying out loud.

The images he'd seen of the South Asian earthquake-triggered tsunami that killed thousands—including families on vacation, lounging around pools—flicked through his mind. He'd been a sophomore in college at the time, and his friend had been on vacation in Indonesia. He'd died in the tsunami, along with his parents and sister.

The entire family. Gone. Unexpectedly.

The tragedy had hit Dax hard, eclipsing the other disasters ruining his life at the time, like his girlfriend dumping him and his parent's divorce announcement.

He hated the unexpected.

Dax sucked in a deep breath, rubbed the base of his throat, then put his hands on his hips.

The tsunami was a memory. The past. The reason he'd decided to study quakes. To save people. To stop natural disasters from shaking and tearing lives apart like fissures in the crusty earth. It wasn't something he talked about, especially not to the girls.

"We're at a lodge, Dad. I think we'd need to go on a safari to see the wild animals." Fern folded her arms and shifted her weight to one side. They'd been begging for him to take them on a safari, once they arrived in Kenya, but he didn't have time for one yet. They weren't here on vacation. He had work to do. People to answer to.

"Should I forward you the article I read about an elephant that kept breaking onto hotel grounds to drink from their pool? Besides, if gators and snakes can make it into toilets and pools in Florida, then I wouldn't be surprised if something more dangerous slinked into a pool out here.

And by dangerous, I mean more dangerous than the two of you."

"Very funny." Ivy grinned. "So, when's Number Seven supposed to get here?"

"That's Miss Melissa, to you. Don't you dare call her Nanny Number Seven. She has no idea how many you've been through. Unless you told her."

"Why would we do that?" Ivy pursed her lips as if to keep from smiling as she dried her hair.

There was that fleeting exchange between them again. Dax pinched the bridge of his nose, then raked his hair back.

Melissa had been with them only a week before he'd signed this contract with Erebus Oil. The contract had been an offer he couldn't refuse. Due to his expertise and reputation as a seismologist, they were paying him more than he'd ever make in research…even more than he'd made on his last two jobs in the petroleum industry. And the living allowance Erebus offered as incentive was helping him afford Tabara Lodge. He'd told them upfront that he'd need a living situation amnenable to bringing his daughters along. That part of the deal had been nonnegotiable. His daughters and their nanny couldn't live on-site in trailers, like the rest of Dax's crew would be doing. He was lucky Melissa had agreed to come with them, and he'd gone over the arrangement with her multiple times. Of course, he had paid for her ticket from Texas, too.

Then he'd bribed the girls.

For every month the nanny stayed, he'd give them an allowance bonus. If their nanny quit, he'd dock their allowance. Reimbursement for his time and trouble. So far, so good.

"*Miss Melissa* should be here tonight. I was about to check for any flight delays when I returned from my meeting, but as luck would have it, I ended up looking for the two of you. You left the room unlocked, by the way. Strike two. Let's go."

"Oops." Fern linked her arm in Ivy's and the two vanished down the garden path toward their room. He heard them giggling to each other. Laughter was supposed to be a happy sound, not a worrisome one. He scrubbed his face and shook his head.

"It's been less than forty-eight hours

since you left home, Dax. Man up. You'll survive," he muttered. A little sleep wouldn't hurt. His exhaustion and pre-occupation with work gave the twins the advantage. How was it the girls seemed immune to jet lag? He needed a nap but didn't dare take one. Unless, perhaps, he kept one eye open.

More laughter rang out as he started down the path after them, only this time it didn't sound like the twins, and it was coming from—

He looked across the pool and beyond an arched stone arbor that led to an out-door, canopy-covered seating area for the lodge's restaurant. A woman with wildly curly auburn hair and an equally radiant smile walked past the tables and mass of fig trees that divided the dining and pool areas, making odd gestures with her arms as she spoke. There. He was right to warn the kids that everyone here was a stranger and some were a bit off in the knocker.

A brood of six blond-haired kids emerged from behind the curve of the lodge's wall, following her like she was the Pied Piper. Okay, so she wasn't talking to herself, but still, one had to be just a tad nuts to have that many kids. He could barely handle two.

He stuck his hands in his pockets and returned to the bungalow. Reassured by the sound of the twins' voices in their room, he went straight for his laptop, hoping the lodge's wifi wouldn't fail him. It was yet another reason he'd booked this place. Most lodges only offered it in the lounge and restaurant.

The first few emails were from Ron Swale, the chief engineer he'd met with earlier at the survey site. The not-so-subtle yet diplomatic reminder that any seismic data Dax and his team collected was for the purpose of analyzing and mapping the possibility of oil pockets in a field extension near Erebus's current wells—not research—had set his blood to simmering. It had taken everything in him not to walk away, but he'd signed a contract and his crew was counting on him for their jobs. He needed the income, as well. The fact was, he'd cleared collecting a little seismic data on his own time with management when he'd signed on for this. He'd never been close to the Greater

Rift Valley region before. Not studying the area while he was here would be like forcing a kid to walk through miles of toys and not be allowed to touch even one.

Ron's condescension might have irked him, but it was guilt that really gnawed at Dax.

Giving up on researching earthquake prediction hadn't been a choice, it had been a necessity. And now any research he did was in the name of serving the oil company.

He knew about the relatively recent uptick in tremor activity in the area, some too weak for anyone to feel, but environmental groups were beginning to make waves. The same anti-fracking environmental groups Sandy used to support. Most oil companies insisted post-fracking water injections had nothing to do with increases in seismic activity.

Dax wasn't so sure. Yet, here he was. That made him an enabler, didn't it? But he had debts to pay off and the girls to raise and working for a petroleum company paid well. Six-figures well, which was more than double what he'd been pulling in before from research grants.

Don't overanalyze. It's a steady job. Just do it. But "doing it" meant he required full-time help with the twins more than ever. He rubbed the back of his neck as he scrolled down the emails in his inbox, finally spotting one from Melissa. He needed her here yesterday. He opened the email, but the knots in his neck only tightened. *You've got to be kidding me.*

"Ivy! Fern! Come in here. Now."

The carved wood door to their room swung open and the two appeared dressed in shorts and T-shirts with their wet hair loose and half-combed out. Their eyes flitted toward his laptop and back up to him, widening just enough to look innocent.

"What's up?"

"Nanny Number Seven quit. What do you two know about this?"

"I thought we weren't supposed to call her that," Fern said.

"I'm a little upset here, so I'll call her Seven if I want to, especially since I now have to take time I don't have to search for Eight." He was sounding just like the twins. He squeezed his eyes shut and inhaled, long and deep.

"He's at a 5.0," Ivy muttered. "We'll live."

"Are you kidding? His neck is red. That puts him at a 6.5," Fern countered.

Dax ignored their habit of using the Richter scale to gauge how mad he was at their shenanigans.

"It says in her email that the giant spider in her purse was the last straw."

"It was fake. Besides, that's such an overused prank, she should have expected it. She's just a wimp. So much for her acting all sergeant-like. All bark and no bite. And she's lazy—anyone who uses that as an excuse to quit doesn't really want to work," Ivy said.

"And you two certainly are a job." He had no doubt the spider had only been a warm-up for the twins. A test. It didn't come close to their somewhat scary creative capacity.

"It was harmless, Dad. We pulled it out of our Halloween supplies. We were just having fun. Fun is a necessary part of raising well-rounded, healthy, psychologically balanced children," Fern added.

Wow. Just wow.

He closed his laptop. Three years and he still had to pause and ask himself what Sandy would do. Only lately, he kept coming up blank. She didn't even visit in his dreams anymore...not the way she had after she'd left him and kept the girls. They had been five at the time.

Looking back, he couldn't blame her for leaving. She'd been right. He'd been too busy chasing after his obsession to find better ways of predicting earthquakes and saving lives. He'd spent more time in tents doing field research than he had at home, protecting his family.

But he *had* tried to make it up to her. He'd been as present as he could possibly be after her diagnosis...but it had been too late.

He checked his watch again. He was supposed to be at the site by midmorning tomorrow to start setting up equipment, laying out geophones and cables. But now he had no nanny and there was no way he was taking the girls to the site. Too dangerous and not allowed.

He stared pointedly at each one. They looked so much like their mother all three could have been triplets, but for the generation gap. Their hair had lightened back to dark blond as it dried, and their hazel eyes sparkled with hints of gold that matched the freckles on their noses. That reminded him to pull out the sunscreen from their bags.

"Ivy. Fern. You need to think before you act. Everything you do has consequences." Now he was sounding like his mother. He cringed. "That fake but—according to your nanny—very realistic spider caused her to scream and jolt. *That* caused her to spill her hot coffee all over her hand and into her purse, which *resulted* in both a burned hand and a fried cell phone, which I'll be paying to replace. Nope. Correction. Which *you'll* be paying to replace."

Ha. There was an inkling of parental genius in him yet. The twins crinkled their foreheads, and the corners of their mouths sank.

"We're really sorry," they said simultaneously. It almost…almost…sounded rehearsed. Like synchronized swimming. Maybe he should look into signing them up for a class. Burn off some of that energy.

"Apology accepted."

"So how do we earn the money to pay for her cell phone? We need jobs, right?" Fern asked. Always the logical one.

Jobs. He hadn't thought that far ahead. Darn it. At their now-rented-out house in Houston, he could have had them weeding for the neighbors. But here? No way were they sticking their hands under shrubs where predators could be lurking. Not that the lodge needed any help with weeding. There were no jobs for eleven-year-olds here, not even lemonade stands or bake sales or… It hit him. *That* was Fern's not-so-innocent point. No job availability. They were trying to get out of paying. Not happening. He scratched the back of his neck and stood up.

"You'll stick to our bargain regarding your next nanny. Behave and you'll get an allowance bonus. Consider yourselves docked for losing Melissa, so you'll have to earn that back, too. And for now, your allowance goes to paying it off. Plus, I'll pay a few extra bucks for keeping your room clean, beds made and bathroom wiped down."

"Sounds fair," Ivy said.

"Good. Now go brush out your hair and get your shoes on so we can get a bite to eat."

The two closed their room door behind them, and Dax leaned his head back against the wall. The tribal mask hanging over his bed on the opposite side of the room scowled at him, as if it disapproved of his parenting skills. This was going to be a long day.

He started to head for his bathroom, but their whispers stopped him. He didn't mean to eavesdrop—or maybe he did. The words he picked up required listening to. It was his parental duty.

"Doesn't he realize?" That was Fern.

"Are you kidding? Maybe there's an advantage to him being too busy to pay attention to us most of the time. It makes it easier to get away with things."

"Yeah, like the fact that, technically, *he's* the one paying for the broken cell phone.

If you take into account that cleaning up is part of getting our allowance to begin with, then add the bonus for doing so, it covers what we were docked and then some."

"And on top of that, we have a little freedom before he hires us a supervisor. But do you think we should get rid of the worms we put in his shaving kit before he opens it in the morning? If he docks us for that, we'll be in the red."

"You're right. He hates worms about as much as Number Seven hates spiders."

My shaving kit?

Dax gritted his teeth and eyed his toiletry bag. He'd always wanted to try the short-stubble look.

God, he needed to focus on his job, not the twins' antics. He needed to be able to work without worrying. He'd made a lot of sacrifices to get through the past few years, but having the twins grow up away from him was where he drew the line.

He'd promised Sandy that he would stay with them. Keep them safe. Their grandparents disagreed with him moving them every time his job took him somewhere for months. They had insisted that the girls required structure and time management. As far as he was concerned, he could provide that. Sticking to a schedule wasn't rocket science.

He just had to find a nanny who could do it.

PIPPA HARPER TUGGED against the stiff leather of her watch band and finally forced it to unbuckle. She shuddered as she shoved the new gadget in the pocket of her khakis and rubbed the imprint it left on her wrist. If anything ranked up there with flies and mosquitoes buzzing persistently around her face or deceptively delicate ants forging a trail up her back during a relaxing nap under the Serengeti sun, it was wearing a watch or following someone else's schedule.

She unfolded a handwoven, flat-weave rug over the dusty, red earth that flowed through the small Maasai village *enkang* and beyond its thorny fence, then stretched out on her stomach and propped herself up on her elbows. The tribe's oldest child, Adia, sat down next to her. At thirteen, she was making huge progress with her fourth-grade-level reading and writing. Pippa was proud of her.

"I'm ready and listening," Pippa prompted with a smile. Adia was used to her relaxed teaching style. Of course, she sat up and gave the lesson more structure when they were writing or doing math, but reading was different. Reading was meant to be enjoyed. She wanted the kids to see that.

Adia opened the book to her marked paged and began reading. Her musical lilt drew Pippa into one of her favorite story-books. The girl had a future ahead of her, so long as her father agreed to let her leave home and continue her education beyond what Pippa could offer. Trying to teach the children of the Maasai and other local tribes—particularly the young girls, who weren't always given the opportunity— was a lot for one person. Thankfully, she wasn't the only teacher who was trying to help. Some well-known people from the university…some who were born in these villages…had programs to teach and give back. But a few people and a couple of pro-grams weren't enough to teach all the rural children in Kenya and the children in the tribes around here were counting on her. She needed more money to help them. She was spread thin, traveling on different days to different *enkangs*. At some point, the girls had to be given the chance to move beyond her limitations.

She closed her eyes and raised her face to the sun as she listened. It felt so much better not to have her watch on. Who needed clocks when they had the sun and stars? Who needed alarms and schedules when all they had to do was listen to the diurnal rhythm and sounds of wildlife announcing everything from daybreak to dusk to the coming of rain?

Rain, fluid. Earth, solid.

The simple facts flashed through her mind the same second that the ground rippled against her like a river current against the belly of a wildebeest trapped during the floods.

She stilled and pressed her palms against the rug, her mind registering fact and logic. *Earth. Solid.* She glanced around. Adia's rhythm hadn't faltered. The others in the village were going about their routines.

The herdsmen had taken their cattle and goats out to pasture, and the *enkang*'s central, stick-fenced pen, where their goats were kept safe from predators at night, stood rigidly against the backdrop of the Serengeti plains. Women were laboriously mashing dried straw with cow dung and urine for the mud walls of their small, rounded *inkajijik*. Simple homes made with what the earth offered. The *solid* earth.

Clearly, she'd imagined the ripples. No one else seemed fazed. Maybe the sun was getting to her. It had shifted in the sky, stealing away the shade that the branches of a fig tree had offered. She took a deep breath and sat up, brushing off her hands, then pushing her curly hair away from her forehead.

"Is everything okay? Should I stop reading? Did I make a mistake?" Adia fingered the rows of red and orange beads that graced her neck, then smoothed her hand across the vibrant patterns of her traditional wrap dress.

"No, no. It wasn't you. I need to get out of the sun."

There was no point in frightening the

girl. Unless... No, she doubted it. She hadn't felt a tremor in forever. Sure, they happened here. She'd studied geology as an undergrad. She knew all about the earth's tectonic plates moving.

She'd felt mild quakes in the past. The Great Rift Valley ran through western Kenya, including the Maasai Mara and the area where the Serengeti ecosystem lay and merged across the border into Tanzania's famous Serengeti National Park. There was more earthquake activity in that region, but minor events happened here, too. Even to the east in Nairobi.

But what had happened a minute ago had been a different, odd sensation. Nothing had shaken. No one else had noticed. Most likely, the sun had made her dizzy. She got up and sat upright next to Adia.

"Okay, you can keep reading. Let's get to the end of the chapter before we stop. That way you can write me a summary for next time."

Adia looked down uncomfortably and bit her lip.

"What is it?"

"I shouldn't ask you for more."

"Adia, if you need something, ask me."

"I can't write a summary. A goat ate the pencil and paper you gave me. I set it down to help my sister when she fell down. And then the goat ate it."

Pippa gave her a reassuring smile. If this had been anywhere else and a student had told her teacher that the dog had eaten her homework, she would have been accused of making up stories. But this wasn't anywhere else, and Adia was as honest and conscientious as a kid could be, which meant a goat really *had* eaten her pencil and paper. She placed her hand on Adia's shoulder.

"Not to worry. I have some extra supplies in my jeep." Pippa reluctantly pulled the watch out of her pocket. She glanced at the time and stuffed the watch away again. "I didn't realize how long we've been sitting here. You are reading so beautifully, you made me forget. And you're at my favorite part in the book, too. It doesn't matter how many times I've read or heard the story, I still feel my heart race when Captain Hook hears the ticktock of the crocodile approaching."

"Me, too," Adia said. She smiled and

marked her page. "Thank you for teaching me to read."

"You're a fast learner. You can do anything you set your mind to. I hate to leave. On my next visit, you can help me teach the little ones, then we can talk about what I mentioned last time." Pippa sighed as she stood. This is why she hated schedules. It didn't seem fair to end class right when a student found his or her stride. Not that this was an official class or standard school, but still. She could remember the day Adia had read her first words when she was nine. Pippa hadn't been teaching formally back then, but she had been donating books to some of the local Maasai villages her entire childhood.

She had taught a few of the kids to read back then because she wanted to. It made her happy. But it took years for her to realize teaching was her passion.

Adia and other children had missed out on lessons when Pippa left Kenya two years ago and spent a year traveling and studying in Europe—an escape she had needed after having her heart broken. But she was glad to be back home this past year. And dedicating herself to teaching children who otherwise had no access to education was more rewarding than she ever could have imagined.

She wanted others to read their first words, too, which was why making it to the tourist lodge on schedule mattered just as much. She had an arrangement with the lodge and the guided children's hikes she provided there allowed her to earn money for teaching supplies. She also hoped to save for a small schoolhouse—or school hut—where she'd be able to teach children from different homesteads all at once, rather than losing so much time driving long distances across the savanna.

The problem was that tourist schedules weren't sun—or Africa-time friendly. Five minutes late and they'd start complaining. Five minutes late was nothing around here, but add an hour or two and she'd have no customers at all.

She had found that out the hard way a few weeks ago. No one had even cared about the fact that a male ostrich had decided to challenge her jeep. And then she'd inadvertently driven too close to a rhino and her calf in the brush. She'd made her escape only to hit a piece of scrap metal in the middle of nowhere that resulted in her having to change her tire. No doubt, the lodge director and tour group parents had thought *she* was making up stories when she'd finally arrived at the hotel.

The trumpeting of elephants in the distance shook the air as if to give her a warning that she would be running late soon. She gave Adia a hug, then quickly scanned the *enkang*. The place bustled with activity, from the familiar act of women grinding corn, to making beaded jewelry and continuing to repair and build their huts. The village would crumble without the tireless work the women did here. Most had never left their clan, yet they had the focus, strength, persistence and motivation that so many students and people Pippa had met during her recent year of travels lacked. People who took the opportunities they had in life for granted.

"I don't see your father. Did you talk to him?" Pippa asked as they walked toward her jeep. She really hoped that Adia's father wouldn't be opposed to the girl pursuing an education in Nairobi. Adia scratched her tightly cropped hair, then fidgeted with the colorful bracelets that ran halfway to her elbows.

"No, not yet. I'll talk to him when you are here next time. With you. Please?"

"Okay. But I don't want to offend him. This discussion is between you. The decision is his." There was a fine line between advocating for a kid like Adia and crossing boundaries when it came to family, expectations and culture. The fact that everyone knew Pippa around here might help a little, but upsetting the tribal leader might put a hitch in her efforts to teach others in the village. She respected the Maasai and this particular family tremendously, and offending them was the last thing she wanted to do.

"Of course," Adia said, following her outside the *enkang*'s fence to where the jeep was parked. Pippa reached into a backpack on the passenger seat and pulled out another pencil and small notebook. She handed them to Adia, gave her a hug and waved as the girl hurried back to her hut.

Pippa settled behind the wheel of her

jeep and looked one more time at her watch. Talk about addictive. No wonder people succumbed so easily to the power of clocks and schedules…and stress and anti-anxiety drugs. How would someone like Adia adjust to that world? Would she lose her bond with and appreciation of her culture? Was Pippa causing more harm than good?

She took a deep breath, and her stomach rumbled as she started the ignition. Her home in the Busara Elephant Research and Rescue Camp was along the way, but she didn't have time to swing by for a bite.

She had six kids booked for the hike, and she couldn't risk being late. There weren't a lot of opportunities out here for her to save up. As much as she hated the outside world leaving its footprints on this majestic land, being near the Maasai Mara meant tourists hungry for a glimpse of Kenya's Serengeti and its wonders—and that meant money.

Funny how the things that annoyed her were the very things that she relied on to achieve her goals. Balance rarely happened without sacrifice. Everything from relationships, marriage and the circle of life that surrounded her proved it. The balance and beauty of the savanna relied on both predator and prey. Death was a necessary evil, but it provided for new beginnings. It, paradoxically, gave hope. She floored the pedal and held her breath till the dust she roused was nothing but a dissipating cloud in her rearview mirror.

She was making it to Tabara Lodge on time if it killed her.

CHAPTER TWO

THE FOOD AT the lodge was better than fantastic and the atmosphere was incredible. Nothing came between them and the outdoors except canvas curtains that Dax was told were only drawn in bad weather. Natural wood covered the ceiling and walls and African art adorned the place. The restaurant opened onto a breezeway that overlooked grasslands dappled with acacia trees and boulders. The view from their table was breathtaking. Dax had been too rushed earlier to really appreciate it. He set his napkin down and looked at the barely touched dishes in front of Ivy and Fern. They'd eaten the chapati flat bread, but the stew hadn't been much more than picked at.

"You have to at least try it."

"I can't identify all the ingredients," Fern said.

"The waiter told you how it's made. Three times."

"Smells...different." Ivy crinkled her nose.

"It's called spices and the stew is delicious, so if you don't want it, I'll eat it." He reached over for their plates, hoping they'd stop him. They didn't. Fine. Their choice.

Living outside of the United States was going to be good for them. They obviously needed to learn to try new things. Houston was full of great, authentic, hole-in-the-wall restaurants, but come to think of it, he couldn't recall taking them to any. When he ate out, it was usually with a colleague at lunch. He added their stew to his empty bowl and took a bite. "You can't live on bread forever. If you're hungry enough, you'll eat."

"Yes, we know. There are starving children in Africa."

"You're *in* Africa."

"We know that, too."

"Have it your way," Dax said, spooning more food into his mouth. Man, the spinach, potatoes and lamb were good.

"I'm a vegetarian," Ivy said. Fern stilled

for a fraction of a second, then pursed her lips and nodded in agreement. Dax set his spoon down and rested his elbows on the table.

"A vegetarian. You, too, Fern? Or did you become one a second ago?"

"We're definitely vegetarians," Fern said.

"You both begged me for hamburgers before our flight here. I recall you eating every last bite, too."

There was no comment. Dax sighed. As if they weren't picky eaters already.

"You do know that even vegetarians don't live on bread? That you'll have to eat more vegetables and beans?" They hated beans, unless they were baked beans that came out of a can and were loaded with sugar. Neither twin made a comment. Stubborn times two. "Okay, then. We can order you vegetarian meals. They had plenty of options that weren't on the dessert menu." He gave them a knowing look. No doubt they were hoping he'd give up on real food and let them order anything they wanted, so long as they didn't starve.

"We're not really hungry anyway," Ivy said. Fern shot her a frown.

"I am," Dax said. "So you'll have to sit and wait while I finish this delicious, savory dish." He took another bite. "Man, this hits the spot. Really good."

Ivy and Fern rolled their eyes and pulled out their e-readers. Their grandmother had bought the gadgets for them last Christmas and got them both international charging kits for this trip. He didn't condone reading during a meal, but right now, if it kept them busy and cut the smart-mouthing he had to listen to so that he could actually enjoy his food, he'd let it slide. Besides, between virtual schooling, e-readers and the occasional movie or game, any pediatric recommendations on limiting screen time were null, void and completely archaic. It had taken him a while, after becoming a single father, to finally figure that out. Nutrition, however, wasn't. Sooner or later, they'd need to eat something. He hated it when they challenged him like this. It was as if they were in a staring contest, waiting to see who'd give in and blink first.

A laugh broke through the monotonous buzz of lounge conversations and clinking of flatware. That laugh. He recognized it immediately and glanced toward the lodge foyer. The wild-haired lady with the six kids, who were all trailing after her again. A person had to have patience to be happy with that many kids to keep in line. He shoved another bite in his mouth and raised a brow. Maybe it wasn't a blissful laugh. Maybe it was a delirious, I'm-going-to-lose-my-mind-someone-give-me-a-kid-break-or-bottle-of-Prozac laugh. He couldn't help but glance back in her direction. Something about her was hard to ignore.

She pushed her hair to the side after giving the youngest kid a hug. She had a clean, natural look about her. Down-to-earth, like Sandy had been. She didn't seem old enough to have six kids, though. Mid-twenties maybe? A couple hurried over to her and began apologizing for being late. Something about the massage they'd been getting. It hit him. Those weren't her kids. Those weren't her—he grabbed his napkin and wiped his mouth, then signaled over to the nearest waiter.

"Ivy, Fern, stay here a minute. Don't go anywhere."

The older fellow approached and started

to refill his drink. Dax waved his hand to decline.

"No, thank you. But would you mind standing here just for a few minutes? If you could just watch over my daughters a moment—" he glanced at the man's name tag "—Alim. I'd really appreciate it. And I won't be long." He didn't dare trust the twins alone again. At least not today.

Alim looked a little nervous when Ivy and Fern smiled at him. He raised a brow.

"Sir, I don't watch children. I have other tables to wait on."

"I'll tip you extra. Just give me five minutes."

Alim hesitated, rubbed a hand over his short, salt-and-pepper hair, then nodded.

Dax narrowed his eyes at the twins.

"Stay put. Read the menu and find yourselves something to eat." That would occupy them. Maybe. Alim grimaced and gave the girls a stern look. Clearly, kids weren't his thing, but Dax didn't have time to worry about the poor guy. He needed to catch Miss Curly Q. He ran out to the foyer, but there was no sign of her. *The reception desk.* Yes. It was near the wide-open archway that served as the lodge's entrance. She couldn't have left without their noting it. He reached the desk in two strides.

"Excuse me. That lady who was just in here. Reddish-brown, curly hair? Does she work here? I noticed she was watching a group of kids, and I'm hoping to hire a baby—a child sitter."

"No, sir." The concierge straightened his uniform and cocked his head politely. "She's not a Tabara employee. She has an arrangement with us to offer the occasional nature hike and mini safari to the young children who visit. It's part of a package we offer to parents who wish to take advantage of our spa."

Dax drummed his fingers on the sleek wood counter. He needed to think. Occasional wasn't going to cut it. He had to catch her before she left.

"Thank you." He ran outside the lodge and stopped to get his bearings. She wasn't hard to spot. She was headed toward a grungy, mud-coated jeep with a bounce in her step. He jogged up behind her. "Excuse me. I'm sorry to bother you."

She spun around and slapped a hand to her chest. Dax held up his hands.

"I'm sorry. I didn't mean to scare you. I thought you would've heard me coming."

"No. No, it's fine. I was thinking about something and...never mind." She looked up at him with glistening, green eyes and cleared her throat. "Can I help you?"

He wasn't so sure anymore. The scare he'd given her wasn't enough to make anyone teary-eyed. Whatever she'd been thinking about was none of his business, but when he saw a person's mood shift so drastically—from laughing and bubbly when they were surrounded by people, to down and withdrawn when they thought they were alone—it pinched at him. Sandy had done that when she was sick. She used to put on a happy face for everyone, not wanting to cause worry, but then he'd catch her alone, depressed and concerned about what would happen to her children after she was gone. He knew pain. He'd masked it plenty of times himself.

"Is everything all right?" He hadn't meant to ask. Asking meant getting involved and trying to help—in short it meant opening a can of worms. He'd learned that lesson with Nanny Number Two. He shifted his stance and practically held his breath.

"I'm completely fine. This is nothing," she said, wiping the corner of one eye. "I got some bad news, but it's taken care of and everything is fine." She smiled, but there was something cloudy and faraway in her eyes.

"Okay." He scratched the back of his neck. No can of worms.

"Okay." She hooked her thumbs on the belt loop of her khakis and waited. "You wanted something?"

"Ah, yes. Yes. I'm hoping you can help me out. I saw back there that you work with kids. I have two girls and—"

"You'd like to book a kid safari. Excellent."

Her face lit up and her smile warmed. She was unassumingly pretty. Just a fact he registered. He was a scientist. He was simply making an observation.

The twins had had one sitter who'd been more concerned with her layers of makeup than with tending to the kids. She didn't last long, not because she'd quit like the rest, but because he'd let her go. He didn't want his girls to become makeup obsessed. At least not for as long as he could help it.

"Would after tomorrow work? Noon-ish? If I could get their names…?" She pulled a mini notebook out from her back pocket, but couldn't seem to find something to write with. "I'm sorry, I had a pencil here somewhere. Oh. I gave it to someone to use."

Noon-*ish*? Just when he thought he'd found someone…a reality check. He had a schedule to keep. *Ish* didn't cut it in his life. She seemed disorganized, too. Great.

Maybe if he went back and spoke to the concierge, the man could help Dax find someone else. Then again, Dax needed to be at work in the morning. There wasn't time to waffle or get picky. He really was desperate for help. Not just any help, either. He needed someone who could deal with the twins and, from what he'd seen, this woman had a healthy dose of patience. Ivy and Fern required an endless supply of that.

"I was thinking more like eight. Sharp."

"In the morning?" She stopped her pencil search.

"Of course, in the morning," he said. Eight at night didn't even make sense. "Look, I should have introduced myself first. Then I'll explain everything. I'm Dax. Dax Calder." He held out his hand and, after a brief hesitation, she shook it.

"Pippa."

"Pippa. That's easy enough to remember. Like that book my daughters used to read. *Pippa Longstocking.* Or something like that."

Pippa's smile flattened and she raised her brows.

"It's Pippa Harper. If you were referring to the book character with braids sticking out at right angles to her head, that would be Pippi. Not Pippa."

"Oh. Right." Dax swiped a hand across the back of his neck. It was the little things that always reminded him that Sandy had been a far better parent than he could ever be.

The girls used to read to *him*. Not the other way around. And they used to accuse him of not paying attention to the story. Clearly, he hadn't. He closed his eyes briefly. "Miss Harper, I'm here on business—long-term-*ish*—and I thought that maybe you would be interested in…" What would she more likely say yes to? Homeschooling them? Babysitting them? Nanny sounded like a career position, and she obviously already had work. "I need help with my two daughters. The nanny I had arranged to come stay with us here in Kenya couldn't make it over from the US, and so I really have to find—"

"A babysitter. I'm sorry. I'm not a babysitter. Good luck in your search and have a nice day." The sparkle in her eyes had dimmed and the softness of her features tightened. She turned on her heel and took long, quick strides toward her jeep. She grabbed a bottle of water and a book from the back seat and hurriedly climbed behind the wheel as he approached.

"Wait. Just give me a second. Please. They're not babies." *They'd be a lot easier to handle if they were.* "There wouldn't be diaper changes or anything like that. The girls are very smart and they don't bite. Their names are Ivy and Fern."

"Did you name them after characters in a novel? Or search through a gardening book?" She flashed him a fake, close-lipped smile.

He stuffed his hands in his pockets and nodded.

"I get it. If I insulted you, I apologize. It wasn't intentional." He looked down the red dirt road that stretched, tired and dry, across the savanna until the tall grasses devoured it. "My wife named them."

"If you and your wife want time alone, then sign up for the spa treatment package and your kids can enjoy a safari hike with me."

"She's dead. Their mother...she died three years ago."

Something shifted in Pippa's face. She blinked and rested her hands in her lap.

"I'm sorry. I just assumed. I didn't mean to be insensitive."

"It's not your fault. You couldn't have known."

"It's just that it wouldn't be the first time I wasn't taken seriously, and it has been a long day. I was being a tad defensive. But the truth is, I don't babysit and I'm not a nanny. I have other things on my schedule and a long drive to get out here. I'm sorry I can't help. Maybe check with the lodge staff."

"I have to go to work tomorrow and I can't leave them alone, nor can I take them with me. I'm begging you to just hear me out."

"You're here for work? Not a family holiday?"

"Yes. And I'll pay well. I need someone to make sure they're safe and keeping up with their schoolwork while I'm gone."

"Schoolwork?"

"I travel for months at a time and don't want to leave them behind, so they're homeschooled. We do some of the classes virtually and some are sent in."

"I know how that works. I was schooled the same way. I grew up a couple of hours from here. An orphaned-elephant research and rescue camp. My mother is a wildlife veterinarian. There aren't traditional schools out here."

This was good. They were connecting. He was getting her on the same page.

"Great. Then you'd know exactly what to do."

"But, as I said, Mr. Calder, I don't baby-sit."

"But earlier I saw you handle that group of kids like a pro."

"I was teaching them about the natural environment here and why it's so important to protect the land as well as the animals from being destroyed by human ignorance and man's greedy actions. Not babysitting."

It did make sense that she'd be involved in environmental awareness, her mother being a vet and all. *Mental note: Tell the twins not to mention his contract with Erebus Oil.*

"I understand, but I would pay you double whatever you're making for tours. And it'd be just until I find a nanny replacement."

"I'm not a nanny, either. I told you, I teach."

"But isn't a nanny like a…a hybrid between a teacher and a sitter?"

She gave him a dirty look and started the ignition.

Pippa couldn't believe this guy. He saw a woman with kids and the first thing he assumed was that she was babysitter material. Now she knew how her Aunt Hope felt when guys who noticed her wearing scrubs assumed she was a nurse instead of a doctor. Oh, and the hair thing. Had he really compared her to Pippi Longstocking? Her hair was hard to control, but that comment had been plain low. She reached up and self-consciously tucked a lock behind her ear as she revved the engine. The corkscrew curl sprang right back out.

His wife had died. Pippa took a deep breath. Her Aunt Zoe had been killed the day her Uncle Ben had returned home from duty many years ago. Being a marine thrown into raising three young kids while mourning hadn't been easy. Pippa had been a little girl at the time, but she remembered how much her cousin Maddie, then ten, had really suffered and struggled with coping after her mother's death. Maddie had been close in age to this guy's daughters, then. It had been Aunt Hope who'd helped them survive that trauma.

Pippa had also grown up around baby elephants orphaned by poachers. It didn't matter that they weren't human. They knew grief. They suffered the loss, too. Pippa hated witnessing that kind of pain.

Dax placed his hands on her door frame. She recalled from his handshake that his fingers were strong and calloused—nothing like the majority of men who stayed at Tabara Lodge, married or otherwise. This place catered to business types in search of an exotic getaway and spa treatments. It attracted the wealthy because one had to be rich in order to afford the rates. Guests here were looking for a safari experience without sacrificing modern conveniences, like flushable toilets and running water. The guests here could likely afford maids and chauffeurs and people to raise their kids for them. Calloused as his hands were, this man was probably no different—after all, he was wearing slacks and a polo shirt at a safari lodge. Outdoorsy people didn't do that. But he did say he was here for work.

"Look, bottom line is that I'm in a bind and desperate enough to pay well. How long are your tours?"

Desperate. That was Pippa. The runner-up. A last resort. Just like she'd been with her childhood friend Haki. He'd considered

her his girlfriend and almost married her...
until his first choice—her cousin Maddie—
had stepped back into his life.

Pippa pressed a hand against the twinge
in her chest. She was over it. She really
was. But sometimes the hurt resurfaced,
like when she'd seen the happy couple
who'd picked up their six kids after the
tour.

A year and a half ago, she'd pictured her
future like that: happily married and ready
to start a family of her own. Not anymore.
Her kids were all the children in the tribal
villages who were counting on her for an
education and more possibilities for their
futures. She tapped her steering wheel.

Fine. It wouldn't hurt to hear him out.
Money was money. Still, she wasn't going
to sacrifice time in the villages to teach a
rich man's children unless it was worth it.
She had not spent the last year and a half
figuring out what she wanted to do with her
life only to get sucked into someone else's
schedule and responsibilities.

She turned off her ignition and looked
up at Dax.

"My tours are three hours. *Ish*. I try to

be on time, but this is the wild and if that means I'm delayed because we come across something the kids should see, then we see it."

"I assume you do two tours in a full day, then. I'll pay you twice what you'd make taking those groups out."

Pippa's pulse scattered, but she bit the inside of her cheek to hide her shock. Good-looking and daft. Definitely not business minded…unless he had more money than he knew what to do with.

"But you don't even know my price yet. Per child."

"Come on. It's a tour. It can't be that much. I know what I can afford. I told you I'd pay well. Deal or no deal?"

She was so going to raise her price just because of his condescension, but heaven help her. Easy money. One week would add up to more cash than she could make in two months. She couldn't even begin to wrap her head around all the school supplies she would be able to afford, and how much faster she'd be able to get a small school built where the tribal children could gather for lessons.

Play it cool, Pippa. She shrugged.

"Let me get this straight. You want me to watch your girls morning till night, every day, until you can get a permanent nanny."

"Permanent...yes."

"Because you're here for..." She never pried when it came to the parents of her tour kids. It wasn't professional to do so. But he wanted her watching his daughters full time and she was getting curious about what he did for work.

"I'm here on business."

Ah. Okay. That was the polite answer for "none of your business." Fine.

He scratched his head, and his chocolate-brown hair stuck out where his fingers had been. His eyes were the same color, and the laugh lines at the outer corners gave his eyes a serene, kind look. Too bad his personality didn't match. He seemed too obsessed with his work to laugh enough for creases.

"Getting a replacement might take a few weeks," he continued. "But yes, you have the idea. I have a schedule laid out for them, so you don't have to do any prep work. Could you be here by eight tomorrow morning? I have to leave by then. All you have to do is stick to the schedule and keep them with you at all times. Trust me, it's just easier that way. I want them safe."

She thrummed her fingers on the steering wheel. Rich and private about his business and out here in the middle of nowhere for work. She had it. Maybe he was a silent partner for Tabara Lodge. That would explain him wanting to keep his identity under wraps and it'd also fit in with his being able to afford Tabara for a long stay. She looked at him.

"How old are they?" she asked. He made it sound like she'd need car seats and safety gates, or pens of some sort.

"Eleven."

"And the other one?"

"Um…eleven." His forehead creased apologetically.

"Twins?"

"Identical. Didn't I mention that?"

"You skipped that part."

"Does it really make a difference? Two kids is two kids."

Then why was that expression "double trouble" so well-known? Pippa studied him, then hugged her book and water bottle to her chest and got out of the jeep.

"Are they around? Maybe I should meet them before I make any final decisions."

Dax glanced toward the lodge and cranked his neck to one side, then the other.

"Okay. I suppose that's a good idea."

He didn't sound convinced.

"After you," Pippa said.

He led the way back through the lodge's foyer and to the dining area.

Alim stood next to a table where two girls sat, one wearing a purple headband and the other a green one. They were otherwise identical and quite pretty. She guessed, by the fact that their eyes were hazel and their dark blond hair was lighter than Dax's, that they looked like their mother. E-readers were on the table next to three dessert plates—one in front of each girl and one between them—all piled with a powdered-sugar-covered *mandazi*. A small ramekin filled with chocolate dipping sauce, typically used with fruit, sat within their reach. That was a lot of fried dough—not to mention sugar—for two kids. What was their dad thinking?

"Enjoying your desserts, girls?" Dax said. There was an edge to his tone.

Both girls immediately sat up straight. Chocolate clung to their fingers and the corners of their mouths and powdered sugar spotted their cheeks and clothes. They wiped their mouths and put their hands neatly in their laps. Well behaved enough. This was going to be easy money.

"Um, yes. They're delicious," the one in green said, biting her lower lip.

"He brought them to us," the one in purple quipped, pointing at Alim.

"They ordered them," Alim quickly said, scowling down at the girls. "When you left, you told them to look at the menu. They said you had given them permission to have dessert. You were gone much longer than five minutes."

"Three desserts?" Dax raised a brow. "I'm guessing the third wasn't mine, considering it's half-gone, too."

"They said they were ordering for their sister. The one you left to go get from your room. I was explaining something to a new waiter and when I turned around, they were eating their sister's dessert. I will have another brought out free of charge," Alim said.

"You didn't mention three girls. I'm positive you said I'd be helping with twins, not triplets," Pippa said.

"I did. Interestingly, I've never met this sister of theirs and I'm pretty sure they haven't, either. Alim, another dessert won't be necessary. I apologize for taking longer than I expected," Dax said, reaching into his wallet.

Alim shot the girls a disapproving look, then held out his palm. Dax put a bill in it. The palm remained extended. Dax frowned at the girls and gave Alim another bill. He'd paid a waiter to watch his kids? Overprotective much? At that age, Pippa had been climbing trees, working with elephants and disappearing into the tall savanna grasses on wild, exploratory adventures.

"Kuwa makini," Alim muttered as he passed Pippa on his way back to the kitchen. Really?

"Ku-what?" Dax asked.

"Oh, nothing," Pippa said. Alim had given her fair warning to be careful. But then, he never did like dealing with children at the dining tables. All things considered, she probably would have pulled a trick for extra dessert, too. Their dad moved the plates next to his half-eaten meal. Not exactly out of reach, but his message was clear. No more dessert.

"We'll discuss this later," he told the twins.

"Hi there. I'm Pippa."

"Yes, sorry. Ivy and Fern, this is Miss Harper."

"What are you reading?" Fern asked.

Pippa held up the cover of the book she was holding.

"A mystery I found in an antiques bookstore when I was in Spain. Apparently, it's out of print and a rare find. I didn't have a chance to start it until yesterday, but it's such a page-turner, I'm already near the end. The best part of a mystery is when you finally get all the answers and all the pieces fall into place, isn't it? What are you two reading?"

Pippa wasn't big on e-readers. Having to rely on generators for power made printed books more convenient out here. And even though she read books on her computer on occasion and could have an e-reader now if she wanted, she preferred to feel and smell the pages. She wanted to be able to read perched on a boulder in the savanna without sun glaring off her screen or the battery dying and having to drive back to camp for a charge. Besides, she taught reading in the villages using print books and liked to be able to share. The Maasai children didn't have electricity. Their children didn't have modern distractions like cell phones or televisions or movie theaters. Just books.

"*History of the Civil War.* It's for homework," Ivy said.

"You two must be diligent students."

"I told you they were smart," Dax said. "Girls, Miss Pippa has agreed to help look after you for a while."

Had she actually agreed? Pippa pressed her lips together and peered at him. He cocked his head and gave her a silent, pleading look. Like his future was in her hands. Okay, then. She was in it for the money. And the girls seemed pretty sweet, too. She'd be reducing their sugar intake drastically, though.

"I suppose we should exchange contact information," she said.

"Yes. Absolutely. I don't have business cards on me, but I can write down a number for when I'm not at the lodge. I should have a satellite phone on me most of the time and I brought one to leave in the bungalow, just in case I need to be reached. If it works. I've been warned reception is spotty."

"It can be."

Pippa set her book and water down on their table and pulled out her mini notebook.

"The bartender will have a pen," she said.

Dax told the girls not to move and followed her to the bar at the end of the room. They scribbled down their info and swapped papers.

"I hope you don't mind my asking you a few questions. I mean, since you're going to be caring for my kids. Normally, I would interview anyone I planned to hire to watch my kids, but I figured if the lodge let you take off with the children of their guests, they know you pretty well."

"Feel free to ask questions, but you already know my name. My vehicle. Where I work and, therefore, my references. I already told you my mom is a vet. She founded the Busara Elephant Research and Rescue Camp twenty-four years ago. The same year I was born. I'll add that my father is a geneticist. I also have a large extended family that includes friends living at Busara or within a few hours of it. Anything else?"

"No wonder everyone seems to know you around here."

There was an awkward moment of silence. Eye contact she wanted to break but couldn't seem to. One of the twins calling out to her dad saved Pippa from the trance.

"I should get going," she said.

"Yes. I need to get back to my girls."

They both hurried to the table, and Pippa picked up her things. She'd planned on sitting under a tree and reading for a bit before heading home, but that wasn't happening now. She wasn't going to risk Dax shirking parenthood and leaving the kids with her before she was on the clock tomorrow. She wasn't going to risk any more awkward moments, either.

"Ivy and Fern. It was nice to meet you. I'll see you tomorrow. Okay?"

"Sure. See you in the morning," Fern said.

"Bye. Let us know how your mystery turns out if you finish it."

Pippa noticed that one of the dessert plates had inched its way a little closer to Ivy. The tablecloth between Ivy and the dish was sprinkled with sugar and had a smear of chocolate on it. The girl grabbed her napkin and wiped the evidence off her mouth and fingers before her dad could notice.

"I will. And you can tell me all about war and battle strategies because history isn't my thing," Pippa said.

"Totally. We can teach you *all* about battle strategies," Ivy said.

Something in the tone of her voice made Pippa a little uneasy. Alim looked over from another table he was serving and gave her a pitiful head shake.

Dax grabbed her hand and shook it while placing his other hand on her back and guiding her swiftly out of the dining hall. Her skin felt warm under his hands.

"Thanks so much. I'll have a partial advance on your salary ready for you in the morning. You won't regret this."

An advance? He was trying to make sure she showed up tomorrow. As for not regretting this, she wouldn't. This one job would change everything. She'd be able to bring an education to so many more kids so much faster. But the sudden twist in Pippa's gut had her wondering who was more desperate about this job.

Dax...or her.

CHAPTER THREE

DAX CRACKED OPEN the girls' room door and peeked in. Two totally precious, harmless angels—when they were sound asleep. He closed the door and padded barefoot over to the small teak writing desk by his bed. Not being able to sleep had its advantages when it came to getting work done. He'd pay for it tomorrow, though. Especially since he had an early morning.

He checked a surface map of the field extension site he was surveying. Most of the data analysis would happen on-site using high powered computers housed in trailers, but he could still work on paper and make notes from here.

His small crew, who'd been working with him ever since he quit research to start up a small company specializing in subterranean mapping for the petroleum industry, were already at the site. Erebus had provided multiple trailers to cover their needs, including housing, meals and one trailer that served as their recording station.

His crew looked all set to start work when he saw them earlier at the meeting with Ron. A part of him yearned to be out there in the field spending nights under the stars like he used to when he researched quakes.

He hated that Erebus and a few other companies had gotten concessions to explore parcels of land in Kenya's wilderness. The region was an environmental wonder. It was famous for its beauty, wildlife and indigenous people. It was also known in his academic circle for its fault line along the Great Rift Valley. Not an ideal place to drill and frack—two things Erebus had already been doing...with government approval, no less.

He could see their tank farms, wells and trucks from the area his team was supposed to map out. In fact, that chief engineer, Ron, had mentioned that if things went well with this project, they might have him do another seismic survey in their current drilling field to map out more definition between the subterranean structures shown in their original models. They wanted to improve efficiency in hitting their jackpots and zeroing in on oil pockets. Dax was building a reputation for himself.

He yawned and rubbed his eyes. He really did need to get a little sleep before his morning commute. Erebus Oil had provided a driver, so he wasn't worried about getting to the site again. He was worried about the girls, though. He would be an hour away, and it was their first day with a new caretaker. Pippa seemed fine, though. Plus, he'd done some checking up on her after she left. He'd told himself it was necessary and responsible to do so. For the twins.

The elephant rescue she'd mentioned had a big website, and most of the photographs on it were credited to Pippa Harper. They were good, too, though he really hoped she'd used a super zoom lens on some of those close-ups. According to some of the lodge employees, she also had relatives with connections in security and the Kenyan Wildlife Service. The twins were probably in safer hands with her out here than with a professional nanny who freaked out at the sight of a toy spider.

He reviewed the list of rules and the schedule he'd laid out for tomorrow. Nothing was missing as far as he could tell. If all went well, they'd be done with their list by the time he arrived back from the site.

I was teaching them about the natural environment here and why it's so important to protect the land as well as the animals from being destroyed by human ignorance and man's greedy actions.

Pippa's voice filled his head loud and clear. She may not have been referring to him at the time, but according to her worldview, he was selling his soul by working for an oil company.

And wasn't he? He'd abandoned his research on earthquake patterns and prediction. He'd forgotten the Dax who'd become a seismologist because he desperately wanted to figure out how to save people. The Dax who believed in climate change, and wanted to preserve the land, sea and sky and all their inhabitants.

Maybe he wasn't destroying any of that directly with this new job, but he was guilty of aiding and abetting. He was using his skills and expertise in reflection seismology to analyze and develop subterranean maps that would in turn tell them where to drill…or even frack if they chose to.

One of these days, he'd have to explain it all to Ivy and Fern and hope that they'd forgive him. He was doing this for them. And as far as Pippa was concerned, she knew nothing about him. She had no idea what it was like to raise the twins alone. He was doing what he had to do. Besides, she drove a jeep, and it sure didn't run on air. Who was she to judge? And why did he care what she thought of him anyway? Why did he suddenly feel guilty?

It didn't matter. She was responsible enough to watch the girls until he found someone else. That's all he needed. So long as she kept the girls safe for the next few weeks, Pippa Harper could think whatever she wanted of him.

PIPPA PROPPED HER feet up on the rattan ottoman, threw a light shawl over her knees and leaned back in the rocker that sat on the front porch of the Busara house.

The full moon cast shadows on the opposite side of the camp, where the old framed tents she'd grown up in still stood, decades later.

Her parents, and Kamau—the other vet who ran Busara—and his wife, Niara—Pippa's mother's best friend—hadn't built the house until Pippa was five years old... right after her father had discovered she existed.

The fact that she still lived here wasn't all that weird. It wasn't like there were apartment complexes every block so she could move out—not that she wanted to move away. The year and a half she'd spent traveling had been enough to stretch her wings and make her miss home. At least that's what she kept telling herself. Maybe if she ever made enough money to invest in herself, she'd be able to build her own cottage nearby. It seemed like a waste of resources, though. There was room here. And whatever money she made, she preferred to donate to her education project or funding wildlife projects, like at Busara.

A lamp from inside cast just enough light through the nearby window for her to read the book in her lap. The house was quiet; everyone was asleep. The rise and fall of cricket and cicada song lulled her into a dreamy, relaxed zone, perfect for reading. Dark. Breezy. Alone. Perfect for a romantic mystery.

She opened her book and vanished into the story. It sucked her in. Page after page. The thrill of not knowing…like that first spark of attraction or first crush. Dax's face flashed in her head and she rubbed at her eyes. Where had that come from? She glanced at the page number and paragraph she'd just read. Nope. She wasn't falling asleep. She'd read that. It had just been an exhausting day, that's all. She shifted in her chair and kept reading.

This was it. The moment of truth. The whodunit. A wild dog howled in the distance, and the brush beyond the elephant pens rustled. Her pulse raced, and she flipped the page.

"What in the name of thunder? No!" she growled.

She double-checked the page numbers. It wasn't a typo. *The* page was gone. The page with the whodunit. She stretched the binding apart just enough to spy the jagged remains of a torn page. White powder shook onto her lap. *White powder. Sugar.* A brown smudge stained the following page. *Chocolate.*

"They. Did. Not!"

The twins had torn out *the* page. Who did that? Who damaged books like that? A rare copy, no less.

"Those freaking girls. I'm going to—" She grabbed fistfuls of her hair and braced her head against her knees. "I swear they better not have thrown it away."

The screen door to the house creaked open and her mother appeared, half-awake.

"Pippa, what in the world is going on? You're going to wake up the entire camp."

"I'm sorry, Mom. I didn't realize my voice had carried. It's just these twins I've agreed to look after. This whole thing might not be worth it. I'm pretty sure their dad knew they were a handful. He lied to me by omission. Alim tried to warn me. I should have listened."

Her mom sat on the corner of the ottoman and put her hand on Pippa's knee.

"Since when do you back down from a

challenge? You seemed so excited about this at dinner and you haven't seen them since you left Tabara. Why the change of heart in just a few hours?"

"They tore my book."

"Ooh, that's bad. Girls their age should know better. You ought to call in first thing and quit."

"Just like that?" Pippa sighed and slumped back when Anna smiled. "Am I ever going to outgrow your reverse psychology tactics?"

"Nope. Because we parents know our kids so well."

Just how well does Dax know his daughters?

"I guess. I just never met a child who would tear up a book. They're evil little monsters."

"A harsh label for girls so young. I love you to pieces, Pippa, but I'm pretty sure a few of my gray hairs were caused by you." She gave Pippa's hand a loving squeeze.

"Just a few?" Pippa tipped her head up and stared at the moon. "I'm sorry I woke you. Go back to bed. I'll be in in a sec."

"Okay. But just remember, Pip, you're

the one in control. This can't be that different from all the tours you've given at camps and lodges in the past. You're the leader. You make the rules and set the boundaries. Maybe these girls need some. Maybe they need someone like you."

"You're right. I'm the one in control."

Her mom nodded as she disappeared through the screen door. Pippa got up, wrapped the shawl around her shoulders and filled her lungs with night air.

You have them at your mercy, Pippa. Don't lose it. Use it.

Civil war history and battle strategies, huh?

She had a few battle plans herself.

And if Dax didn't like her methods, he was on his own.

CHAPTER FOUR

DAX CLOSED HIS laptop and hurried to answer the knock on the bungalow door. She was ten minutes late. Even five wouldn't have been acceptable, but he was desperate and his ride was waiting. And he'd been hoping for a few minutes to go over the schedule and to set things straight...like not being late and not letting Ivy and Fern out of her sight.

"Girls, I'm getting ready to leave. Come out here." He cleared the ten feet to the door in three strides, then opened it and stood aside.

Miss Harper smiled brightly and marched right past him. He glanced at his watch, just as she turned around.

"Sorry I'm late, but I'm all set to go now," she said. She was beaming, as if taking care of his daughters was the most exciting thing in her life. Her green eyes sparkled the way Ivy and Fern's did when they were having fun. They lit the way Sandy's used to, simply because she loved life and lived each moment like a celebration, even before the diagnosis. He loved his daughters, but their idea of fun was probably not the kind Pippa would appreciate. Unless she was *that* bored, living out here in the middle of nowhere. "Where are they? I hope they have comfortable shoes. I have the best day planned," she said, tipping her head at him expectantly.

She had planned the day? No, no, no. *He* had the day planned. *Just get back in control.*

Dax held up a finger, but she spoke before he could get a word out.

"You're standing very still for someone who needs to be somewhere. I've got this. You're already late, so go on. You can leave now."

He was late? Well, yes, he was, but only because *she* had been late first. Was getting Pippa to be on time and follow a schedule going to be that much work? His temples throbbed. He really did need to go. He tugged at his collar and motioned toward the girls' room.

"They're in there. Ivy, Fern! Come on out here a second." He turned back to Pippa. "About the time—"

"Oh. Zebras," she said with a brush of her hand. She helped herself to the view outside the window. Was that supposed to be an expression...like "Oh whatever"? She was so not going to dismiss him that easily.

"Look, Ms. Harper, I need you to be on time. The girls have to stick to their schedule or they'll fall behind. You can't plan their day without reading their lesson plans. As I explained, they're homeschooled, so you've got to stick with my plan. If I can't count on you, say so now." From his research, he knew she was trustworthy on the not-a-criminal front, but trustworthy and dependable didn't always go hand in hand. He needed a nanny who was dependable and punctual. And resilient.

"Mr. Calder. I can't control the wild herds."

She pulled an elastic out of the pocket of her jeans and proceeded to gather her wind-blown hair into a semitidy ponytail. A curly strand escaped and fell across her face. She tucked it behind her ear and put her hands on her hips. The curly lock fell back against her cheek.

"What?"

"The zebras. I had to wait for them to escape."

"Wait a minute. Escape what?"

"They were being chased by a lion and I wasn't about to slow them down. I stopped my jeep and waited. I'll admit, I didn't just sit there. I mean, who could pass up an opportunity like that to take photographs? But I did drive here as fast as I could once they passed. And they did get away. The zebras, I mean. Not that I want the lion to starve. She probably had cubs to feed. But I certainly didn't want to witness the kill. You know what I mean?"

No, he didn't. But, boy, could she talk. And he kind of wished said lion wasn't out there hungry. Not with his daughters being escape artists.

"I don't know where this zebra crossing happened, but the girls aren't allowed anywhere near there. I don't want them in any sort of danger, got it?"

"You do realize where we are, right? Wild animals aren't restricted to one area. This isn't a zoo."

"I get enough snark from my kids. I'm fully aware that this isn't a zoo, which is why maybe you should stick around the lodge, especially for the first day, and see how things go. Look. I'm running late. I have a schedule printed out here," he said, grabbing the sheet of paper off the small desk and handing it to her. "Also, I'd prefer it if you and the girls didn't touch any of my paperwork or printed maps. You shouldn't have to remind the girls. They know my work is off-limits."

"Yes, sir," Pippa said, taking the sheet with a salute. "I'm not a nosy person. Your work stuff is safe from me." She scanned the schedule. "Is this really how their day is supposed to go?" She scrunched her face at him and held the sheet up?

"Yes. That's why it's called a *schedule*. I don't have time to argue. I'm paying you to stick to it, okay? And keep a close eye on them."

"It's the only kind I keep. I'm sure they'll be fine. They're not the first kids I've worked with, and they seemed so well behaved that I can't imagine their being any trouble at all. And can I just point out that you're the one who begged me to watch them?"

He noticed her gaze shift, and he glanced over his shoulder. The twins were standing behind him looking as innocent as could be. He couldn't argue in front of them, particularly if the argument was *about* them.

"I'll leave you all to it, then. Ivy. Fern. Be good. Ms. Harper. The schedule."

"Yes. The schedule. And please don't call me Ms. Harper. It makes me sound like a prissy schoolteacher. I prefer to go by Pippa."

The girls giggled, and Fern stepped to his side and looped her arm in his.

"Don't worry about us, Dad. We'll listen to Miss Pippa and get all our work done."

"Right. Good."

He didn't believe it. But he didn't have a choice except to leave Pippa to the lions right now. He zipped up the duffel bag that held a spare pair of jeans and a T-shirt, in case he needed them and grabbed his laptop. His hard hat and utility vest were already on-site. He glanced at his watch again.

"There's a satellite phone on the desk with the number where I'll be. See you later," he said, heading for the door.

"Oh, wait. One more thing before you leave." Pippa stepped close to his side and lowered her voice. "How do you tell them apart?"

PIPPA SHUT THE door behind Dax and leaned back against it. Ivy stood with her arms crossed and a smirk on her face. Fern rocked on her heels with her hands clasped behind her.

She was so going to make them pay for the damage they'd done to her book.

She smiled.

"So, girls. Let's take a look at what you're supposed to be doing. Um, let's see, no history today? Did you finish that book you were reading?"

"Yep," Ivy said, collapsing into a wicker lounge chair and kicking her feet up on the matching ottoman. "Did you finish yours?"

Ivy gave her sister a look, but Fern stared boldly at Pippa. *Ivy is purple and Fern is green. Right.* Boy, was this going to be fun. *Not.*

Their dad had her worried there. He did not look happy when she walked in late, and if he fired her before she even started, she'd be out a lot of money. Not to mention the page from her book. Only she wouldn't be the one really losing out. This was about the kids out there who needed a teacher, not about her or the two kids in front of her who took what they had for granted. She stood as tall as she could.

"No, I haven't finished mine yet." It wasn't a lie. She hated lies. Lies ruined lives. Lies caused pain. These girls had better tell the truth about the book page. She wasn't going to let on that she knew about it just yet, though. Nope. Getting mad would only feed their entertainment. "How about starting with social studies?"

"But we're supposed to clean our rooms first. That's what we were doing when you got here, and we're not quite done," Fern said.

"As long as it's done before your dad gets

back, I don't see a problem with changing things up."

"But the schedule says—"

"The schedule says that you have a social studies paper to write, so I say let's get the essays done so that we can go do something social. Besides, flexibility is an important lesson when it comes to living in this world. Consider it part of your lesson."

Ivy and Fern looked dumbfounded.

"Do you have kids? Are you married?" Fern asked.

Pippa's stomach recoiled and she fought to keep the prickle of self-doubt that still plagued her every so often in check. *Almost.* She was over it…past it…but the betrayal and heartbreak that had changed her life and all her future plans still had a way of creeping out of the darkness and grabbing her by the ankles.

Changes. That's all it was. She was feeling uncertain because this was a new job and it was reminding her subconscious of how grueling changes could be. She stood her ground.

"No to both questions. Why do you ask?"

"Because every nanny we've ever had

was either a spinster type who couldn't wait to get away at the end of the day, or single and anxious to leave for their dates," Ivy said. How many nannies had they had? Maybe she was better off not knowing.

"Wrong," Fern said. "There was the one who loved being around, but not because of us. She was crushing on Dad."

Oh, for crying out loud. She wasn't crushing on their dad…even though she had to admit he looked really good dressed ruggedly in jeans, a T-shirt and work boots.

"I assure you, I'm not here because of your dad. He's not my type." No one was her type right now. The last thing she needed was another relationship. But it wasn't hard to read between the lines of what the girls were saying. The twins felt second-best. Boy, did she know that feeling. "Listen, I have things I do other than helping take care of the two of you, but when I'm here, I'm here. You have my undivided attention and I hope I have yours."

Their lips twisted and they folded their arms. Interesting.

"So, you're going to sit and watch us write essays? Isn't that boring?" Fern asked.

"Yeah," Ivy added. "The nannies we've had before usually leave us to do our work…since we're so responsible and all… and they go get coffee or something. You can go if you want and come back when we're done."

Pippa went over to her bag and pulled out her book.

"I won't be the least bit bored. I plan to finish reading this mystery so that I can loan it to your dad. I figured he might want to read it while he watches you guys swim at the pool."

"He doesn't read mysteries. He prefers scientific magazines," Fern said.

"Science? I thought he was in business. Those types tend to prefer magazines like *Forbes* or *The Economist*."

"Um…yeah. Land business," Ivy said, frowning.

"Oh. Okay," Pippa said. That explained his outfit today. Maybe he was a developer or an architect looking to build another safari lodge in the area. The idea of overdeveloping this wilderness made her cringe. They already had enough lodges and camps. She wasn't going to ask his kids behind his back. It wasn't right. "Well, if he likes science, this book has a lot of scientific evidence in it. I'm sure he'll love it."

"He'll never read it," Fern insisted.

"Yes, he will. He told me he wants to borrow it." A huge, massive, unforgivable white lie. "What's the fun in a book if you can't share what you're reading with someone? Like you two, both reading the same history assignment so that you can discuss it."

The twins glanced at each other and Ivy nibbled at her bottom lip. At least *she* seemed to have a conscience. Wait a minute. Dax had told her that Fern was the more timid one. Ivy, purple. Fern, green. Hmm.

"Grab your assignments and let's sit at the patio table. It's too nice of a day to stay in here. We can head out after that." Pippa waited for them to gather their things and followed them out. The day was warm with a slight breeze that carried the scent of jasmine toward them. A perfect day for daydreaming. She sat and flipped the book open to just enough pages before the missing one to keep them on edge. Twenty minutes later, neither had written as much as a word; they'd merely fidgeted and passed notes. From the corner of her eye, Pippa watched the one she was beginning to suspect was Fern squirming, but Ivy kept nudging her with her elbow and scowling at her to stop.

"Oh, gosh, this is getting good," Pippa said, as she flipped another page. She looked up. "Sorry, I didn't mean to say that out loud and interrupt your work." She resumed reading.

"Um, we sort of—" Fern jolted when Ivy kicked her under the table.

Pippa slapped the book shut and stood.

"I know what you did. I'm totally on to you two."

"You are?"

"Yep. I can see that you sort-of-never-really did your reading yesterday, right? Which is why you have nothing to write about."

The girls' shoulders relaxed.

"That's right. I mean, we were reading, but didn't finish," Ivy said.

"You weren't really reading. Were you?" Pippa asked. She turned to the one in the purple headband. "Tell the truth, Ivy. Fern probably has better grades and does all of your essays for you, right?"

"That's not true! My grades are just as good as hers," the real Ivy to her left immediately countered, then froze.

"I thought so. How about wearing your own headbands?"

The girls reluctantly traded all purple and green accessories.

"How'd you know?"

"I didn't. Not for certain, at least. Thanks for the admission, though. Care to admit to not reading, too?"

Ivy made a face.

"Is that how it's going to be?"

"No—actually..."

"Shut up, Fern," Ivy said.

"Hey, you two. No need for that. I just want to hear if you did or didn't read the history book. Because if you didn't, I have an idea that'll give you something to write about, and it involves a whole lot more adventure than sitting around here," Pippa said.

That got Ivy's attention.

"But Dad said to stick to the lodge." As

if Ivy cared about rules. A lion's roar startled the twins.

"Don't worry. It's not close by." She stood and tucked her chair in. "What your father said was that I had to keep an eye on you and help you get your lessons done. We'll be doing that. I mean, really, now. Don't you two *ever* have fun?"

DAX WIPED THE sweat from his forehead and adjusted his sunglasses and hard hat. The afternoon sun beat down on the back of his neck.

Meeting with Ron again that morning had gone smoothly enough. Unexpectedly, he'd brought a younger engineer along with him—Steven—and assigned him to help out with Dax's team. He also produced the general timetable for fracking activity in the adjacent field that was getting pumped. Dax had asked for the information yesterday, so that he could make out any interference activity in his readings. So now as he had a team of three of his own men—Syd, Lee and Alberto—plus two drivers, a cook and Steven…all provided by Erebus. Right now, Lee was in the trailer recording station checking all of their computer systems and programs. Syd and Alberto were helping Dax lay out geophones in straight lines and at even intervals, pressing their spiked ends into the dry soil like small lawn sprinklers, only without the sprinkler mechanism. He surveyed their work every thirty feet or so to make sure the grid line were getting laid evenly. Good 3D mapping and data depended, in part, on their geophone grid.

Steven carried over the cables Dax requested so that he could begin connecting the geophone receivers.

They'd be doing this for days. And they had to get the grid set up before they could bring in the Vibroseis trucks to send acoustic waves below the earth so they could start receiving data on subterranean structures based on those sound waves hitting them. That's when the real work would begin for Dax—analyzing data via computer programs and mapping out what sat deep beneath their feet.

Seeing all those readouts and fine lines kicked his pulse up. He got to see things the average person didn't…structures and formations thousands of feet down. A different kind of wilderness or undiscovered frontier...far from human touch, yet not impervious to human impact. Much like the Serengeti.

He stretched his back and looked westward. A chorus of wildlife calls echoed through the area as if protesting man's invasion. They were answered with the sound of a truck engine roaring to life.

He was selling his soul, all right.

Before Sandy died, his time in the field had been invigorating. Seeing activity on the seismograph readings had fueled him to do more. To chase what his colleagues claimed was beyond his reach—to come up with a way to accurately predict the big ones. A way to warn people when an earthquake was about to strike.

And now, here he was in the sweltering heat, at the beck and call of someone else. Gathering data that paid the bills, but betrayed his conscience. He was betraying his friend Josh and all the others who had died with him.

He paused and looked at the dappled landscape. A herd of gazelle grazed in the distance, and the cry of a hawk pierced through the air as its shadow swept over him.

It was no secret that Sandy had been a vocal environmental activist in her college days. It was how they had met. She was spearheading a relief fund-raiser for earthquake victims, and after the tsunami, he'd needed to do something more than just wallow in grief. She had pulled him through. She had even continued to volunteer for nonprofits before getting pregnant with the twins. And how had he repaid her? By leaving her to take on the bulk of raising two preemies and eventually toddlers so that he could figure out how to save them all in the future, rather than embracing them in the present.

What would she think of him now?

If she was looking down on him, she'd know he was doing what he had to do. She'd know he was still paying off the medical bills from their premature twins and those that had piled up during her cancer treatments. That he was doing what he had to do to give the girls a more stable life and save for simultaneous college tuitions in the future. He was doing what Sandy had wished for—for him to stop chasing after what had become an obsession. For him to just be a "normal" husband and father who came home every night to spend it with his wife and kids.

Well, maybe lugging the girls to off-the-grid locations wasn't what the average dad did, but he was never far from them. He came home to them every night. He could only hope she knew that and that it somehow comforted her.

He swallowed but his throat stuck. He trudged over to his jeep and pulled out his thermos and took a long drink. Steven glanced over at him, and Dax held up the canteen to signal that everyone should take a water break, too.

"You guys are efficient," Steven said, taking a swig from his own canteen.

"We know our stuff. It's why we're here," Dax said. There was something about the guy he didn't like. "I also have to make it back to the lodge in time for my nanny to go home tonight."

Pippa wasn't around to hear him call her a nanny, and he wasn't about to mention her by name. If as many folks knew her and her family in these parts as she claimed, it would be better for him not to complicate things with the people he answered to at Erebus. How long of a drive did Pippa say she had to get home before dark?

"Oh, yeah. I heard you brought kids along. Most of the guys out here are either single or have their families living in Nairobi. They go see them on weekends. Except those whose families aren't in Kenya. It's easier that way, and when the family is far away, the site workers never have a problem with working overtime."

Had Ron Swale fed Steven that line? Dax knew all about working overtime. It wasn't happening anymore.

Long, geometric shadows stretched from his equipment to where they stood, as the sun dipped a couple of degrees lower.

"I do have kids here and not staying on-site is what works for me. We'll still have all the mapping done on schedule."

"I get it. Sort of. I'm not married nor do I plan to be. I've gotta hand it to you, juggling it all."

"Yeah." Dax didn't want to talk anymore.

Working in silence suited him just fine. Especially around guys who did *not* get it. "I have it down to a science."

PIPPA WATCHED AS Ivy and Fern joined the circle. Hesitant at first, but seemingly enthralled by the Maasai girls' dress and, particularly, their earrings. Etiana handed each twin a beaded bracelet, and Ivy's face beamed.

"Thank you so much. You made this yourself?"

"Yes. I made one for Pippa once, too, because she taught me to read. She's a special friend and now I have two more special friends." She smiled at Ivy and Fern.

"Thank you, as well," Fern said, slipping on the bracelet. "What's your favorite book?"

"Oh, whichever one Pippa gives me to read. Each one is a different experience. A journey I can't take except in a book. I wished to give you a special gift to remember me by with those bracelets, but the most precious gift I have ever gotten is a book…and learning to read it. We have no bookstores here. If it weren't for Pippa…"

She glanced up at Pippa and pressed her hand to her heart in gratitude. Ivy and Fern looked at each other, but instead of conspiracy or mischief on their faces, there was shame.

"Someday you'll write your own book," Pippa told Etiana.

"And you can bet that we'll buy copies," Fern said.

"And we'll have to find you so that you can sign them for us," Ivy added.

Etiana's face wasn't the only thing that lit up. Pippa felt her heart do somersaults. They were getting it. They were finally understanding.

"Me? Write a book?"

"Well, if you want to. You can do anything you set your mind to. Doctor, lawyer, teacher, filmmaker or even an astronaut. The world is your oyster," Pippa said, walking over and sitting next to them. "Same goes for you, Ivy and Fern. And all the children here."

Ivy hesitated, then reached into her backpack and unfolded a piece of paper. *The page*.

"We're really sorry. It was a stupid thing

to do, but we weren't thinking at the time. We took this page out of your book, hoping you'd be irritated enough to leave us be—"

"Yeah, like the others did," Fern added, referring to their other nannies. Had they wanted all their nannies out of the way? Pippa could come up with only one reason why they'd want that—to force their dad to spend more time with them. It was the only thing that made sense, other than a fear of Dax replacing their mother. Or maybe he didn't talk to them about her enough. Or maybe they were clinging to their dad because they were afraid of losing him, too.

"But messing up your book was a bad thing to do. I wanted to tell you what we'd done before you got to the page and found it missing."

Fern nodded in agreement. Etiana smiled sympathetically.

"Girls, I reached that page long ago. I'm not the kind of woman who gives up. Especially not on those she cares about."

Their foreheads crinkled and lips parted.

"You knew?"

Pippa nodded.

"And you didn't quit?" Fern asked.

"Or tell Dad on us?" Ivy added.

Pippa shook her head.

"She has what we say in Swahili is *moyo mwema*, a good heart." Etiana said.

Ivy frowned and didn't say anything else.

"The page can be taped in. Just don't ever destroy a book again. And maybe you'll enjoy reading it after I'm done. Unless you already read the missing page and know how it all turns out." She turned to Etiana. "The girls and I have to head back before I get in trouble for taking them too far away from the lodge."

"We won't let Dad get mad at you," Fern said.

"Yeah, we've got your back," Ivy said, but something in her eyes made Pippa wonder if the twins weren't the type to give up, either.

"So long as you don't drop anything like a spider down my shirt," Pippa warned.

"We'd never do something so awful," Fern said, looping her arm in Ivy's and heading to the jeep. They waved back at the other children who'd made up the circle.

"I like them," Etiana said.

"Maybe I'll bring them to visit again," Pippa said, marching after them. She waved again from the jeep and headed for Tabara.

"We heard you tell Dad about the zebras and lions. Will we get to see any?"

"Eventually, I'm sure. Just keep your eyes peeled. Can't guarantee we'll pass them today. You two still have those papers to finish."

"I was hoping you forgot," Ivy said, yelling over the engine noise. Fern held tight to the door frame.

"I never forget. I have the memory of an elephant."

She stepped on the gas, and the girls squealed as she hit a rut in the dirt. Maybe if they got their adrenaline kick on the ride, they'd be less likely to pull stunts at the lodge.

They made it back in plenty of time and everything on the list was done. Dax, however, was still not home.

"You don't think he got lost, do you?" Fern nibbled at her thumbnail as she held out a piece of tape for Ivy with her other hand.

"No, I'm sure his driver knows his way

around. He probably got caught up in work." Pippa didn't need to check her watch to know she'd never make it to Busara before dark at this point. And he'd been mad at her for being late this morning?

At least she'd only been late by a few minutes. Not almost an hour. And her being late didn't keep him from heading to work, whereas she was going to be stuck at Tabara for the night.

She wasn't afraid to make the drive after dark, but she had enough experience and common sense to know that making the drive alone in the dark wasn't worth the risk. Nocturnal predators...and even illegal poachers...came out of the shadows at night. It was one of those things she would have done two years ago, worrying her family to death in the process, but she wasn't the same person anymore.

"Or maybe caught up at an elephant crossing," Ivy joked, as she held Pippa's book page in place and took the tape from her sister. Pippa chuckled.

"Or that."

The door to the bungalow finally swung open and Dax shuffled in, easing his bag through the doorway and setting it down. He looked sun kissed and utterly wiped out. The girls ran over and gave him a hug. He kissed each one on the top of her head and squeezed his arms around them.

"Hey, you two. Sorry I'm late."

"We thought you'd been eaten by lions," Ivy said.

"Seriously?"

"No." She and Fern giggled and went back to mending the book. They may have teased him, but Pippa could see there had been a tension in their faces that was now dissipating.

"I'm sorry," Dax said to Pippa. He had the decency to appear ashamed after giving her the third degree this morning about being on time.

"So, now you understand sticking to the minute around here is harder than it seems," Pippa quipped.

"Only, my delays were caused entirely by humans, and had nothing to do with zebras and lions. I'll pay you for the extra hours, of course."

"I have no doubt you'll keep track of it all. I do have a schedule to stick to, though.

I can't have you running late all the time," she said, hoping he caught the jab. She fetched her backpack from next to the desk.

He looked up at the ceiling and put his hands on his hips.

"It's dark out."

"I can see that."

"I realize this is my fault and that you live in this area and know it like the back of your hand, but isn't driving a couple of hours to get home too dangerous right now?"

"Yes. It is. Which is why I'll be reading in the lounge area."

He walked over to where Ivy and Fern were smoothing out the crumpled page they'd taped up. They quickly shut the book and stood in front of it.

"What happened to the book?" Dax asked. His eyes narrowed, and the twins' got wider.

"I had a mishap with it and Ivy and Fern kindly offered to help me fix it. You have great kids. Thank you, girls," Pippa said, taking the book from them. Their chests sank and shoulders relaxed as they glanced at each other.

"Oh. That was nice of you to fix the book." He sounded as relieved as they looked.

"I'll see you all in the morning," Pippa said.

"Wait. You're planning to read in the lounge all night?"

"Yes." Pippa shrugged. "I'm sure I'll fall asleep, but I doubt anyone will mind too much. Just don't do this to me every night."

"Tell her she can stay with us tonight, Dad," Fern said.

"You can stay with us," Dax said, almost too quickly.

Pippa stared at them and blinked.

"I don't think that's a good idea. You need to spend time with Ivy and Fern, and it has been a long day. I'm sure everyone's exhausted."

"I'm sure you are, too," Dax said. "And sleeping on a chair in the lounge isn't right. I can't have you do that because I made you late."

She'd be in a chair either way. The bungalow-style suite had one separate bedroom with its own bath—the room the twins were sharing...and it had only two twin beds in it. The other bed was in this main room, with only a small sitting area to the side and a separate small half bath. Staying in the same room, even if it was in a chair, with Dax was not going to happen.

"But there aren't enough beds, so I guess she'll have to," Ivy said.

They all looked at her. Someone was protective of time with her dad. At least Ivy was on the same wavelength as Pippa. She slung her backpack onto her shoulder, ready to leave.

"Ivy, there's always enough room when it's needed." Dax gave her a pointed look, and the girl didn't answer back. He turned to Pippa. "You can stay in the twins' room with them. You'll have more privacy that way. I can move this mattress in there for you."

She knew he meant privacy with respect to him. She appreciated that, though she wasn't sure the girls wanted to spend the night with her after she'd been looking over their shoulders the whole day.

On the other hand, a lot of people passed through the lodge at night, and she wasn't familiar with many of the employees.

Sleeping here as opposed to out in the common area would be safer. She'd have to radio Busara to let everyone know not to worry or to expect her.

"You don't have to give up your bed. I've done plenty of camping. I can sleep on the floor in the bedroom."

"Leave that up to me," he said, as he took the decorative, woven pillows off his bed so that he could move the futon-style mattress. Pippa dropped her backpack and tried to jump in and help support the mattress, but he'd already lifted it, balancing it to his side, and was halfway through the bedroom door. His strength was…unexpected. He didn't look brawny, but the way his biceps flexed against his shirt clearly indicated he didn't spend his days behind a desk.

"Okay, then," she said, twisting the corner of her lips and splaying her hands to Ivy and Fern. "I hope you don't mind. I promise I don't snore."

That earned a grin from Fern, but not from Ivy. Pippa sighed. How could she explain that she wasn't a threat when it came to their dad? Not only was he not her type—nor she his—she wasn't trying to infiltrate their family unit. Dax had come to her for the job. He was the one who'd been late and created this situation.

"Whatever," Ivy said.

"It'll be fun. Like a slumber party," Fern said, elbowing her sister.

Dax stepped back into the room.

"It's all set. I'm pretty sure there are enough towels in that bathroom."

"Thank you. I think I'll just retire early, if you all don't mind. Ivy, Fern, don't worry about waking me when you're ready for bed. Just go about your normal routine. I'm a deep sleeper."

An hour later, when they did slip into the room, Pippa was lying on her mattress engrossed in the last pages of her book. No one said anything, and she didn't look up. She heard the girls cleaning up and then climbing into their beds.

They turned off the lamp between their beds, but the smaller one near Pippa remained on. She finished the last page and took a deep breath, relishing that sublime feeling that always came over her when she finished a good book. She reached up and switched off her light, then curled on her side, nestling her cheek against the pillow, her lids heavy with the images from the story. Moonlight streaked across the room, giving it a dreamy glow. A clean scent from the pillows enveloped her. It wasn't soap. It was too warm and heady for soap. It was Dax's shampoo or maybe his cologne.

"Miss Pippa?"

"Yes, Ivy?" Pippa turned her face up to distance herself from his scent.

"Thanks for not telling Dad the real reason we were taping your book."

She'd earned a little of Ivy's trust. Something settled across her chest like dust motes dancing in a moonbeam.

"No worries. Get some sleep."

With that, she quietly moved the pillow out from under her head and set it as far away as she could reach, then she tucked her arm under her head and hoped the mystery she'd just finished would fill her dreams, so there would be no room for the mystery of Dax.

PIPPA WAS GETTING a headache. Dax had left for work early, since she'd stayed over and he didn't have to wait on her arrival. Sleeping over had made the day seem even longer and more trying. She'd lost count by early afternoon as to how many times the twins had tricked her by switching their color-coded accessories. They'd even played the parts, and in retrospect, she should have picked up on the fact that "Fern's" snarkiness was a bit off.

Right now, trying to remember who was who when they'd completed different homework assignments, including online tests, was making her temples pound. She pressed her fingers against her eyes and squeezed.

She needed to straighten this out before Dax got back. She'd tell him because it had to do with their studies, but she wanted to show him she'd handled things, too. She had a reputation to uphold at the lodge, and the last thing she needed was word getting out that she was incompetent or couldn't tell kids apart. Granted these two were identical, but still, they were individuals with enough personality differences and expressions that she should have noticed. Maybe if she'd slept better her instincts would be sharper.

Don't think about their dad so much.

Her conscience needed to shut up. That was so not the reason they were able to mess with her. She wasn't distracted. She was worried about his opinion of her.

"Miss Pippa?"

"Quiet." She held up a finger without looking at them. They'd used up her patience. She had them each sitting on opposite sides of the room studying on their e-readers.

"But we're sorry," Fern said. "Really sorry. Research shows that identical twins like to exchange roles. It helps them to explore their individuality."

Seriously? Pippa turned and raised a brow at her.

"It helps them to trick people, is what it does. I've seen *The Parent Trap*." On DVD, years ago, at her uncle and aunt's house in Nairobi since there was no TV at Busara.

"That movie wasn't about individuality. It was about the twins trying to be matchmakers to get their parents back together," Ivy said. "Trust me. We're not trying to play matchmaker for you and Dad."

Pippa's cheeks burned like molten

magma rising to the surface. Any second she'd blow her top.

"I certainly hope not," she said.

"Don't bother, Fern. She probably doesn't care about our emotional development. She barely knows us, so why should she?"

"I *do* care. But you two don't seem to appreciate whether I'm nice or not nice. Or whether we follow your father's schedule like military cadets or throw in some flexibility and weave in some fun. I'm starting to understand why he has you under strict rules."

The satellite phone she kept nearby rang in that moment, and she grabbed it.

"Hello." She kept her eyes on the girls.

"It's Dax. I'm just checking on Ivy and Fern."

A parent's sixth sense.

"They are—" She eyed them both and caved. They looked nervous. Vulnerable. She could remember being in their position a time or two at their age. "Everything is under control."

"That implies something wasn't," he said. "What happened?"

"Nothing. I just got their colors mixed

up for a bit, but that's all straightened out now. We're good."

"I see." There was a pause. "You're sure?"

She took a deep breath.

"I'm totally sure. You deal with work." *I'll deal with you monsters.*

"Okay."

She disconnected and faced the twins.

"You told on us."

"Not really. He guessed. I could have said a lot more but didn't." Because she was a masochist…or a saint. Or she simply hoped to get through to them.

Ivy and Fern glanced at each other and put their readers down.

"I guess you're right," Fern said. "Why didn't you?"

"Because everyone deserves the chance to make things right."

"Or she's probably waiting to tell him in person," Ivy said.

"Not true. But if he asks directly, I won't lie."

"Told you," Ivy said to her sister.

"That's what our last nanny said, too. She was always trying to brown-nose him."

"Yeah. Our mom died when we were little and our other nannies never liked us. They were mean and ugly," Ivy said.

"*She*'s not ugly," Fern whispered over her shoulder.

"Shh." Ivy scowled at Fern. Something passed between them. A look. An expression. Something Pippa couldn't quite decipher.

"And they never played with us. Not even board games, or doing fun things like playing hairdresser or painting our toenails," Fern added, after another look from Ivy.

"Yeah. They were dictators," Ivy said. "See, I did read my history lesson."

They looked at her through their lashes. Were they exaggerating to get sympathy? The girls glanced at each other. They really did seem sincere. So that's why they hated nannies. No wonder they had to resort to entertaining themselves—the wrong way. She rubbed her forehead and sat down. How could she lose her patience with them after what they'd been through?

"Girls, I'm sorry about the nannies you've had before, and especially that you lost your mother. I know that was painful, and I'm sure you miss her."

Ivy swallowed before frowning and tried to gather herself. Fern's nose turned red. Pippa saw both of their eyes fill with tears. They weren't faking now.

"Not having our mother around is the worst," Fern said.

"How about we forget serious stuff for the rest of the day and do whatever you want?" In all honesty, Pippa's head hurt too much to think about their schedule.

"Anything? Really?" Ivy asked.

"Really. As long as it's not dangerous. Your father would kill me. My headache is bad enough without my worrying about him trying."

"Can we play girl spa? We could fix your hair and give you a head massage the way they do at the hairdresser's."

"They do that?" She'd never had her hair professionally done. Not even in Europe.

"Yep. Nanny Number Five said so," Fern said, then covered her mouth.

"Number Five? Do I want to know what number I am?"

"It doesn't matter. You're the only one we've had on this continent," Ivy said, matter-of-factly.

They took her by the hands and led her to their bathroom.

"We should do this before Dad gets home. He's not a girl, so having him here will spoil the fun," Fern said.

They pulled up a wooden chair near the sink for her to sit on. Pippa complied. No harm in letting the poor girls enjoy themselves a little. Everyone needed a break now and then. Plus, maybe this *would* get rid of her headache.

"Just lean your head back and relax." Ivy lifted Pippa's curls over the edge of the basin. "Now close your eyes and enjoy the spa treatment."

"This is so much fun. I'll paint your nails after we wash your hair," Fern said.

"I'm in charge of hair washing. Fern, get me that *really good* conditioner we bought when grandma took us to the mall. The expensive stuff. You know?"

"Uh, oh yes. That stuff is really, *really* good."

"You don't have to use anything expensive on me. Don't waste it. My hair is impossible no matter what," Pippa said.

"Your hair is fantastic. Wild. Free. Love it," Ivy said. "I really want to dye mine pitch-black, but maybe I'll go auburn like yours and get a perm."

"Don't get a perm. You'll ruin your hair. You both have such beautiful hair."

She listened as the water ran behind her head and felt like she was melting as Ivy gently sluiced it over her hair. It was so good and soothing. It was a warm day, but they'd opened the patio doors and the breeze coming through hypnotized her.

"Here's the shampoo and conditioner. Fancy stuff," Fern said.

She relaxed as the girls giggled and massaged her head. Had they never done this for previous babysitters? Because, man, this was worth all their escapades put together.

"This conditioner is supposed to be left in for fifteen minutes, but we'll paint each other's nails while you relax here," Ivy said.

They massaged something cold and thick into her scalp.

"What's this stuff made of?" she asked, her lids heavy.

"Oh, a mixture of nutrients and minerals. They soak into the hair and make it healthier. It's called 'Nothing-Like-It Curly Hair Remedy.'"

"Well, if it tames my curls, I'm game."

"It'll do just that. Trust me. Your hair won't fly anywhere after this."

"Okay, now we're going to do our toes and we'll come back to rinse your head when it's done."

"Just nap," Fern said. "It'll help your headache."

"But you two will stay in the room, right?"

"Of course. We'll try to keep our voices down, though, because of your headache. Or we'll just read."

"Okay. I must admit this feels good."

It did. Enough that she dozed in and out of consciousness. The pain in her temples was gone. No more throbbing. No more noise…

"Do you know where the twins are?"

That voice was anything but breezy and ethereal. She opened her eyes, and Dax was staring down at her with a bewildered look on his face. She shot up and looked around the room. How long had she dozed off? Awhile, if Dax was home. Oh, God.

"They were just here. Ivy, Fern!"

Dax just stared at her.

She stared back.

"I swear they were here. In this room. They just wanted to do girl stuff and they'd been so...good... I let them convince me to be a guinea pig so they could play spa and—"

"You volunteered to be a guinea pig? For my twins?"

"Well...yes." Was there something wrong with that?

Dax's face reddened and he braced his hands on his hips.

"You were supposed to be watching over them and teaching them, not using them to get your hair done."

"Oh, no." Pippa suddenly had total recall. She reached up and touched her head. Her hair felt hard. She tried to tug a strand from her scalp, but it didn't budge. She glanced in the mirror and gasped. Mud. They'd plastered her hair in thick, clay-like mud. The kind the Maasai built huts with. Her head looked like a badly built *inkajijik*. "This was supposed to be conditioner. They were going to rinse it out." They'd tricked her again. Evil nannies, huh?

Remember you're doing this for the money. Think of how far it will go to fund a school, all the books you'll be able to buy for the village children.

"You have no idea where they are and you're still worried about your hair?" he hissed.

"No! I'll find them."

"With your head like that?"

"I couldn't care less about my hair. I had a headache and…never mind. I swear they can't be far. Kids explore the lodge all the time on their own. They'll be okay. I'll find them."

She started to move past him. She'd be the laugh of the lodge, running around with mud on her head, searching for them, but that was the least of her worries. She'd fallen asleep on the job. Her reputation was ruined, not to mention she'd just blown her chance to earn more money for her school. Surely, Dax would fire her over this.

She took a deep breath and squeezed her eyes shut in frustration. He was eyeing her like some science experiment gone bad, but she wasn't trying to impress him with her looks. She didn't care if he found her unattractive. She absolutely didn't. Men were the last thing she needed in her life right now, and this one came with the equivalent of twenty kids packed into two.

What bothered her was the fact that she'd lost any respect he might have had for her. He'd see her as someone who needed to be taken care of, rather than a grown, responsible woman. Just like Haki had.

Haki had always acted as if she was a danger to herself. Like he had to rescue her from herself. And he'd ended up being her greatest danger. She'd given him her heart, and he'd crushed it in the worst way possible. She hadn't been enough for him. She wasn't even enough for Dax as a nanny.

How would anyone take her seriously if word got out about this? The lodge might pull its agreement with her to run the children's safari. Sleeping while supervising kids was a liability. No income would mean no money for her school.

Giggles emanated from the living room area, and she heard the words *mud head* and *napping nanny*.

"They're here? You knew?" She could

feel her cheeks heat up. Her temples were starting to throb again.

"Would I be standing here with you if I didn't?"

Pippa's jaw ached, and she unclenched her teeth.

"No. You'd be out there searching for them. Like I was about to do."

"You wouldn't have had to do that if you'd stayed awake while you were on duty."

God help her, she didn't have to put up with this. She needed to leave.

"I'll get out of your hair." She closed her eyes again. Had she really just said that? "I mean, I'll leave immediately."

Dax sucked his cheeks in and started for the bedroom door. A chuckle escaped him as he left, followed a few seconds later by a loud and firm "now."

Ivy and Fern shuffled through the doorway. They looked behind them, presumably to Dax in the other room.

"We're sorry," Ivy said, pursing her lips. She and Fern exchanged a smile. They knew their dad couldn't see their faces. "We'll help you wash it out."

"I'll wash my own hair." How she'd manage that without clogging the drains and having the lodge kick them all out, she had no idea. "I can't use the bathroom for this. I'm going to have to wash it outside. Please find me a container to carry the water out. I'd get one myself, but I don't think this look is the guest image Tabara Lodge is after."

Dax appeared behind them.

"You two go get the pitcher in my bathroom and the bin by the desk." They obeyed and he tucked his hands in his pockets as he faced Pippa again. "I don't know what to say. I'll make them earn the money to pay for a professional who can help you. I mean for your hair…not a therapist. Well, maybe hair therapy. Like the kind at the spa here. Not that—"

"I'm not the one who needs help. Besides, I thought I was fired."

"Did I say you were fired?"

"No, but I assumed after this that you wouldn't want to see me here again."

"I don't want you sleeping while you're supposed to be watching them, for your safety and theirs, but you're not fired." He scratched his jaw and cocked his head. "Look, I know they can be a handful and they're masters at pranking. I can't blame you entirely for what happened."

The girls returned to the bathroom with the supplies and Dax turned on the faucet. Pippa marched outside and sat on one of the patio chairs with her head hanging forward. She caught an upside-down view of a couple in the next bungalow staring as they walked by. The girls ran back and forth from the bathroom, getting water and pouring it on her head to wet the mud. It started to glob and drip onto the ground.

She had no pride left. She couldn't possibly get any more embarrassed than this.

Then Dax showed up with another container of water and began rubbing the mud out of her hair himself.

CHAPTER FIVE

DAX LEFT BEFORE breakfast the next day. He figured the earlier he left, the sooner he'd get back. And the sooner he got back, the less chance Pippa would have to stay the night again.

He'd barely been able to sleep the night she'd stayed over, and it wasn't because he'd slept on the floor. Like her, he'd camped out plenty of times over the course of his career, taking seismic readings well into the night. Not in the past couple of years, sure, but it hadn't been the floor that had kept him up. His back was fine. It was his brain that was weak.

He couldn't seem to grasp what it was about her, but she kept popping into his head last night. Her scent had lingered in the room long after she'd escaped to the twins' bedroom. It wasn't the noxious perfume Nanny Number Five had worn until he broke down and told her it triggered his migraines. Pippa smelled of mangoes and something citrusy, light and fresh. He liked it. That scared him.

He didn't want to be thinking about her. He sure as heck didn't need to be. He had enough to worry about.

He hadn't missed the look on Ivy's face when he'd invited Pippa to stay. He'd also heard her protest loud and clear. His girls were determined to chase Pippa off, just as they'd done with all their previous nannies.

But from what he could tell, Pippa Harper wasn't easily fazed. She hadn't even ratted on them about the torn book. Oh, he'd noticed the crumpled book page. He'd have bet money it hadn't been an accident. The fact that she'd kept that to herself spoke volumes about her.

He pinched the bridge of his nose. Then there was yesterday and the mud fiasco. He'd thought for sure she'd quit on him, but she didn't. She had shown up right on time this morning. She was either stubborn and tenacious or patient as a saint. Whichever it was, it meant she was good for the twins.

And that was the only reason he wanted her to stick around.

Except washing her hair had been so… personal. He could still feel the softness of her hair in his hands and the warmth of her skin lingered long after he'd held her arms to steady her when she'd risen from her head-down position too quickly. He rubbed his palms against his jeans and tried to focus on setting out more of the geophone grid. They had another four square miles to cover before they could start using the Vibroseis trucks.

He leaned over and pressed another geophone stake in the ground as his crew laid out a parallel grid line. The seismic data he'd looked at when he'd arrived early this morning was also bothering him. It had nothing to do with their survey, but he wondered if the fracking in the adjacent drilling field had had any bearing on it.

Despite Ron's comment on day one, Dax had set up his own equipment—a separate seismograph, high precision GPS and a few other basics. He hadn't brought anything like lasers or strain gauges that he'd used in research before, so data would be limited, but to come out here near the famous Rift Valley and not get any readings would have eaten away at him. His team knew it, too. They also knew not to let Ron, Steven or anyone else touch his personal equipment when he was at Tabara.

Syd, Lee and Alberto were the ones who'd handed him a cup of coffee this morning and the readouts they'd registered after he'd left yesterday. There were definitely tremors in the area. Some crust movement was expected so close to fault lines, but compared to older data he'd seen for the area, there seemed to be an increase…a few anomalies that correlated with Erebus's fracking schedule.

He set up another geophone and straightened out to work the tension from his neck. Their cook stepped out from the food trailer and signaled lunch. Dax grabbed his sandwich and headed to where his "personal" readouts were. He ate as he examined the data his seismograph had registered.

Steven walked over and glanced over Dax's shoulder at the readout.

"It's not enough to mean anything," Steven said. Clearly, he'd noticed the kick in the readout, too. Interesting that he'd hadn't really studied them, yet he was ready to brush them off so quickly.

"I'm not so sure. I think it's worth watching. If you look at the schedule of Erebus's water injections, then compare it with the timing of the anomalies shown by these readings, the seismic activity is more than a coincidence," Dax insisted.

"But it's not statistically significant. You're new to this area. We get activity all the time. Most of it goes unnoticed by the average person. But occasionally we hit four Mw's. You may have seen a correlation here, but it's only data from one night. You need more than that."

Dax nodded, not because he was conceding, but because it was clear Steven was going to turn a blind eye in order to be loyal to the company. Dax wasn't from Kenya, but he'd done his homework. He'd studied past Mercalli intensity scale records and even records from as far back as when the Richter scale was used, as well as more recent—and more accurate—moment magnitude readings. Yes, readings from one night weren't enough—obviously—but to brush it off wasn't right. Dax had good instincts. He knew when something was worth following up on. He felt it in his gut the way some people could sense a storm brewing before the clouds arrived. He lived and breathed quakes. But he also had two girls he needed to support.

"You're right," Dax said. "Just excited to be back in the field. I've always loved this stuff. Gets the blood pumping. I wasn't going to jump the gun. Just pointing out interesting activity. It shows our instruments are working, at least."

He'd keep gathering data until he amassed enough to prove there was a concern, then he'd report it to the chief engineer, as protocol dictated.

"True. Always good to get a baseline. You know you love quakes when you get a rush from a readout." Steven laughed. "And, hey, I didn't mean to come off strong there. I've just been out here awhile."

As an assistant. Dax wanted to point that out, but decided he'd let it go for now. Sometimes there was a benefit to keeping quiet and taking note of the people you were dealing with before setting your foot down.

It was going to be a long day.

PIPPA KEPT LOOKING in her rearview mirror. Having Ivy and Fern sitting behind her in the back seat of her jeep made her a little nervous, but she had stopped the argument over who got to sit up front by telling them they were both banned from the front all week because of the stunt they pulled on her yesterday. She eyed them again as she drove along a dirt road that ran through the savanna grasses toward an *enkang* just under an hour away. Had they switched headbands again? She narrowed her eyes at them, but they seemed more focused on the scenery and giraffes in the distance than playing tricks. She needed to keep them distracted.

"Do you want me to pull over so you can get a better look through your binoculars?"

"Yes, please." Fern nodded and held on to her pair. "Do we have to stay in the car?"

"Absolutely."

"Over there. What are those? They look like deer with curvy horns." Ivy pointed to a herd of animals gathered near a mass of brush.

Pippa slowed and pulled to a stop beside a rocky outcropping that cast shade over them. She looked to where Ivy was pointing.

"Those are impala."

Both girls aimed their binoculars and focused in on the animals.

"Oh, and you see that acacia tree, the one that's shaped like an umbrella? Look to the right of it." She waited for them to spot the two rhinos.

"Wow," Fern said.

"That's pretty cool."

"They are cool, but not cool tempered. It's a good thing we're not too close," Pippa said.

"That horn is incredible," Ivy said.

"That, it is. But it also puts that bull at risk of poaching. It's really sad and unimaginable what poachers kill for. Some people think a rhino's horn has medicinal powers. Others just want to carve them like they do elephant tusks. So, poachers hunt the rhinos down and kill them for the horns. Illegally. These animals are being threatened to the point that, when you're all grown up and have your own kids and grandkids, you might be telling them stories about the time you went to Africa and saw a real live rhino or elephant before they went extinct."

"Oh my God. Really?" Fern said, the corners of her mouth falling.

"That's so depressing. Maybe we should become vegetarians for real. Are you one?" Ivy asked Pippa.

"Yes, but the nonjudgy kind. I have some family and friends who are vegetarians and some who aren't. But even the people I know who aren't vegetarians only eat meat or poultry that has been treated humanely and fed on pasture their entire lives. It's about doing what's best for all life on earth and the environment as a whole. There has to be balance in all things. The more you look into it and dig into both views, the more you'll see that becoming a vegetarian is a complex decision. And, by the way, it's a personal choice, too. You may be identical twins, but you're two distinct individuals and you each have the right to make your own decisions."

Fern lowered her binoculars and gazed off into the distance.

"Got that, Fern? You, too, Ivy?" Pippa asked softly. Fern finally nodded.

"Yes. Got it," Ivy said, keeping her binoculars glued to her eyes. She was a proud one. Independent. But Pippa could tell she was listening. She needed to hear it.

"Quick, look there, past that boulder," Pippa said, lightening up the conversation.

"Elephants!" Fern jumped up onto her knees. "Wow. Ivy, can you see the babies?"

"Man." Ivy sighed as she spotted them. "I can't believe anyone would kill them."

"I wish we had cell phones so that we could take photos," Fern said.

"Yeah," Ivy said. "Dad's punishment yesterday was to tell us we can't get cell phones until we're sixteen now. I'm not worried. He'll forget he said that in a month."

That was Dax's punishment for mud in her hair? Curious.

"You do know you don't need a phone to have a camera, don't you?" Pippa asked.

"Well, yes, but no one has just a camera anymore. It's kind of silly. Why bother if you have a phone that can fit in your pocket?" Ivy said.

"Unless you're a professional, maybe, but she's right. Cameras are old-fashioned. You wouldn't use a giant box computer from the '80s if you could have a thin laptop would you?" Fern pointed out.

"I disagree. Sometimes old is better, or at least special in its own right. For example, a phone wouldn't be able to zoom in enough to take a photo of those elephants. The clarity would suffer, too, especially when taking night photos or capturing a full moon on a clear night out here in the middle of nowhere. Maybe I should take you two camping so you can see for yourselves."

"We've been camping with Dad," Ivy said.

"Ah, but have you camped in Africa's wilderness surrounded by lions and hyenas?"

The girls tucked their chins in and shook their heads as if that might be a little too daring.

Pippa pulled her camera out of a case in her backpack.

"This, my dears, is a real camera. Not old enough for film, but still old. And, Fern, I do take photos for my family's elephant rescue, Busara, so I guess in some ways, I'm a professional. It has great zoom, too. I'll let you try it, but first let me snap a shot of that baby elephant with its mother. It's so perfect. The lighting is magnificent. I like capturing happy moments, too, you know? Not just the sad ones, where the babies are orphaned. People need to have hope and see the beauty in life. One of you keep an eye on the herd so we don't lose sight of them."

Pippa turned in her seat and switched the camera on. It didn't respond. She tried again. The herd was moving away, though neither girl was warning her. She glanced up at them and they were watching her apprehensively. She tried the on button again. No luck. The herd moved behind a distant copse of trees and underbrush. Completely out of view.

"No! I missed it. My batteries must be bad. I replaced them recently. They shouldn't have died on me so soon." She rested her forehead in her hand. Overreacting wasn't going to make that shot happen. This was what life was about. Missed opportunities. But the shot she'd wanted wasn't just about the animals; it had also been about the composition of the boulders, trees and clouds. It had been the shot she'd been after for months. The one she'd pictured in her mind. The one she'd been planning to take and frame as a gift for her parents' anniversary.

Ivy stared down at her lap. Fern slumped down next to her, looking miserable and biting her lip. Ivy never did that, she'd noticed. Ivy picked at her thumbnail when she was nervous. She stopped picking at it, reached into her pocket and pulled out the batteries.

Pressure filled Pippa's ears. She glared at the girls and grabbed the batteries from Ivy's hand.

Breathe. Breathe. Breathe.

"I cannot believe you two," Pippa said, as she put the batteries in the camera and returned the camera to its case. She stepped out of the jeep and slammed the door behind her.

"Get out. Both of you."

Ivy and Fern looked at each other wide-eyed, then back at her as if she couldn't mean it. They didn't move.

"Now!" Pippa yelled, pointing at the ground outside the jeep. Her voice caught in her throat. She never yelled. She never lost her cool, especially not with kids, but these girls were possessed or something. She gripped her hair back from her face and let the sun sting her skin.

The girls climbed out of the jeep slowly and stood very close to one another. Fear crinkled their faces. Guilt sliced through Pippa, but fury and duty won out.

"You can't leave us out here. That's child abandonment and abuse," Fern said.

"Yeah. Like in *Hansel and Gretel*. Dad would kill you a million times over," Ivy added, her voice shaking.

They thought she was going to leave them out here? Not a chance. She was angry but not insane or abusive. But she'd allow them to assume what they wanted. Letting them simmer a little bit might teach them a lesson.

"Riding in my jeep and taking these outings is a privilege. I don't have to put up with your antics. We can stick to your strict schedule like hardened sap for all I care," she said, raising her voice and pointing at each one. "I have *never* in my life dealt with more disrespectful, manipulative, ungrateful and infuriating children than the two of you."

They didn't say anything, but tears brimmed in their eyes.

"That shot was perfect and I missed it, but what bothers me more is the fact that you touched my camera. You tampered with an item that doesn't belong to you and you have no right to touch. You might think it's just an old camera and no big deal, but it is a big deal to me. You have to learn to have respect for things that don't belong to you, and that starts now. A person learns respect of another's belongings as a child so that it hopefully impacts decisions they make later…even things like choosing not to kill a rhino and steal its horn. That camera is special to me. It was given to me by my father and to him by his adoptive parents. He was adopted as a teenager because he lost both of his birth parents. And my father didn't know I existed when I was born, but the love he and my mother had for each other brought us all together and made us a family. I was taking that photograph as an anniversary gift for them. Because I love them and respect them and because family is important. Because a father or mother's relationship with their child is important. But I missed that photo because you two needed to pull another one of your inconsiderate, selfish pranks. Don't you ever stop and think before you act? Couldn't you for once pause and consider the consequences of your actions?" Pippa stopped ranting to catch her breath.

The twins looped their arms and Fern buried her face in Ivy's shoulder. Ivy swiped a tear away with the back of her hand. Pippa paced. What in the world would it take to get them to change their behavior? Kids didn't act out like this without reason.

"Look, I'm not trying to get revenge here by making you cry. Seeing you upset doesn't make me happy. I don't want to sit here and lecture you, but I'm trying to make you understand that you're not alone in losing your mother. I have family members who've gone through what you've gone through. My father lost both of his parents. My cousins lost their mother, just like you did. And all of them ended up with the gift of second moms who love them to the ends of the earth. Yet, they all still honor and remember their first moms, or dads. So, if all these pranks you're playing are because you're afraid that a nanny will take your mother's place, you can stop it because nobody can do that. Nobody. And if your pranks are to get your dad's attention, is having him frustrated and stressed or upset the kind of attention you want? If you love him that much, stop doing this to him. Give him a chance. He loves you both. That's why you're here and not off in some boarding school. Think about that."

Neither one responded. She'd said enough. She felt drained.

"Get in the jeep...and remember it's a privilege." She climbed into the driver's seat, and Ivy and Fern rushed into the back seat, clearly relieved that she wasn't leaving them out here to get eaten alive.

She started the ignition and resumed course for the *enkang*. They'd be there in less than fifteen minutes. Maybe that would be enough time for the twins to process all that she'd said.

She rested her elbow on the door frame and let the wind wrestle her hair. She did slow down and point out a herd of gazelle at one point. The girls looked but didn't lift their binoculars. Maybe she'd gone overboard. What did she know? Sure she'd been a girl their age once, and yes, she worked with kids, but she wasn't a parent, let alone one of twins with double the emotional baggage load. She shouldn't have raised her voice, but man, they'd worn away at her last shred of patience. She let the wind fill her lungs, and she held her breath for a moment before exhaling. No, she'd done and said what she had to. The girls needed guidance and boundaries for their own good.

Did Dax understand where they were coming from? Had he just given up? Or maybe he didn't understand the concept of tough love. She refused to believe that he didn't care.

Dust plumed around the jeep as she made a sharp right around the jagged remains of a tree and pulled to a stop outside the Maasai homestead's thorny fence.

"Miss Pippa? We're sorry about the camera," they both said.

They'd apologized before for previous pranks. She had no idea if they were being sincere this time or not. Actually, she believed they were always sincere in the moment. They just had short-term memories when it came to life lessons. Which is why she was thinking that maybe a more hands-on approach would stick better. Mud for mud, in this case. She turned slightly in her seat and faced them.

"Thank you. But remember, actions speak louder than words, so show me that you're sorry by never doing something like that again."

She motioned toward the circle of domed huts fashioned with a practical blend of mud, straw and cow's urine and topped with thick, thatched roofs. The familiar aroma of *ugali* getting stirred and cooked into warm grits mingled with the raw, green scent of grass, earth and goats. "This is a different village from the one I brought you to last time. I've known this family since I was a baby. If you help me review the alphabet with the younger children, we can do something fun and different afterward."

"Like what?" Ivy asked.

"Like getting tattooed. One of the fifteen-year-olds here is very good at it. She tries to insist it's in exchange for my lessons, but I usually bring something like a supply of sugar or tea."

Ivy's eyes widened with interest. This was the girl who wanted to dye her hair black. She also wore a purple headband, which meant they hadn't tried to switch identities on her today.

Fern didn't look as convinced.

"We would get in trouble. And don't they use needles to make tattoos? I'm not going anywhere near a needle."

"This is a special kind of tattoo. No needles involved. I wouldn't do that to you. Have you heard of henna?"

The girls shook their heads.

"Well, you're going to learn about henna tattoos. Just don't put it in your hair. It looks like the mud you put in mine, only this stuff on your light hair would turn you into flaming redheads. I don't think your dad would be amused."

"Oh, I don't know," Ivy said, nudging Fern.

"No, girls. Just. No," Pippa warned. The twins exchanged conspiratorial glances. "Consequences. Remember?"

"Whatever," Ivy said. "I'll be old enough to do what I want, eventually."

"Key word, eventually. Not on my watch."

The villagers spotted Pippa, and they called out her name. The sound carried toward her, rising and falling like the soft hills and valleys to their west. She waved, then began filling Ivy and Fern's arms with the supplies she'd brought as gifts.

"Come on. They're waiting for us."

"Do they speak English?" Fern asked.

"Most of them do, along with Swahili and Maa. The kids you'll be working with do for sure."

"You mean we'll actually get to teach?" Fern asked. Her eyebrows lifted, and she looked up at Pippa as their hiking boots crunched against the dry ground.

"Of course you will. I didn't bring you

along to daydream. And I expect you to earn the reward of body art." That didn't sound quite like she'd intended. Dax really would kill her if he heard her encouraging them to alter their bodies. Even their little ears were plain as a baby's bottom—unlike the adorned lobes of the young Maasai girls who were hurrying toward them. One of their mothers nodded and flashed a bright, white smile in greeting as she sifted through grain. Her earlobes, stretched impressively by large loops, swayed as she tossed the small stones she found in the grain onto the ground near her.

"How do we say hello?" Ivy asked.

"Sopa." The girls repeated the greeting after her. She figured one word would be good for now. "It's also tradition and respectful to ask how the children are doing, if you're speaking to a grown-up. Children are extremely important to the Maasai. If you get the hang of *sopa*, I'll teach you the rest."

Ivy's forehead creased at the mention of children being important. Pippa tugged her braid playfully and put a hand on her shoulder. Did Ivy doubt her and Fern's importance to their dad? Boy. These two, for all their bravado, were confidence starved.

"I brought extra teachers today," Pippa said to the children who ran up to them. "This is Ivy and Fern." Nashipi, one of the older mothers approached behind them. *"Sopa. Kasserian ingera?"* Pippa asked. "These are for you as a thank-you for letting Jaha do henna for us later," she added, handing the tea and sugar over to her. Jaha was Nashipi's fifteen-year-old daughter.

"It is not necessary. It makes me happy, like you make the children. But I must say that a few of the children have been ill. My youngest grandchild is tired and resting. Nika is tired, too, but perhaps it's the heat."

Pippa looked over at Nika, one of Nashipi's grandchildren. She seemed fine, if a bit fatigued. She'd make note of the kids' attention span and any obvious health issues as she taught them.

"Okay. I'll try to see when Dr. Hope will be out this way."

Pippa's aunt, Dr. Hope Alwanga—now Corallis—was a pediatrician who routinely made medical trips into rural areas to provide care and vaccines to the tribal children. She had met Pippa's Uncle Ben after he'd lost his wife to an accident the day he'd returned home from the marines many years ago.

He'd been left with a newborn, a toddler and Pippa's cousin Maddie, then ten, who'd stopped speaking when her mother died. Hope had not only helped them deal with their tragedy, she and Ben also ended up falling in love. It was hard not to love Hope. She was so giving, and many of the tribal families counted on her. Many wouldn't have medical care without her. She'd definitely want to know if some of the children here weren't feeling well.

"For now, should we set up inside or out? There's a lovely breeze in the shade. How about the tree?" Pippa asked. An ancient acacia sprawled just outside the homestead's fence near the entrance, casting a shadow just large enough to shade the entire group.

The beloved tree won by a majority.

Ivy and Fern were surprisingly excellent helpers when it came to the lesson. Kids really made great teachers for their peers, and the benefits went both ways. Even Fern sat straighter, with her shoulders pulled back and that flicker of tension that she always seemed to have in her face faded away. Pippa was quite impressed. The two pranksters had a responsible side. Who knew? She wished Dax could witness it.

But as the lesson went on, she became concerned by the attention span of some of the other kids. At first, she thought maybe it had something to do with the twins' being there, but with the warning Nashipi had given her, she couldn't discount it so easily.

Apart from her concerns, the lessons went well, and hearing Ivy and Fern's voices harmonizing with the sweet lilts of their new friends as they read aloud stirred something warm and blissful in Pippa's chest.

She watched now, as Ivy and Fern sat still, mesmerized by the ornate patterns getting painted onto their left ankles.

Jaha was quite skilled at henna for such a young girl. It pained Pippa to know that— as good a reader as Jaha was—she didn't want to leave her family for higher schooling. Even Nashipi had tried convincing her, but Jaha insisted that she didn't want to leave. She was a shy girl. The bottom line was that at least she had a choice. At least her grandfather, the *Laibon*, the medicine man here, had said that he'd let her go if she wanted. That wasn't the norm in the Maasai villages, but he'd known Pippa's family a long time now.

"This is so not on our schedule," Fern said. She grinned at Ivy, who seemed too enthralled with the design process to look up.

"Call it art class." Pippa spooned the olive green muddy goop into a fresh bag made of thin hide with a tiny bit of the corner snipped off. "When you're done with your ankles, I'll draw bracelets on you, then you can do my wrists after yours dry a little, so they don't ruin. How's that sound?"

"Awesome. We really get to try doing this? This is so much better than playing with makeup." Ivy admired her ankle and thanked the artist. "Do you really do this all the time, Miss Pippa?"

"Only when I *have* time. It's tradition here to paint henna tattoos for weddings.

The brides get elaborately decorated. It's pretty incredible and requires patience."

"I can totally be patient for something like this," Ivy said.

"Yeah. I can't believe we've been sitting here so long. It doesn't feel like it's been that long at all," Fern added.

"That's why they say time flies when you're having fun," Pippa said.

"It's so true." Fern grinned.

"Are you going to do this when you get married, Miss Pippa?"

Wow. That hit a nerve. Ivy had no way of knowing about Pippa's ex. She couldn't have meant to open a wound.

But after Ivy's question, Pippa couldn't help but wonder. Would she have celebrated her wedding with traditional henna designs…had Haki not left her? Would she be looking forward right now to going home to him at the end of the day? Or would she have been robbed of that joy because she knew, somewhere deep down, that he'd turned his back on his soul mate. Could she have ever been confident in his love after her cousin Maddie had reentered his life and she witnessed a connection between them that she could have never competed with?

She glanced quickly at the twins and back at her bag of henna. Confidence. It was tricky, wasn't it? Something the twins needed to build. Something she strove to instill in the Maasai girls she taught. And, yet, it was something that still wavered in her.

Maybe if Haki had been The One, she wouldn't have had to question any of this. Things happened for a reason…even floods and droughts. Her heart was suffering from the latter, but she'd deal with that any day over having it cracked and shaken to the core again.

"I don't know, Ivy. Maybe. Some things are better left to decide in the moment. Like right now. I'm deciding, in this very moment, what to draw on each one of you."

"Any chance we can get our ears pierced like the other girls? Not the giant stretch loops. I'm just asking for a tiny hole," Ivy hedged.

"That's up to your dad, not me. I'm betting he doesn't even allow makeup yet."

"Only nail polish."

"Makeup is overrated, in my opinion. Don't be in any rush," Pippa said.

Pippa took Ivy's wrist and smiled as she began designing a vine with leaves twisting around the girl's hand like a bracelet. Ivy watched intently, then held up her hand and admired the intensely dark brown of the wet design.

"Don't let it smear. You need to keep your arm and hand still. If you twist your wrist, it'll mess the design up. Let the henna dry a bit and you'll be able to move a little. The longer we leave it on, the darker red the tattoo will be."

"I want it as dark as possible," Ivy said.

Pippa chuckled.

"I bet you do. You're next, Fern." She took the other girl's hand and made a tattoo bracelet of longer, multilobed fern leaves. Fern's face lit up.

"I love it! What about yours? Are you seriously going to let us paint on you after what we did to your hair? You'd trust us to tattoo a design on you? What if we mess up?"

"I trust you."

Ivy's and Fern's lips parted. They looked at each other, then back at her.

"For real? Even after all we've done? Like to your camera?" Ivy asked.

Pippa sucked in a grounding breath.

"Sure." Was she? How bad could it be? Whatever they marked her up with, it would fade. Eventually. Right now, the lesson they were getting in trust was more important.

That...and the fact that they wouldn't be able to switch bracelets.

DAX SET HIS things down, hugged Ivy and Fern, then almost collapsed in the chair by his desk—almost. Heat crawled up the back of his neck when he noticed their wrists.

"Girls, to your room, now. I need to talk to Pippa."

Their faces sank. They glanced at Pippa for courage, and she motioned for them to obey.

"You're overreacting," she said, the minute their door closed.

"You have no business telling me that. What in heaven's name made you think that tattooing my daughters was okay?

Who does something like that without a parent's permission? What next? Ear piercings or purple and green hair?" He ran his fingers through his own and stood akimbo, towering over her. She'd covered his girls in body art!

"Red hair almost happened, but I stopped it. On *your* account. They would have matched your ungodly shade of crimson right now, though. Maybe I should have let them do it."

"I'm being serious."

"So am I. You know, I had my ears pierced when I was only a year old. I never understood the whole issue some parents have with that."

"Hard to understand a lot of things if you're not a parent."

"Hard to understand preteen girls if you've never been one."

She was killing him. Why had he ever crossed paths with her? And what about her made him keep coming back for more? Masochism?

"They're henna tattoos. It's all natural and it's not permanent. Have you even bothered to look at them? Ivy on Ivy and

ferns on Fern. And they can't take the tattoos off and switch them around like their
headbands or clothes."

He stood there and stared at her. He
didn't know what to say. That's what this
was about? Beating them at their own
game? He took a deep breath and gazed at
the floor a minute. Maybe she wasn't or-
thodox, but she also hadn't given up on the
girls. She hadn't quit and run off, like all
the others had. And a minute ago, they'd
actually looked to her for guidance before
leaving the room. A huge turnaround compared with the mud head he'd walked in on
yesterday. He scrubbed the stubble along
his jawline.

"I realize they're not permanent. That's
not the point." Okay, so he hadn't really
known they'd fade. They didn't look like
regular inked tattoos, but then, those came
in colors, too.

"Okay, what *is* the point? That they're
not allowed to have fun? That unless you
approve the next molecules of oxygen they
breathe, they should suffocate? Because, let
me tell you, if you keep this up, they will.

You'll end up with teenagers who can't wait to get away from home."

"That's not what I'm doing. I'm trying to raise them right." He squeezed his eyes shut for a moment, then looked aimlessly around the room. Anywhere but at Pippa. "You took me by surprise."

"Yeah, I picked up on that," Pippa said, folding her arms and shifting her weight impatiently.

"You weren't trying to teach them a lesson, then?" he asked, sitting down and leaning forward on his elbows.

"I'm not that petty. And if that's what this was about, I wouldn't have let them put designs on me, too." She turned her arms so the inner sides faced up. She had a trail of flowers from wrists to elbows and what appeared to be a small elephant on each wrist. She'd sacrificed her skin to connect with the twins? Not that he'd really call it a sacrifice. He had to admit, he was raising budding artists and the designs looked good on her. They seemed to go with Pippa's personality. Even matched her auburn hair. Henna tattoos. Totally something Sandy would have done. Maybe that's why it had hit him so hard.

"Not permanent?"

It was meant to be a rhetorical question. She'd already said that they weren't. But she was standing too close now and he had to say something to justify the fact that he couldn't seem to stop looking at the smooth skin of her arm.

"It'll fade over the next week or two, maybe sooner because we didn't leave it on that long. I'm sorry, but it was an in-the-moment thing."

Being in the moment. When was the last time he'd tried that? Sandy had always been that way: creative, expressive and spontaneous.

But he didn't have that luxury. The twins were his responsibility. He had promised Sandy in her last minutes that they'd be okay and he wouldn't let anything bad ever happen to them. Sure, they'd had their fair share of scraped knees and flu bugs, but nothing worse.

They heard the shuffle of feet behind the bedroom door. Pippa took him by the hand and pulled him up, then yanked him quickly outside the front door, presumably for privacy. She closed the door behind them and let go, but he could still feel her hand in his. She was standing close again. Close enough that she could lower her voice to barely above a whisper and he was still able to hear every word...every breath. He couldn't help but notice the way her lips moved when she spoke.

"Look, Dax, maybe I don't have kids of my own, but I wasn't that different from Ivy and Fern. I don't know what it's like to lose a mother, I'm lucky for that, but I do understand being spontaneous and free. My parents used to call me a little monkey. I did my share of disappearing and other stunts that gave them heart attacks. But I was simply trying to spread my wings and discover who I really was, knowing I had this safety net if I stumbled. You're not even letting Ivy and Fern stumble. Here they are, identical twins, who need to embrace who they are as individuals. They want your approval. They want to be assured that they're more than just the twins to you."

"Of course they're more than that. You

can't pass that judgment on me when you've just met us. I don't care if you've taken a million kids on hikes or if you went and got a PhD in psychology, or even raised ten kids yourself. You still wouldn't know my daughters and me well enough to tell us—tell *me*—what I'm doing wrong. I hired you to watch and teach them, not to judge and psychoanalyze my parenting. Maybe this arrangement was a bad idea." He started to reach for the doorknob, but she put her hands on his arm.

"I'm not judging. I'm trying to help. Isn't that what you needed?"

"Help. Yes. Stage an intervention? No." He was still mad. He really was. But he made no attempt to draw his arm away from her hands.

"I'm sorry if I overstepped. I'll stick to what you're paying me to do."

She let go of him.

The slap of reality hit him in the face. He'd needed it, too. Which bothered him to no end.

Never once had he stood this close to anyone caring for the twins. Never once had he felt drawn to a woman since Sandy.

Not even a tiny bit. And not only because it wouldn't have been professional. He'd learned his lesson: let a person in and he'd only be opening him and the twins up to loss and heartbreak and agony.

He was human. He was bound to feel attracted to a woman sooner or later. That's all this confusion broiling in him. He was irritated with the way she challenged his requests and seemed to see right through him, but he was attracted to her for the very same reasons. It was killing him. It wasn't right.

But he, of all people, knew that he couldn't handle any more loss. He had the twins, and worrying about anything happening to them was more than enough to weigh on him. Whatever energy seemed to pass between him and Pippa every time they were in the same room was a one-way figment of his imagination.

Besides, Pippa said it herself. She was helping him only for the money. No wonder she was putting up with the girls' pranks. She wasn't sticking around because he affected her or was stuck in her head the way she'd managed to stick in his. She wasn't here because the twins were special to her.

It was for the money. Money drove everyone. It was the universal motivator.

After all, money was the reason he was working for an oil company, so he couldn't judge.

He put his hands on his hips and took a small step back to put some distance between them. She splayed her hands, and her soft face creased.

"How can you not see it? They're desperate for your attention. Not in a responsible-parent way, but in a 'there's nothing in the world that matters other than hanging out with you' way. You're right… I've only just met them. Yet, I can see it all as plain as day. Doesn't that tell you something?"

"They're my life. I take them everywhere I go. Why else do you think they're here and not with their grandparents? The one thing I promised their mother before she died was that we'd stick together, the three of us, and I would never give them to someone else to raise."

"Is that what all the rules and schedules are about? To make you feel like you're raising them even if they're with a nanny all day?"

"That's out of line. I'm not the first parent to work all day. I'm still their father. It's my job to keep them safe and to make sure they stay safe even when I'm not around."

"You can't control everything, Dax. You can't shelter them and then expect them to survive in this world. They want their dad to sometimes let his guard down and throw caution to the wind. I mean, haven't you ever done something like jump in the pool with your clothes on just to make them laugh? Haven't you ever played hooky and told them to ignore their studies for a day so the three of you could have fun? That's all they want."

"My job is to give them what they need. Not what they want."

"Your job includes their emotional well-being. They miss their mother. I may be wrong but I'm guessing they miss the way you were when she was alive. When we were doing the henna, they told me you weren't always around when they were little, but that when you were, your time together was the best."

He felt sucker punched. The girls had never mentioned that to him. Did that mean they trusted her more than they trusted him now? Had he really built a wall between him and his daughters? Maybe they remembered things that way because their mom had been the hands-on parent, so when he was at home, he could enjoy them without any burdens hanging over him. He was the good-cop parent. When had he become the bad cop?

He scrubbed at his jaw and rested his back against the wall by the door. Pippa bridged the gap between them and took his hand again. She meant it as a gesture of comfort and understanding, no doubt, but something in the way her fingers wrapped around his made it about need and connection and wanting something indefinable that neither of them had to give.

"You're the most important person in the world to them, Dax. They love you to pieces. They just want you to be yourself."

"I'm not sure that's good enough."

"It has to be."

CHAPTER SIX

TWO DAYS AND not an incident. The girls had actually been behaving and Pippa... she seemed to be mellower than usual. Like she was making a point to follow his rules and not overstep.

So why did the last forty-eight hours seem stagnant and boring?

Dax looked around and checked the girls' room. No one was around. He'd come home early, but according to the schedule, they were supposed to be wrapping up an online math test. He set his stuff down and noticed a handwritten note sitting on his desk.

Gone swimming.
—Pippa :)

Like giant smiley faces made playing hooky okay. Faces like the twins drew on notes.

He checked the patio door in the bedroom, relieved that they'd at least locked it behind them. He went outside and made his way down the path through the garden to the pool area. The normal chatter of monkeys scampering through the canopy of trees with hoarded fruit, birds fluttering to their nests and the occasional trumpeting in the distance of wandering elephant herds was drowned out by the cacophony of human squeals and arguments before the pool even came into view. He rounded the path and stopped at the pool gate.

The family with all the kids he'd seen Pippa taking on tour the first day was there, too. All of them were in the water except for the father, who sat drying off in a lounge chair with a drink.

Pippa and the girls hadn't noticed Dax yet. He was about to call out when the ball everyone was playing with got bumped over the edge. Pippa hoisted herself up onto the edge of the pool, then stood and padded over to the ball.

Dax tried not to watch her. He even made an effort to keep his eyes on his daughters in the crowded pool, but his gaze kept straying to Pippa. She wore a navy blue one-piece that didn't reveal much, other than the fact that she was captivating in an unassuming, simple, natural-beauty sort of way.

He rubbed his eyes between the pad of his thumb and forefinger and scratched at the base of his throat as he walked to the end of the pool where the other parents sat.

"Dad! We're winning!" Fern and Ivy called out when they saw him.

"Hey!" Pippa shot him a huge grin and waved, then served the ball.

He couldn't exactly call them out of the pool or make a big deal about the change in the schedule…not in front of everyone. Besides, they really were having fun. When was the last time he'd taken a day off to just relax since they'd gotten here? For that matter, when was the last time he'd taken a real weekend off? One where he didn't bring work home?

"Go Team Twins!" he yelled out, giving them a thumbs-up. Granted, they did have a few members from the other family on their side to even things out.

"They are a competitive bunch," the

other father pointed out, nodding to Dax. "You should have seen the volley between my wife and yours right before you got here. I swear they kept it in the air for at least ten hits."

My wife and yours?

Dax scratched the back of his head and winced uncomfortably at the sun. Should he let it go? No. No. It was a small place and Pippa worked here. What if the assumption spread? He cranked his neck to one side and rubbed at the knot forming there.

"They're…um…definitely having fun, but she's…um…not my wife," he said.

"No? Oh, sorry. Something in the way you two looked at each other when you got here…and those twins. I just assumed."

"No worries. She's watching my daughters temporarily. I was in a bind because of work." Dax pulled up one of the garden chairs and took a seat.

Squeals erupted from the pool, followed by laughter.

"Honey, did you see that?" the man's wife called out. Her kids high-fived her.

What would it be like to have someone

calling him "honey" or "sweetheart" again? He missed the way Sandy used to infuse those words with love before they split up. They'd been a team, or so he'd thought. The reality was he hadn't been there for her until it was too late. He'd taken so many things for granted. He didn't deserve anyone calling him "honey" or loving him the way Sandy once had. Pippa's face flashed in his mind, and he quickly blinked it away.

Team Twins was starting to fall behind, but for a good reason. Pippa kept passing the ball to either Ivy or Fern so one of them could take the shot across the red rope they'd strung across the pool as a makeshift volleyball net. She may have enjoyed a little competition briefly with this guy's wife, but she wasn't making the game about her. She wanted the girls to have a chance. She was going out of her way to boost their confidence. He watched as Fern started to give Pippa the ball to serve, but Pippa shook her head and told her she could do it. Something shifted in Dax's chest. It had to be gratitude. Nothing more. She was a teacher. Good teachers did that sort of thing with kids.

"Game over!" one of the blond boys called out. His side cheered.

Ivy and Fern smiled and congratulated the others, but the excitement had dulled in their eyes. Pippa double high-fived them and thanked the family for the game.

"Enjoy the rest of your afternoon," Dax told the dad.

"Yes, you, too," the father said, glancing at Pippa, then lifting the corner of his mouth assumingly. "You know, kids have good instincts about people. She's great with your daughters...and I don't think the way you two looked at each other was nothing."

"It's really not like that."

"Maybe it could be. I almost lost my chance out of sheer stubbornness. Look what I'd have missed out on," he said, nodding toward his family before joining them.

Dax turned away. Did boundaries not exist out here? A sharp pain shot through his temple, and he rubbed at his clenched jaw. There was nothing between him and Pippa. Nothing. They hadn't known each other long enough for that. He walked over to where the twins were climbing out of the pool and handed them their towels. Pippa was climbing out after them. He tossed a towel to her while keeping his attention on his daughters.

"You two played like pros," he said.

"You're exaggerating. We lost." Ivy dried her face and hair.

"Not all games are about winning or losing. You all seemed to be having a great time."

"Yeah, it was fun," Fern said.

"I thought you both did great—great playing and great sportsmanship," Dax said.

"They were awesome. We'll have to do it again. I hardly ever get to swim. I'm not a guest here and I'm always working, so I don't get to use the pool. This place is like a small oasis. We don't have such luxuries at Busara or most places around here. Besides, if we did, the elephants would think it was a watering hole," Pippa said, earning laughs from the girls.

"But those kids said they're leaving tomorrow," Fern said.

"Then we'll have to get your dad in the

pool to play on a team with one of you," Pippa said.

"We'll see about that," Dax said. "Shower time. Then I brought you girls something."

Ivy and Fern took off for the bungalow.

Pippa had wrapped the towel around herself, so it was safe to look at her. Little drops of water glistened on her damp hair, and one dangled from the end of a curl before falling and sliding down her shoulder.

"I know this wasn't on the schedule, but they did their—"

"Thank you. For doing this," he said, then he left her standing there speechless and—as far as he was concerned—totally off-limits.

PIPPA FINISHED DRYING off and changing in the twins' bathroom. She looked in the mirror and frowned, leaning in for a better look. Why hadn't she noticed the freckles on the bridge of her nose before? Did freckles make a person unattractive? With all the sun she got out here, she'd be blessed with wrinkles before thirty, too.

She stood back, frowned at herself and

straightened her T-shirt. Since when did she care about being attractive? *Never. I never had to.* That was it. Playing in the pool with all of those kids and seeing the way that ten-year-old boy kept smiling sheepishly at Fern brought back memories. Their curious, innocent glances at one another had pulled a stitch on an old wound, and it had taken all she had in her to focus on the game and not let that wound bleed out.

She and Haki had grown up side by side since birth. He'd been the guy next door—or the tent next door, in her case. Her looks had never mattered to her because he'd known her at her best and worst…and sometimes even better than she knew herself. She'd never dated anyone else. But he'd moved on. And here she was now, worried about freckles? Why?

Dax.

No. No way. She wasn't going there. In all honesty, yes, he was attractive, and despite his annoying need for a schedule, there was something endearing about the way he ruffled his hair whenever he was unsure of himself.

None of that meant anything, though. None of it was important. Life was about pursuing her dreams and helping other young girls to have the confidence and means to pursue theirs. Life was about feeling empowered without anyone acting as a crutch for her. It would be hypocritical and self-defeating to worry about her looks all of a sudden. If she ever did find the courage to fall in love again, she wanted it to be with someone who didn't care if she had freckles, wrinkles or scars. It had to be with a man who loved and respected her mind, soul and free spirit—henna parties and all.

She pushed her rampant curls away from her forehead, but that only brought back the memory of Dax washing her hair. Her freckles faded behind the sudden flush in her cheeks.

You do not like him that way. He's no fun.

But he needs you.

Haki had never really needed her. It felt good to be needed.

She heard Ivy and Fern in the main room arguing over who could open something. It had to be whatever Dax had brought them. She took a deep breath and escaped from the bathroom mirror.

All three were leaning over the desk as he opened a sample box and laid the cover aside. Clearly, he'd settled the argument by opening the surprise himself. She had to hand it to him—smart move.

"They're totally cool, Dad. What's this one called?" Ivy asked. She pointed to a gray rock with slightly pink hues.

"That looks like rhyolite," Pippa said, craning her neck over Ivy's shoulder. Fern shot her an inquisitive glance.

"We haven't seen that one before."

"It's an igneous rock," she said. "The kind that are formed when lava cools quickly. We have volcanoes here in Kenya. You're standing along part of the Great Rift Valley as we speak."

"Cool," Ivy said.

"Exactly what I was going to point out," Dax said, cocking his head and studying her.

"I'm sorry. I didn't mean to jump in—"

"I didn't mean to imply that you had. It's totally fine. It's just that rhyolite isn't one of those rocks the average person knows the name of," he said.

"Maybe I'm not average," Pippa said. Was she flirting? Being coy? So what if she was? Besides, it didn't hurt to show him she had brains, too.

Dax tried to keep from smiling, but failed and cleared his throat instead.

"No, I suppose you're not."

Ivy and Fern fingered the different rock samples and held them each up to the light.

"I know this one. Pyrite. Looks like gold," Ivy said.

"I knew it, too," Fern said.

"I'm sure you both did," Pippa quickly added.

"I suppose you have to know this stuff to teach kids about the land on your tours," Dax said.

Ah. He assumed she knew about rocks and volcanoes because she had to keep the kids entertained on the tours. Not entirely off base. She picked up the rhyolite and rubbed the pad of her thumb along its surface.

"Actually, my undergraduate degree is in geology."

"No kidding."

She shrugged. It was a male-dominated major. She got that.

"Hard to believe?" she asked.

"Not at all. It's just that you're so…unexpected."

Was that good or bad?

"Well, I didn't end up pursuing it. Wasted time, I guess." For more than one reason. She'd picked a major on a whim because she wanted to be with Haki when he'd gone off to study veterinary medicine. Time wasted on many levels. "I love the subject and everything to do with the land here, but I didn't figure out until later that what I really wanted to do was teach. I love working with kids, especially teaching them how to read. It's like… I don't know…giving them a second set of wings. The first set they get at birth because all kids are angels, but the second set allows them to soar through life. Reading opens doors."

"Nanny Number Three insisted we were little devils," Ivy said.

Pippa couldn't help but laugh when Dax grinned.

"Maybe she was seeing angels in disguise." Pippa gave them a conspiratorial wink.

"For what it's worth, I'm a firm believer that education is never wasted," Dax said.

Pippa fought the urge to hug him. She had always considered the years she'd spent studying for her degree as wasted because she associated them with her broken relationship with Haki. She'd followed him to Nairobi and picked the first major that occurred to her. All that mattered at the time was being near him. But Dax was right. It hadn't been wasted. It hadn't been all about Haki. She'd earned a degree. An education. She swallowed hard and wrapped her arms around her waist.

"Thank you for saying that," She said.

"He always tells us that. Especially when we complain about math," Fern said, setting a rock down and picking up another.

"Yeah," Ivy said.

"It's true. Even for math," Dax said, giving their braids a playful tug. It was good to see him—them—like this. For all his rules, Dax's heart was in the right place.

"We'll never use math in real life, though," Ivy said.

"I use it all the time. Tons of it. I'm going to bet you will, too, at some point," he said.

"We're not going to study earthquakes or do surveys like you do," Fern argued.

"Shh! You're going to ruin everything, big mouth," Ivy muttered, slapping a hand over her eyes.

Pippa stilled. *Land business?*

Something dark and distant seemed to wash over Dax's face.

"You're a seismologist?" Why didn't he just say so from the start? Why lie about it?

"Hard to believe?" The corner of his mouth twisted.

"No? Maybe? I'm just surprised. You'd said you were here on business and I was given the impression you didn't want to say more. Then the girls mentioned land business and, no, I wasn't digging. A lot of business types come out here intent on setting up the next-best lodge, or capitalizing on the demand for safaris and such. I just assumed it was something like that. Maybe an investor or even an architect, maybe. I tend not to ask parents of my tour kids what they're here for. It's prying, you know? I took what you told me at face value."

I trusted you.

"Well, now you know. And you, Fern and Ivy, don't have to follow in my footsteps unless you want to. You can grow up and chase whatever makes you happy," he said, turning the attention on them.

Pippa caught herself staring at him. Her lips parted, but nothing came out. He was encouraging his daughters the way she did with the Maasai girls. She appreciated that, but at the same time, he seemed anxious to change the subject. Why?

"Are you doing some type of research out here?" she pressed. "Are we in for a big one?" She recalled the strange ripple she'd felt when Adia was reading. Maybe it hadn't been her imagination or the heat.

"Why would you ask that?"

"It's just that, for a seismologist, you don't have much equipment. Only your laptop and that duffel bag."

"I have a team. They camp at the research site in trailers. None of them has kids."

"Then why didn't you say so?" *Business...*

land...seismologist... It hit her out of no-where. "Oh my god. You work for the petro-leum industry. You didn't want to tell me because I made my family's stance on en-vironmental issues clear. But you needed my cooperation." She shook her head in dis-belief. "I don't know what to say or think." She pressed her hands to her eyes.

"Girls, why don't you two go wash up for dinner." He closed the sample box they'd been looking through. The twins glanced at each other. "Now."

Pippa waited for the twins to disappear into their room. No doubt they'd be listen-ing in, but they knew more than she did anyway.

"Which one? Which oil company?"

"Erebus Oil." Dax sat at the edge of his bed and had the decency to look upset with himself.

"Erebus. Darkness and shadows. Born from chaos. How appropriate."

"I'm sorry I didn't say something sooner," he said.

"Why in the world would you become an earthquake expert only to go work for a company whose actions increase tectonic activity? It makes no sense."

"Why would you get a degree in geology and not use it?"

"Maybe money doesn't motivate me."

"Maybe you don't have the same responsibilities that I do. Besides, I remember your finding my money very convincing when I approached you about watching the twins."

"I save every penny I make so that I can build schools in Maasai *enkangs* to give the children an education. Particularly the girls. Many of them come from such traditional families that they can't leave their tribe to pursue an education. They often don't have the rights or the skills to determine their own futures. I want to change that. The time I spend teaching in rural villages is meaningful. I consider those children—girls who would otherwise be married as soon as they hit puberty...girls not much older than yours—my responsibility."

Dax bore his eyes right through her.

"So *you* follow the moral path and I don't."

"I think you can make that call yourself," she said. Blood was pounding in her ears.

Why was she taking whom he worked for so personally? Because she cared about the environment? Because she cared about how the twins were being raised? Or was it because the Dax she'd been building up in her head, the one she'd been falling for, had suddenly vanished and the real one was standing in front of her? She glanced back toward the room. She heard a shuffle and whisper. "We shouldn't be discussing this now."

She didn't have the energy to argue. She felt drained and disappointed in everyone and everything.

Dax worked for Erebus. Her entire family had joined forces with local and international environmental groups in a failed attempt to keep Erebus from acquiring the rights to drill in the area years ago.

And it was obvious Dax had instructed the twins not to say anything. Everyone had kept the truth from her, just like Haki and Maddie had tried to keep their feelings for one another from her.

She had been utterly humiliated back then. She'd been such a fool. So maybe it was a good thing she'd found out now who Dax truly was. She didn't think she could survive losing her dignity again. This was the reminder she needed.

Her heart was off-limits, and she planned to keep it that way.

"I have to go now. It's getting late."

She rushed out and closed the front door behind her, then leaned against it and let out a breath.

He'd lied to her. Lying by omission was just as bad to her. She covered her face. Had she imagined the pull between them? Was she still just as inept at reading men as she'd been when she thought Haki wanted to marry her? He'd lied to her by omission, too, only it had been about his feelings. She had zero tolerance for lying. If she had one requirement in a guy, it was honesty. She needed to extinguish even the tiniest bit of curiosity she'd had about him. From now on, she wouldn't so much as put her hand on his arm.

She started toward the lodge's foyer and the exit. She had a long drive ahead of her.

And she needed it to purge her head of Dax.

DAX SLUMPED DOWN on the edge of his bed. He'd really screwed up this time. The look of shock and disappointment in Pippa's eyes just about killed him. Ivy walked out of her room and sat in the desk chair across from him.

"I thought you told us never to lie."

"I did. I still do."

"Then why did you ask us not to say anything about the company you work for? Which for the record, Fern almost did mention it to Pippa. She can't help herself."

"I can so help myself," Fern said, coming out to join them. "I didn't say *where* he worked. Just what he *does* for work. There's a difference," Fern said, joining them.

"I'm not lying, girls. Sometimes you don't have to divulge private information. That's not the same as lying. It's simply not anyone's business."

"But she's not a stranger anymore. And now she might not come back," Fern said. Her chin quivered.

"I know she's not a stranger. I had every intention of explaining everything after I saw what a good person she was. A friend.

I guess I held back because I didn't want to disappoint her. She comes from a long line of environmental and animal advocates. They tend to frown on the oil industry. Honestly, girls, I don't know if she'll quit or not."

"You really think she'd leave us? Even after the time we've spent with her?" Ivy pulled her heels up on the edge of the chair and hugged her knees.

"Think about it, Ivy," said Fern. "Mud in her hair, the batteries, the—"

Ivy made big eyes at Fern.

"What batteries?" Dax asked.

"Nothing," they both said. Too quickly.

He narrowed his eyes at them. Had they been up to their usual pranks again?

If they had been, it said a lot that Pippa hadn't bailed on them yet. She hadn't mentioned any misbehavior. *The henna.* She'd handled things herself with the henna. He rubbed his palms against his jeans. What if she didn't return? Ivy and Fern would never forgive him. They'd never connected with anyone else the way they had with Pippa. Then again, she wouldn't be in their lives forever. The twins knew they'd be heading back to the United States when Dax's contract finished. Still, he hoped Pippa wouldn't quit. The last thing the twins needed was to feel unworthy or that anyone they liked...or loved...would disappear on them the way they always had in his own life. It was enough they'd lost their mom.

"I'm sure she really likes you two. What she's upset about has nothing to do with you. If she quits, it's my fault, not yours." The girls sat there quietly with sullen faces.

"Hey, you two. How about we go get dinner and not worry so much? She didn't say she was quitting when she left. She has tomorrow off. I bet she'll miss you too much to quit."

They looked at him with a glimmer of hope.

"Okay then. Let's go," he said. He got up, and ruffled the tops of their heads. "Front door or back and around outside?"

"Outside for sure," Fern said.

"Hang on. Can we take the two stones with all the mica?" Ivy asked.

"I guess. So long as you don't throw them at anyone—or anything." The girls had a tendency to pocket the samples he brought them as good-luck charms. It made him happy that they actually got excited about his bringing them rocks. It had become a tradition over the years. Odd gift, but it somehow mattered.

Ivy whispered something in Fern's ear, then they grabbed their samples from the box and pushed past him into the garden.

"You two aren't up to no good, are you?"

"Us? Come on, Dad. You heard Miss Pippa. We're angels." Fern sent him the sweetest smile. He was going to have gray hair before they turned thirteen. Thirteen. Heaven help him. How was he ever going to survive the teen years?

The aroma of cumin, cardamom and something mouthwatering he couldn't quite identify wafted through the air and enveloped him. He was starving. The girls had to be, too. They'd stuck to this vegetarian thing of theirs, but were still being picky about eating. He was tempted to use bribery just to get them to try something spicy and new.

They grabbed a table in the outdoor seating area, and Dax stretched his aching legs out and crossed his ankles. The sun was hanging low, and the first streaks of red cut across the sky like threads of saffron spice.

"There he is," Ivy told Fern. She motioned toward Alim, who was standing beside a young fig tree, still bushy in size. The waiter was plucking ripe figs and putting them in a bowl that he carried in the crux of his arm. He seemed to sense the presence of the twins and looked over his shoulder apprehensively. He winced, and Dax bit the inside of his cheek to keep from smiling. The girls, seemingly oblivious to Alim's lack of enthusiasm for their presence, waved madly at him. He trudged over.

"I'm actually not on duty, but I'll have a waiter come to your table right away."

"Wait, we have something for you. Hold out your hand."

The poor guy looked at them like they were nuts.

"I don't trust you. I value my hands."

Dax chuckled.

"Think of it as a test of courage," Dax said. "I doubt they'd do anything too atrocious right under my nose. Right, girls?" He gave them a pointed look.

"We're not playing a trick," Fern said.

"Come on. We have a present for you," Ivy said.

Alim unfolded his free hand slowly and held it out palm up. The girls plopped their mica rocks in his palm. He stared down at his hand.

"These are rocks. You're giving me rocks?"

"Not any rocks. They sparkle. We've decided that you've got sparkle, too. You just don't like showing it, so you pretend that you're a dull rock," Ivy said.

"But you're not, really, and you can't stop us from being your friend," Fern added.

Alim cleared his throat and raised a brow.

"Is this because I know where the desserts are kept?" The girls shook their heads in disbelief. Dax shook his head at the girls' smooth skills. Man, it was easier to catch on when one wasn't their target. To his surprise, Alim's face softened for a fleeting moment and he pocketed the stones. "Thank you."

"Are you picking those for the kitchen?" Dax asked, eyeing the bright green figs.

"Not just for the kitchen. We are preparing for the arrival of Djimon Barongo."

Dax had no idea who that was, and apparently, Alim could tell.

"He's a well-known official. He likes to bring his wife here on holiday once in a while. But we have plenty of figs to go around. Help yourself." Alim held out the bowl, and Dax took a fig.

"You girls should really try these," he said. "They're sweet. It's just fruit."

"You haven't had figs?" Alim asked the girls.

Dax peeled back the soft skin and split his open, revealing the bright red flesh glistening with dew-like drops of honey. Its fresh, sweet scent made his mouth water.

"Try them," he said, holding out the halves. The twins declined. Alim smirked at them.

"And here I thought you two were courageous. You act so daring, yet you won't taste a piece of fruit. You're like lionesses who roar but don't know how to hunt," Alim said.

"What's the big deal? Maybe I'm just not hungry," Ivy said.

"The insides remind me of monkey brains." Fern made a face, and a small vervet monkey cackled at her from a nearby mango tree as if he understood.

Dax finished off his fig.

"So good."

"One bite and I'll ask the chef to fry potatoes for you," Alim dared the girls. "Plain, like your American french fries," he said.

That got their attention. Ivy went first with a small bite, then Fern.

"They're actually good."

Alim gave Dax a nod.

"If you'd like the usual, I'll go let them know in the kitchen."

"Yes, thank you. And please have the chef put extra eggs and beans on their salads for the protein."

Alim walked off, fiddling with the stones in his pocket. Ivy and Fern grinned.

"He likes us…and we're getting fries."

CHAPTER SEVEN

A PART OF Pippa was relieved that she had a day to herself, but another part of her missed Ivy and Fern...and Dax. She hated that she missed him.

Maybe she was falling into her old pattern of one-way relationships and codependence. Like with Haki, who had been more in love with her cousin Maddie than he'd been with her.

But at least she'd been in a relationship with Haki. Everyone had known they were a couple.

She didn't have a relationship with Dax beyond their business deal. So why was she letting her mind wander in that direction? Why did she feel let down and more disappointed than she had a right to be? She pulled her jeep to a stop near Adia's homestead and yanked fistfuls of her hair as if the tug at her scalp would wake her up and make her more sensible.

He's just not that into you. And you're not into him. He's not right for you.

Right.

Good thing they wouldn't be around each other today. He could spend time with his daughters and she could get back to prioritizing the children in the area.

She tucked her keys in the pocket of her khakis, walked over to Adia and gave her a hug.

"How have you been?"

"I'm good. And you?"

She kept her arm around Adia's slim shoulders, as they walked toward the teen's mother and the other women who were grinding corn. It struck her how vibrant life here always seemed to be. There was a zest in everything the villagers did, from the rhythm of their work, to their traditional jumping at weddings and celebrations to their colorful clothing and jewelry. It was such a stark contrast to Dax's life with the twins, or at least Dax's part in it. The twins' escapades were essentially repressed zest.

She caught sight of the single book that Adia was holding onto the way one would hold something precious. A reminder that maybe the girls here were repressed in a different way. Maybe life here buzzed on the surface but underneath it all there were issues. Marrying young. Female excision, though it was illegal. Lack of educational opportunities. Two different worlds, yet, she wasn't so sure getting through to Adia's father would be any easier than getting through to Dax.

"Sopa," Pippa said to Adia's mother, Lankenua, when the other woman came to greet her. "I brought some supplies to take a sample of your water, if that's okay, after Adia's lesson. Some of the children north of here haven't been well. Dr. Hope said she'd noticed the same in another area in the east, and asked me to take some samples for her. Just to rule out water contamination."

"Why would there be contamination?" Adia's mother asked.

"It's groundwater. Many things can affect it."

Even when the drought season left the

land looking desiccated and dead, there were rivers and streams that ran deep beneath the surface, fed by mountains like Kilimanjaro or Mount Kenya. Fresh, underground spring water, yet something as unnoticeable as a minor tremor could cause contaminants to leak into it. Just like dealing with loss tainted a person's life and changed its course forever after.

Her last visit here flashed in her mind. She could have sworn the ground had rippled beneath her, but at the time she'd chalked it up to sun sickness. But maybe it *had* been a tremor.

"Don't worry, if no one has been ill here, it's probably not a concern. I'm just taking it to compare with the others." She really hoped it would turn up clean.

"Of course. Do what you think is necessary," Lankenua said.

"I will, thank you, but first let's go take a look at your essay, Adia. And then we'll talk to your father, as I promised."

"Thank you." Adia smiled and put a hand to her chest. "I hope he listens."

Pippa hoped so, too. But if she couldn't get through to Dax about giving the twins more freedom, the chances of her changing the mind of a Maasai warrior about letting his daughter move away were slim.

Lankenua and the other women glanced pitifully at Adia. Pippa's stomach churned. Was Adia's father arranging a marriage for her? Oh, God no. She knew it was the norm in the Maasai villages for girls to marry in their midteens, but when Adia's father had approved her learning to read and write, Pippa had thought he'd taken on more progressive views.

"Is he still here today?" she asked. This couldn't wait any longer.

"Yes. He is talking to the boys about warrior training over there." She pointed toward the far side of the *enkang*, outside the fenced perimeter. To interrupt Adia's father's lesson would be disrespectful, but then most everyone here had known Pippa for years. Even Adia's father had a tendency to overlook her persistence, blaming it on the fact that, since she wasn't Maasai, she didn't know any better.

"I'll be back," she told everyone. From the expressions on the women's faces, she suspected that Adia was unaware of what-

ever was going on. "Wait here. I promise
we'll still have time for our lesson."

"I need to gather more wood," her mother
said. "I will accompany you, Pippa." She
left her corn grinding and walked ahead
of Pippa toward the gate. They cleared the
fenced area, and Pippa doubled her step,
picking up sticks to help.

"Tell me what happened," she pleaded.

"He says her marriage was arranged long
ago and that it is time."

"No. He can't marry her off. She's too
young and smart and she has such a bright
future ahead of her. You know that, don't
you? Why would he suddenly change his
mind after letting me come to teach for so
long?"

What bothered Pippa most was that, unlike in Jaha's situation at the other village,
Adia didn't want to get married yet. She
longed to go to school and study a career.
She'd told Pippa so, many times.

"He doesn't explain all of his decisions.
He did say the man has done well with
his land and cattle, despite the rains that
haven't come for us. He can provide a good

dowry for her. Her father said we need the cattle so the family doesn't suffer."

Money. A mixed blessing. A double-edged sword. It gave a person the power to do both good and evil. It was a necessity in so many ways. The world ran on it—a fact that wasn't changing anytime soon. But where was the tipping point between need and want? Between giving and taking?

Pippa needed money to build a school and to buy supplies for children. Her family at Busara needed money to help support the care and rescue operations that had saved so many orphaned baby elephants. Her Aunt Hope earned a good income as a doctor, but she was driven to help others and donated time and funds to bring medical care to rural areas in need. But what about major companies that based their decisions on earnings without considering repercussions or the people impacted? Or the dangers of cutting corners out of greed? What about people who were easily bribed…even some in politics or government whose decisions affected so many? She had no doubt money played a role in companies like Erebus getting land concessions and drilling rights. And even closer to her heart, money was the drug that drove poachers to kill.

Then there were those heart wrenching gray areas. Impossible choices…like Adia's father, Chaga, having to decide between one child's future or the entire family's well-being. She thought of Dax. Had his decision to work for Erebus been one of sacrifice or greed? Or somewhere in the gray shadows between the two? No…in her heart of hearts, she knew he was a good man. A father.

Pippa took a deep breath and closed her eyes. Money was complicated. Heck, life was complicated. She pushed Dax from her thoughts. She needed to focus on Adia. The girl's entire future was riding on the fact that a dowry would help her family. Was the village suffering more than she'd noticed from the drought this season?

The earth crunched beneath her boots as they made their way around a copse of elephant pepper trees. There was Chaga, looking regal with his orange-and-red shawl and long wooden staff. He appeared almost old enough to be Adia's grandfather, but it wasn't unusual for extremely young girls to be married to older men. It had happened to Adia's mother. How old was the man Adia had been promised to? The sound of her footsteps made him look up. The stern set of his face indicated that he knew and expected her protest.

"Sopa. Kasserian ingera?"

"The children are well, Pippa. And your family?" His accent was heavy, but his English was good. He traveled on occasion to the city to trade or sell handmade goods or crops. It was one of the reasons Pippa suspected he'd been more open to her teaching than the heads of some of the other villages.

He turned his staff against the dry ground. Pippa wanted to point out that Adia was still one of the children, but she needed to convince him, not make him defensive. He was a good man within the framework of life as he saw it to be. He loved his family. That, she didn't doubt.

She knew, respected and appreciated the Maasai culture—she'd grown up surrounded by it—but there were certain aspects to *every* world culture…every society…that needed changing. Some things simply weren't right.

There had been a time when hunting trips had been organized for the sole purpose of kidnapping wildlife for zoos. Now, that practice was considered inhumane and horrific. That's what education did. It opened the mind. It even opened the heart. The children out here deserved that chance. Educating the village girls would help their people in the long run.

"My family is good, thank you. I'm sorry to bother you, but can I speak to you for a moment? It's important."

Adia's mother hung back, busying herself with collecting kindling, but she kept well within earshot.

"I expected this," he said, studying the sky as if it had warned him of her arrival.

"Please. Hear me out. I understand these are hard times, but you've been so kind, letting me teach Adia. Don't let that end."

"You don't run a village. I see things. *Meitang'e oltung'ani olkikuei leme olenye.*"

Pippa understood well enough thanks to her Aunt Hope and Hope's brother, Simba, always trying to outdo each other with old tribal wisdoms. *A person doesn't itch from a thorn that's not his*. Adia's father didn't believe she could understand his burdens or the troubles of the village.

He tipped his chin as if he'd had the last word. He should have known her better than that.

"I do understand that times are difficult, but letting Adia and other children pursue an education could help the village. There is much to learn about agriculture. Or perhaps one of them will go into law and be able to speak on behalf of the Maasai and their rights. Or they could share their earnings with you to help when the rains don't come. Let her go to a real school. She'd be of more value to you educated than married off so young. You could make a difference for all Maasai children with this one decision. *Esuj erashe ng'ejuk emusana. If an idea is good, it will be copied.*"

He grinned widely and nodded at her in appreciation of her familiarity with the saying.

"Memut elukunya nabo eng'eno," he said, shaking a finger at her to make a point.

"*One person's mind can't hold all the knowledge out there.* Perhaps, but even a little makes a difference. *Menang' silig kewan.*" She folded her arms and waited. *Facing backward does not perform itself.* She loved that one. Initiative mattered. Even the smallest act is as important as a big one. "You don't need Adia to marry in order for your village to survive."

His mouth moved as if he was mashing her words. He reached up past the giant, beaded loops that dangled from his ears and scratched behind them. His eyes creased in thought.

"The city is expensive." He ground the end of his staff in the dirt again. Relief washed through Pippa like a flooded river during the rainy season. He was considering her plea. She couldn't let him change his mind. She also needed to help him preserve his pride.

"Adia has gotten a scholarship. She doesn't know about it yet," Pippa said. She didn't know about it, either, until she made it up a second ago. It wasn't a lie. As a teacher running her own rudimentary program, she could create a scholarship on a whim if she wanted to. The dilemma would be in how in the world she'd cover it. As it was, she was barely saving enough for a schoolhouse.

"Her school, paid for?"

"Yes. *Edoorie enker modooni nkuta.* Right?" *Even a blind sheep might chance across rainwater.* It meant that good luck could happen to anyone. It was happening to her right now...a woman being listened to by the leader of an exceedingly patriarchal tribe. She hoped that luck would pass on to Adia.

"Perhaps the suitor and his cattle were meant to be our good fortune. A gift from Enkai."

"But didn't your god Enkai choose the Maasai as the wise ones? Perhaps he trusts you to make a wise choice. Perhaps this decision is like a warrior's test. It's even possible that he had our paths cross and brought me here to teach your children for a reason."

He turned and stared intently at her, shifting once to adjust the way his *shuka* draped over his shoulder.

"It is my decision," he said unequivocally.

"Yes. It is." She had to give him that, just like she'd done with Dax, even when she didn't agree with his stringent schedule for his daughters.

"She will not marry now."

Tears welled behind Pippa's eyes, and the pressure in her chest pushed against her throat. She swallowed hard and tried to remain composed. From the corner of her eye, she could see Adia's mother covering her mouth and turning away.

"*Asante*. Thank you. Your wisdom makes you a great Maasai leader."

"May Enkai bless us all," he said. He smiled and trudged off toward his drying field of corn.

Adia's mother rushed over and gave her a hug.

"You are a special one, Pippa."

She didn't want to be special. She just wanted to make a difference...and doing so meant following through. She pushed her hair back from her face, but it sprang forward again.

She'd promised Adia a scholarship. Now she had to figure out how to fund it. Do first, think later. It was her worst fault. Maybe she needed to learn a lesson herself.

CHAPTER EIGHT

PIPPA RAN HER hand along the trunk of Busara's newest orphan as he stood on shaky legs in one of the wooden stalls reserved for those in critical care. The baby barely had the energy to curl its length around her arm, but he tried.

It broke her up inside every time her Uncle Kamau had to rescue another baby. Knowing that the little ones were terrified and traumatized by witnessing the slaughter of their mothers ate away at her insides.

She'd lived here, at Busara, since her birth, and yet the pain and utter disbelief that anyone could rip a family apart for the sake of selling ivory on the black market never got easier. Cruelty was never okay. Children and parents…families…getting ripped apart like that was wrong on so many levels.

"He's still weak, huh?" Pippa asked her mother.

"Yes, but at least he doesn't have any external wounds to contend with," Anna said. Dr. Bekker had done surgery on one too many orphaned elephants over the years. Many had their legs gouged by snares and some even got caught in the crossfire of arrows or bullets. Still others, like this one, slowly starved next to their mother's dead body.

"Do you want to name him yet?" Anna asked her.

Pippa didn't miss the *yet*. Pippa had been naming the babies ever since she learned to speak. Her parents as well as Haki's used to warn her that giving an animal a name too soon or growing too attached would only make it harder if he or she didn't make it. It was too soon to know if this young elephant would survive. She didn't care.

"How about Duma?"

"Cheetah? I don't think he'll ever run as fast as that, even if he fully recovers." Her mom laughed.

"No, but maybe the name will inspire

him to grow strong and healthy enough to dream that he can," Pippa said.

"Fair enough. Let me know if he drinks any formula," she said to the keeper, who stayed close by Duma's side. All of their rescues had their own keepers who cared for them night and day, often sleeping on a cot in the same pen if the baby needed extra attention or was suffering from PTSD.

The whole thing made her think of Ivy and Fern. How had they handled losing their mother? How many nights had Dax held them close to keep bad dreams from plaguing them? Who had comforted him?

She followed her mom out into the afternoon sun and waved as her brother, Noah, and Haki's brother, Huru, jogged out to where Kamau and his team were restocking their field medical unit. They'd both gotten so tall in the past year. At eighteen, Noah was probably done growing. She couldn't believe he'd be leaving for college in the fall. And Huru, at seventeen, was already taller than Haki, though his shoulders weren't as broad.

"Are the boys going on a round?" Pippa asked.

"So I'm told. I'm not sure either of them will have the stomach for injuries the field unit comes across, but we'll see. I'll catch you inside in a bit," her mom said as she headed toward the supply tent.

Pippa looked back over at Noah and Huru. Those two were more into art and law than medicine of any kind. All teens loved adventure, though. Kamau was a well-known field vet in the area, and he'd been instrumental in helping Anna establish the camp back when it was nothing but a few tents.

The only one of the children she'd ever seen him take along as a teenager had been Haki. Then again, Haki had wanted to follow in Kamau's footsteps. He'd ended up in veterinary school. He'd worked diligently at Busara, too, until he'd broken up with Pippa.

Now he and Maddie were living in Nairobi, just until he finished working on his PhD. In the meantime, she practiced law there. Something about seeing his younger brother, Huru, climb into the front passenger seat sent a gutting pain through her. Memories poured out like blood from a nicked vein. She bit her lip and pressed her hand to her stomach. She hated how the pain would come back without warning. She was over the breakup. She really was. Haki and Maddie were destined to be together. Those two were soul mates if such a thing really existed. She'd made peace with it all, at least on some level.

But there was a deep, dark hole inside her that was too far out of reach to heal. A place that held the shattered pieces of her confidence and ability to trust anyone with her heart. She'd trusted both Haki and Maddie. Mads had been more than her cousin. She had been her best friend. And now Pippa was nothing more than a broken and discarded third wheel. Alone.

She forced herself to look away, but everything here had a part of Haki in it. The wooden table where he always played chess under the tree. The old, framed tent where they used to nap as toddlers. The front porch of the main house built many years later, where they'd sit and talk well into the night when they were older teens.

Mosi, the camp's persistent mascot and resident vervet monkey, scampered around her as she approached the house. He squealed and held out his hand, then squealed some more when she held her empty palms up.

"I'm sorry. I don't have anything on me right now."

He ran up the tree that flanked the porch and made a face at her. She made one back and entered the screen door.

"Is that you, Anna?" Niara, Haki's mother and Anna's best friend from the day they met, both single and struggling to cope with their first pregnancies, smiled when she saw Pippa.

"Mom said she'd be here soon."

"I was just going to show her the article I finished for the website. I used that photograph you captured a few weeks ago of the rhino giving birth."

Pippa walked over and looked over her Auntie Niara's shoulder at the screen. She quickly read through the post.

"I love it. It gets to the heart of what we do here."

Niara closed the window and got up, pulling Pippa along with her to the kitchen. Anna may have founded Busara and remained its most famous veterinarian, but Niara was the matriarch of the place. Not only did she contribute to Busara's website and fund-raising initiatives, she was also an amazing cook.

"Honey, you have that look in your eyes again."

"No, I don't."

She tipped her chin down and eyed Pippa.

"You can't fool me. Sit. I'll make some chamomile tea. It'll calm you."

"I'm fine, Auntie. I swear."

She was fine. The moment of pain had passed like all the others before it. It had been worse when she'd first returned home after living in Europe for a year after the breakup. The fact that Busara was home to both her and Haki and their respective families made it impossible to escape the memories entirely, but she'd learned to cope. Sort of. Spending long daylight hours teaching and, now, taking care of the twins helped.

"Well, it won't hurt you to drink it." She set a pot of "safe" water to boil for tea and took a bag of homegrown and dried chamomile out of the cabinet. "How is this job you have with the twin girls going?"

Her mom had asked her the same question earlier.

"Fine, I guess. They've settled down a bit."

"Anna told me about the henna. You always were creative."

"Their father wasn't too thrilled with my creativity, at first."

"And now?"

Now? Dax hadn't brought it up since. Come to think of it, he had stopped harping on her as much about running late, too. Maybe the savanna's slow and undulating energy had tempered his mood. The important things in life really stood out when you were surrounded by life and death and the natural cycle of things.

The important things in life. Like telling the truth.

"I guess he got used to my ways."

Niara smiled as she poured water into two mugs.

"He trusts you now." She placed a mug in front of Pippa and sat down at the large wooden table that could seat ten at a time.

It had been hand built for both families, since they shared the main areas of the house and had separate wings for their bedrooms. Everyone here dined together at the end of the day. It was a tradition. A coming together. One she used to share with Haki.

Trust. Did Dax trust her? Maybe he did with the twins, but apparently he didn't trust her enough to tell her the truth. Why couldn't she just get him out of her head?

"I suppose. I hadn't really thought of it that way," Pippa said.

Dax did trust her. Niara was right. He'd barely mentioned their school schedule lately. He never questioned her about taking the girls to the villages. Or what she did with them all day. How she kept them safe. It was humbling. It was an honor. A wave of warmth spread through her chest, and she hadn't yet sipped her tea. A man like Dax letting go of some control was no small thing, and the fact that it concerned his daughters made it monumental. He trusted her.

But he'd lied.

Haki may have cared about her, but he'd worried about her too much. He hadn't trusted her to be able to take care of herself, let alone keep anyone else safe. He was a good man. An exceptional one at that. But he could never seem to forget the carefree, spontaneous child he'd grown up with enough to see the woman she'd become. And yes, she still hated rules and boundaries, something that drove Haki crazy in terms of potentially endangering herself out in the wild, but that didn't mean she was reckless. She was just overly courageous.

"You're lost in thought."

"Oh. I'm so sorry," Pippa said, blinking and taking a sip of her drink. "I'm tired, and there has been so much going on. Instead of getting to rest on my day off, I feel like my mind is in overdrive."

"Those girls must have made quite an impression on you if you're thinking about them instead of relishing the time off."

Their dad was on her mind, too, but no way was she going to point that out. She wasn't even sure if she should tell her family what he actually did for a living. What if they discouraged her from returning to care for the twins? Her issue was with their father, not them.

"They are not easily forgotten," Pippa said with a smirk.

"You should bring the girls out here. Let us meet them. Let them see the elephants. They'd love it."

"I should."

"Yes." Niara took her mug over to the sink and washed it out. She hesitated, then leaned on the counter and gave Pippa a knowing look. "You should bring their father along, too."

PIPPA HAD SLUMPED her entire body over the sink in Dax's half bath as soon as he'd left for work that morning. Then she'd splashed water on her face to calm her nerves and wake herself up. It did nothing to quell the unsettled feeling in her stomach. She hadn't slept much last night because the fight between them over his work kept playing over and over in her head. She needed to push through the fatigue. The last time she'd fallen asleep on the job, Dax had ended up washing her hair. That wasn't happening again. Not ever.

But here she was, hours later, struggling to stay awake. The girls had also been acting subdued and almost too focused on homework all day. Pippa walked back to their room after using the half bath, since Ivy was in the other bathroom, and found Fern crouched face down on her bed. Her shoulders shook with sobs. Ivy was curled up beside her sister, like twin fetuses nestled against each other in their mother's womb.

Ivy looked over at Pippa.

"Why won't you just leave now! Get it over with. You're no different from the rest. They always leave. Even Mom left. Just go." Her last words came out on a soft, despondent, agonizing sob. Stoic Ivy, crying. Pippa felt her chest rip open.

Their nannies always left, but wasn't it because Ivy and Fern had wanted them to leave? They'd pushed every one of them away. They had done everything they could to try to scare Pippa off, too. And all this time she'd been so sure it was only because they'd wanted Dax to themselves. They wanted a father who was present.

But that wasn't all, was it? *Even Mom left.*

Pippa covered her mouth and swallowed back salty tears. It had never been about pushing anyone away. It was about testing them to see who would leave. They'd tested her, and she had almost passed. Almost.

She started to sit next to them, but both girls scooted off and onto the floor between the two beds.

Fern sat in the corner gasping between sobs. Ivy's face was scrunched painfully tight as her tears fell silently.

Pippa moved around the bed and sat on the floor with them, grabbing their hands when they tried to move away from her again. She tugged them down and wrapped her arms around them both.

How could she promise not to abandon them when it wasn't in her control? Even if she stayed for however many months Dax was assigned to work here, they'd eventually move back to America. Pippa's life was here. Letting them get this attached to her had never been her intention. She'd never expected to love and care for them so deeply. She kissed each one on the top of her head.

"As long as you're in Africa, I'll be here with you."

"But we heard you tell Dad that he needed to find someone else soon," Ivy accused. She tried swiping her face dry, but more tears fell.

"This is all my fault," Fern wailed. "I shouldn't have said anything. My big mouth."

"It's not your fault, Fern. I would have found out sooner or later. Honesty means a lot to me. You're not a big mouth. You just love the truth."

"I didn't mean to make you mad, Fern," Ivy said, trying to steady her breath. "Or you, Miss Pippa."

"Girls. No amount of mud in my hair or identity tricks or stolen batteries is going to scare me away. You're too special to me. You've made this summer the best I've had in a long time, and no matter what the future holds, or wherever you are, I'll always be here for you. That's just the way it's going to be, so you can both stop fighting it."

"We can still be friends after we move back home?" Ivy asked.

"Absolutely. There's that little thing called technology. It has its pluses. Maybe you dad can set you each up with email accounts so that you can contact me as often as you like."

"You think he would?" Fern asked.

"It never hurts to ask. And I have a feeling he'd say yes," Pippa said.

They snuggled against her, and she sat there with them until the sobs softened into hiccups and their eyes closed. She leaned back against the side of the bed and stroked their hair gently as they slept in her arms.

Here she was asking them to be strong, but she wasn't even sure she'd be able to cope when it came time for them to go. Was this what it was like to be a mother? To worry and hope and love a child as if your life depended on it? To be ready to sacrifice that life in an instant if it meant protecting that person?

She finally understood part of the reason why her mother had been determined to keep Pippa's birth a secret for so long… and why her father had been determined to raise her when he found out she existed. Thank goodness they'd come to realize that they not only loved her, they loved each other.

Ivy and Fern's parents would never be together again. Dax was all they had. Her family at Busara were all the orphaned elephants had, at least until they got older.

Her lids felt heavy, and the sound of Ivy and Fern's soft breaths was sedating. A few minutes of sleep. That's all she needed. Just a few minutes.

CHAPTER NINE

TODAY WAS THE DAY. Dax marched through the dry grasses, careful not to disturb any of the cables or geophones they'd laid out. The receiver grid was finally complete and they were ready to start registering readings.

He hadn't been planning to be here. He'd even warned his crew of the possibility of his nanny not showing up and that he might have to stay with his daughters if she didn't. But Pippa had come that morning.

Something overpowering had gripped his chest when he opened the door and saw her standing there. She'd simply said that she was there because she'd given the twins her word. He didn't care that she was there for the twins and not him. Just seeing her again was enough. And it wasn't because he had to work. In fact, a part of him wished he was back at the lodge with them now.

Three Vibroseis trucks sat in line waiting for the green light to begin inching their way along the grid, while stopping at intervals to pound vibrations into the earth. The seismic reflections generated were what Dax needed for developing maps. He preferred this technique over dynamite charges because it didn't pose a chemical threat to the environment. Ironic, since he was surveying for an oil company. At least he was doing what he could do to mitigate damage. Not that these massive trucks didn't leave a trace. There would be surface damage, for sure. There was no way around it.

His team had their computer systems running and ready to take in data. Dax started to put his ear protection on but stopped. The truck hadn't turned their engines on, yet he could feel ground vibrations.

From the way the entire crew startled and looked around at each other, they were all feeling it. The tremor increased in intensity slightly before it suddenly stopped.

Less than a minute and just strong enough to feel.

Even Steven looked up and held out his hands for everyone to wait, in case the shaking resumed, but it didn't. The quake was brief and fairly weak. Had Pippa and the girls felt it back at the lodge?

"Hold off on the test," Dax called out. Now wasn't the time to have the trucks sending acoustic pulses down. It wasn't the time to gather readings for the mapping, either...but Dax sure as heck wanted to see what his seismograph had picked up. "Don't try to tell me that one wasn't worth noting," Dax said to Steven.

"That was definitely not one to ignore. They're disposing down at the field. I was just there earlier," Steven said.

Dax wanted to curse but bit his tongue. Steven had volunteered the information, but Dax still didn't trust him entirely.

"Ron told me he'd pass my concerns to senior management about the readouts we were getting," Dax said. That was when he'd gotten suspicious readings the first few days he was here. This tremor was a game changer.

Hydraulic fracturing generated anywhere from hundreds of thousands to millions of gallons of wastewater per well that had to be disposed of somewhere. So the company routinely injected the wastewater into holding cells dug deep into the earth, a method already under fire back in the United States.

Most of his colleagues had believed there was a link between wastewater injection and an increase in earthquake activity for years now. Studies were finally starting to come in showing a strong link.

But what concerned Dax was whether Erebus would risk trying to reach oil trapped next to a fault. That had a high risk factor for causing tremors or even larger quakes. Were they doing that now? Were the tremors from fracking to access oil where the permeability was low, or from wastewater injections? Either way, they were far too close to a fault as far as he was concerned, but that's what happened when decisions were left to bureaucrats and science was ignored.

Oil companies hired seismologists all the time to help them find the best drilling locations. But environmental groups and those in academic research also wanted experts to back them up—seismologists who would give expert testimony and evidence on their behalf. In effect, counter studies.

And he was walking a tight rope between money and morals by being here. He knew in his gut what they'd just felt was related to the injections. He wasn't an idiot.

"Guys, come with me. I want to see this," Dax said to his team. He purposefully looked to his men…not Steven. He needed to see whatever had been recorded during the tremor. He needed a sign. Was this a precursor event? An isolated one?

God help him…were the twins safe? They were with Pippa. She knew the land. She understood geology. If she felt something or thought they were in danger, she'd protect them. He didn't doubt that for a second. But he wanted to be with them right now. All three of them.

"I called our main office," Steven said, running over. "They want a report by the end of the day. Marked confidential."

Steven had called? Who? Ron Swale, or someone else? And why'd he go over Dax? Man, the guy irritated him. And it wasn't just because of his loyalties. He was passive-aggressive and a subtle manipulator. Dax spared Steven a quick glance.

"It's the only way I send them," Dax said. He'd make his own call. He wasn't going to overlook his protocol just because Steven had overstepped.

And if he didn't get a response—or he didn't get the response he wanted—he'd take matters into his own hands.

Sandy's face filled his mind.

She'd given up on him because he'd become obsessed with figuring out how to save lives, to the point that he hadn't been living his own...at least not with her and the babies. She'd left him because he'd immersed himself in his research.

Yet, now he couldn't help but sense her disapproval, even in spirit. The environmental advocate in her would have hated this. If she were alive and well right now, she'd probably leave him all over again for giving up his soul to Erebus. To darkness.

Guilt settled in the pit of his stomach like black sludge. God help him, he felt like he really was caught in some dark realm between earth and Hades. He couldn't seem to do anything right. Pippa's face replaced Sandy's, and her words came back to him. Sandy had begged him to be there for the twins, and Pippa was telling him he wasn't there enough.

And his own conscience said he needed to do whatever it would take to halt Erebus's drilling. At least until experts could figure out what was going on before it was too late.

True, he'd decided to work with oil companies because he could earn more. But he had needed that money to support his daughters. He'd made that career choice, now he had to live with it. But had he made the right one? What kind of example was he setting for the twins? Money over morality? Short-term results over long-term consequences?

He needed to make things right.

He wiped the sweat from his neck with a small rag he kept in the back pocket of his jeans. The air was dry and the sun was merely warm, but every cell in him felt like it was simmering beneath his skin. Maybe his instincts were trying to warn of a larger quake in the future. Or maybe it was his conscience burning him up.

If the universe was testing him, he was failing miserably.

He removed his hard hat, raked his hair back and replaced the protection.

Pippa. He'd had a handle on things before she'd entered their lives. He'd been doing fine with raising the twins, hadn't he? Well, apart from the high nanny turnover.

He blinked up at the sky and hoped the guys would think he was deciding whether or not it would be safe to proceed with the trucks.

The nannies. Sandy used to say that everything happened for a reason. He hated that saying. It meant that the death of his friend and even Sandy's passing had a purpose...that all the losses he'd suffered had been necessary.

It wasn't. Not to him. It was as senseless now as it had been then. But a part of him couldn't help but wonder if the departure of each nanny had led them to Pippa. Or Pippa to them. No. He was losing it. That sun had to be hotter than he gave it credit for. Or maybe the tremor had shaken up his senses. The stress of working among people whom he disagreed with fundamentally was getting to him. He was also a hypocrite. Even Ivy and Fern had called him out on lying about his job.

But they weren't parents. Someday they'd understand that everything he did, he did with them in mind. He lived to give them better life.

If only life wasn't so complicated.

DAX LEANED BACK and raised his legs onto the empty wicker chair on the other side of the garden table as he peeled another fig. The air was heavy with the scent of fruit. He watched as Ivy and Fern picked mangoes from a small grove of trees on the outskirts of the lodge perimeter, with Alim's guidance. They were growing on the old waiter.

Dax ate the fig and began peeling a banana. He'd gotten back less than an hour ago. Finding the three of them napping together and seeing the twins' puffy eyes had hit him hard. The twins had woken up, but he'd managed to get them out of the room without waking Pippa.

He owed her an explanation, if she'd listen. She deserved more credit than he'd given her before. He'd never met anyone with such grit and strength.

"I'm sorry that I fell asleep."

He jolted as she came out of the bungalow. He quickly put his legs down to free the chair.

"No problem. They were actually still sleeping next to you when I got home." *Home.* Since when was this home?

"Is that your new nanny?"

"Alim?" Dax chuckled. "Don't let him hear you say that. He might have a heart attack. The twins do seem to have chipped away at his gruff exterior, though. I guess sometimes they use their powers for good."

Pippa cracked a smile, but it was weak and a little sad. Dax leaned forward and pulled out the chair next to him.

"Please, sit down, Pippa. Give me a minute to explain."

"I reacted badly yesterday," she said, taking a seat. "What you do for a living is none of my business. I was just caught by surprise and…it's not important. The point is I promised the girls I'd stay on as long as you need me to. For their sake."

"Pippa. There are things I need to say. Things I need you to understand, and I want to explain while the girls are out of earshot."

She picked at her nail, then tried to tuck her hair behind her ear, but the corkscrew lock sprang back out. He loved the way she flinched with irritation every time a lock of her hair did that. He loved her hair. It was perfect for her. Wild. A little unruly. Beautiful.

She reached for a banana from the fruit bowl Alim had brought out. Dax rested his elbows on the table. He didn't want her to see him as the bad guy. He didn't care what anyone else thought, but Pippa's opinion mattered. It just did.

"I've lost a lot of people in my life. My parents announced they were getting a divorce right after I graduated from high school. Pretty much around the time my high school girlfriend broke up with me. Then my sophomore year in college, my best friend and his family were killed in the infamous South Asia quake and tsunami.

That was a lot to deal with for a twenty-year-old."

"That's why you decided to study earthquakes?"

"Yes. I made that decision then and there. But then my junior year, I lost my first college girlfriend to an accident. I think that's when I became obsessed with trying to protect people in my life and people in general. I eventually dated again and met Sandy. We got married as soon as I graduated from college. I was trying to create an unbroken family for myself. Something to hang on to. The thing is, Pippa, I lost my wife long before she got sick."

Pippa frowned and cocked her head.

"You were divorced?"

"Legally separated, but we were headed for divorce. She left me almost a year before she was diagnosed. I wasn't around enough. I wasn't helping enough. I thought I was at the time, but I understand now what she meant. I wasn't present. At least not the way she needed me to be. So she finally figured, why have me around at all? She was a lot like you. Environmental advocate. Nature loving. She told it straight, and she was almost always on target.

"I was only twenty-three when the twins were born. I don't think I was emotionally ready for it. After all I'd been through, I felt it was my calling to try to figure out a way to protect Sandy, my kids and others out there. I *was* in academic research. Research geared toward earthquake prediction. I was working on my master's when the twins were little. I was overwhelmed, so much so that I couldn't see how much Sandy was carrying on her shoulders.

"But when I found out she was sick, I did go home. I halted my research and stayed in Texas to care for her and the twins. I didn't leave her side for six months while she went through treatment. In her last days, she said that she loved me. That she forgave me. That all she wanted in order to die peacefully was to know that I would never leave the twins again. She didn't want them losing both their parents, which is what she said would happen if I tried to deal with her death by burying myself in work the way I had dealt with death before.

"I didn't deserve her forgiveness, but I

kept that promise. I began doing contract work in the oil industry. Working for oil companies meant earning a lot more than I ever could in research. Sandy's medical bills had piled up because I didn't have good insurance, not with the minimal funds I had for research. I needed a steady job to pay those bills, take care of the twins and always have them near me. That, Pippa Harper, is why I'm here working for Erebus. Not because I want to. Because I have to."

PIPPA'S EYES BURNED with tears. For him. For the girls. Her chest tightened. She was ashamed with herself for assuming he was just a man after the highest-paying job. She swiped her nose with a napkin and bit her lip as she looked off toward the girls in the tree. Whatever high branch Pippa had been hanging on all this time, she felt as if the tree under her had just been chopped down.

"I'm so sorry, Dax. I'm an idiot for thinking the worst of you."

"You're not an idiot," he said, shaking his head. "You couldn't have known. I'm the one at fault for keeping Erebus from you. I was so desperate for help that when I found out how active you and your family were in protecting wildlife and the environment, I figured you'd peg me as the enemy, as you put it, and you wouldn't consider watching my kids. I admit that. But that was only at the beginning. Things changed after that and I knew I needed to tell you the truth. I just didn't know how. I was afraid we wouldn't see you anymore. I can't be more honest with you than that." His face flushed a little.

Pippa picked at her thumbnail. If life hadn't unfolded this way, she wouldn't be sitting here with Dax at this moment. She wanted to take his hand in both of hers and make him understand that she wished all his pain could go away. But she didn't dare.

She glanced at Ivy and Fern. No wonder they acted the way they did. They had probably learned to act out in order to get what they wanted from each parent when Sandy and Dax were apart. And then they'd lost their mother and began focusing on trying to earn the attention of the only parent they had left. That's why they had started testing everyone to see who they could count on to stay and not abandon them. They had so much in common with their dad.

"I guess you're right about the fact that I might not have helped you, had I known about Erebus. I'd have missed out on a lot," she said.

He smiled and looked at the girls laughing with Alim.

"We'd have missed out," he said, looking back at her.

She cocked her head at him and this time she didn't look away.

"Thank you for that," she said.

"Can I trust you?"

"Of course," she said. Where was this going?

"I need you to know something else." He cleared his throat, braced his hands together on the table, then exhaled, as if deciding whether what he was about to say would be a mistake. "I'm telling you this in confidence. You need to keep it to yourself because it relates to my work."

"Okay." She frowned and shifted her chair closer to the table.

"I haven't lost my moral boundaries,

Pippa. I swear. I may be working for Erebus, but I'm not going to cower if I see something wrong or if I suspect dangerous activity."

"You're telling me this because you already suspect a problem."

"Yes."

Pippa let out a breath. She knew it. Ever since the company had gotten clearance to drill using fracking methods, she knew no good would come of it. There had to be a link between what they were doing and an increase in tremors in the area. Her gut told her they were also responsible for the sick children in the Maasai villages. She didn't care if Erebus had been cleared in the past of wrongdoing. Something was going on.

"Dax, is what they're doing increasing seismic activity? Are your instruments actually picking it up? Do you know if what they're doing could contaminate underground water supplies? Could—"

He put his hand on her forearm to stop her.

"Back up. What are you saying? Has there been water contamination in the area? You know this for sure?"

"Only suspicions. A couple of years ago, in a village not far from the drill site, my aunt who's a doctor noticed an increase in child illnesses in nearby villages. This was after Erebus got the green light to drill and began fracking shortly after that."

"I wasn't with them at that point."

"I know."

"We tested the village wells for contamination. One tested positive for elevated metals, only that got brushed off as a result of normal tremor activity. And, trust me, it all got reported through the proper channels. Apparently, they'd had an inspection and their wells weren't compromised. At least that's what the reports said. But recently, while teaching, some of the women told me about issues creeping up again. I sent samples back to my aunt. I don't know the results yet. I've been feeling tremors, though. I didn't used to. At least not this often, and I've been here all my life."

"Did you feel a tremor today?" he asked.

"No. Why? Did you?"

Dax nodded and scratched the day-old stubble that shaded his jaw.

"The company is fracking very close

to faults, and that makes me cringe. Even without faults, I'm against it. Not only is the risk of groundwater contamination too high, it uses a lot of water—anywhere from hundreds of thousands of gallons to millions of gallons per well."

"That's unreal," she said.

"And when you look at a place like this, with a drought plaguing the region and people's farms and livelihood affected, it's also sickening," he said "I've seen an increase in seismic activity in the data. I've felt it, so I do think it correlates to Erebus's fracking. I had been taking readings for my own records and research—not initially because of Erebus or anything like that—but my crew and I saw correlations. I told the chief engineer today. He said he'll pass it on to his superiors. Not sure I trust him though, so I plan to look into it more myself. Especially with what you're saying about possible water contamination."

Pippa couldn't believe it. He was on the sly? And here the twins said he didn't like mysteries.

"Wow. Did the twins by any chance inherit their gift for sneakiness from you?"

He waggled his brows and chuckled, as he let go of her arm. She wished he hadn't.

"Probably. I guess that means if you can handle them, you can handle the likes of me."

They both froze, and color rose up the back of his neck and clear to his forehead.

"I totally did not mean to imply that I had any interest in a—"

"Of course not."

"I mean, I do…or would…but—"

"But I'm not your type. I get it. You're not mine, either."

"I know I'm not, but Pippa, for the record, you *are* my type."

"I am?" Goose bumps trailed down her arms and right through her henna tattoos.

"Yes. And I can't deny there's something happening between us, but…" he started.

There was a *but*. Why did there always have to be a *but* in her life?

"I messed up a relationship once, Pippa. I can't go through that or put anyone else, or the twins, through that again. We won't be here after this contract is over. It wouldn't make sense to explore what this is between us. Not when I have to consider the twins.

I don't want them hurt. They're already attached to you. If they got their hopes up that you'd always be in their lives, only to find out it couldn't happen, it would devastate them."

Pippa was still stuck on the fact that he had been feeling something between them, too. She wasn't crazy.

"A lot of things don't make sense. Not everything has to be logical or have a scientific explanation to make sense. I love your daughters. I wouldn't want to see them hurt either," she said.

She did love the twins, but she was afraid to feel anything that strong for Dax. Maybe she was using the twins as an excuse to back away. Maybe they both were. Even if she did feel something for him, admitting it would be stupid. He'd just made it clear that exploring this tug between them couldn't happen. She was not going to pursue a man who didn't think she was worth the risk of jumping into the unknown...of facing the unexpected.

You're so...unexpected.

His words rang in her ears. She needed to get up. It was time for her to leave.

"Some things do have to make sense," he said.

"You're right. I totally agree. I'm glad that's out in the open so we're clear on how things stand. I'll focus on watching the girls, and you deal with finding out what you can at work about the minor quakes we've been having. If my aunt finds out anything about contamination in the water wells, I'll share it with you, too."

"So, we're okay?"

How dense could he be? Time to move on. She stood up and put on a composed face.

"We're totally okay."

CHAPTER TEN

PIPPA SAT CROSS-LEGGED across from Ivy and Fern on the handwoven blanket they had spread out on the ground just outside their bungalow. In the center of the basket lay a wooden bowl filled with tiny beads in various colors, and another one with slightly larger ones. She cut a strand of thin wire and proceeded to string it with tiny beads, as the girls did the same.

"I love doing this," Ivy said, running her fingertips through the glass beads before picking one out. "Feels like sand."

"Mmm-hmm. Melt sand and you make glass." Pippa didn't falter in the rhythm of her stringing as she spoke.

"Really?" Fern swirled her fingers in the bowl.

"Yes, but it's seriously hot stuff. Nothing you'll be doing on a stovetop."

"Why do the Maasai love wearing so many colorful beads?" Ivy asked.

"Yeah. I wondered that, too," Fern said, picking a blue bead and threading it.

"They wear them to show many things, including the strength of the bearer, the stage of life he or she is at, such as warrior-hood or marriage. They make wide neck-laces, or collars, that go from their neck down to their chest for a bride, and the way the beads are strung represents their dowry, which in most cases involves cows."

The girls giggled. Pippa smiled, but she thought of Adia and felt relieved that she wouldn't be wearing such a necklace any-time soon.

"They occasionally also give the jewelry as a gift to show gratitude."

"Have your friends ever given you beaded jewelry?" Fern asked.

"I've gotten a few over the years, and each one is special to me." She eyed the twins' handiwork and smiled. "You two are naturals. I have an idea if you want to make a gift for your dad. You can take both of your strands and make a double-strand bracelet. It's like a friendship bracelet, only it'll represent the two of you being with him, always."

The girls' eyes widened.

"Show us how to combine the ends," Fern said. Ivy held her strand out in agreement. Pippa helped them twist their ends together and had them choose a medium-sized bead to cover the knot.

"Have you ever felt your pulse in your wrist?" Pippa asked them. They shook their heads. She set down her work and demonstrated where to press their two fingers between bone and tendon. "Feel that?"

"Yes! Cool," Ivy said.

"That's your pulse. The beat of your heart." Much like sensing a tremor far from the epicenter of a quake, Pippa thought. "When you tie this bracelet around your father's wrist, it'll be right up against his pulse."

"Can we make more?" Fern asked, as they finished the ends of the bracelet and lay it down on the blanket before them.

"Sure. I promised that you'd have fun if you passed your vocabulary and spelling tests. I keep my promises." Pippa went to work completing her necklace strand.

She heard the rustle of a branch and all three looked up. Alim was setting a plate at a small table and chairs in the shade. He caught them watching, grumbled and walked away, leaving the dish. Ivy jumped up and ran over.

"He left us those triangle doughnuts!"

"Mandazi," Pippa said.

"Mandazi," the girls repeated.

"Did he really leave them for us?" Fern asked, taking a bite out of one before the answer came.

"I believe he did."

"Why is he so grumpy all the time?"

"Well, he doesn't really talk about it, but one of the other hotel staff members once told me that he'd lost his wife and kids in an accident."

"Is that why he never smiles around us? Do you think we remind him of his kids?" Ivy asked.

"Any child probably reminds him of the ones he lost. Sometimes adults can feel bitter about things. Like wondering why someone else has something we don't."

Like why Maddie and Haki have each other.

The thought made her uncomfortable. Was she jealous? All this time, she'd chalked her emotions up to pain. But pain and bitter jealousy were two different things. She didn't want to be jealous. It was such a greedy emotion. She'd always been open-hearted and genuinely happy for others.

She kept stringing as the girls snacked on the pastries. The beading was therapeutic. The rhythm and monotony was meditative.

Finished with their treat, the twins wiped their hands and rummaged through the bowl for more beads.

"You know, we could make jewelry like this when we're back home in America, and sell it in the neighborhood or online, if Dad lets us," Ivy said.

An entrepreneur.

"You could, I suppose. How long did your dad tell you you'd be staying in Kenya?" She wasn't fishing, but the mention of going home struck her. She knew they would be going home sooner rather than later, but she never expected to feel disappointed about it.

"A month or two," Fern said. "Here, give

me your end while I tie mine off," she told Ivy.

"That's a very pretty bracelet," Pippa said. They'd made another "twin" band.

"Hold out your hand," Ivy said.

"Me?" She held her arm out, and the girls wrapped the bracelet around her wrist and tied the ends.

"We made it for you...so that you don't forget us when we return home," Fern said.

Pippa couldn't speak. Pressure built in her nose, and tears stung the rims of her eyes. She sniffed them back and parted her lips, but no words came out. She held her arms out and let the girls come in for a hug.

Alim wasn't the only one they had gotten to. Pippa was going to be crushed when they left.

Dax stood behind the screen door and watched as his girls hugged Pippa. Their bowl of beads tipped over, but she didn't mind. She lay back with her arms cradling Ivy and Fern, then the three of them spread their arms out on the blanket and seemed content to just soak in the moment. He'd been standing there long enough to see how good she was with them and how much they seemed to like her. They were happy.

A lump rose in his throat, and he swallowed hard. He hadn't seen the girls so content since Sandy had passed away. He wasn't even sure how many moments like this one he'd missed because he wasn't around to catch them.

Is that what he was doing for *them*? Working to the point of missing out on their lives? Was dragging them along wherever he went really best for them, or was it a half-assed way to fulfill a promise?

He pushed open the screen, and the three of them jumped up at the sound.

"Dad!" Fern scrambled to her feet and was the first to give him a hug. Ivy was close behind. Pippa's gaze met his, and for a fraction of a second, he imagined her being next, but he quickly shook the thought away.

"You seem to be having fun," he said.

"Oh." Pippa quickly began scooping up beads. "We weren't wasting time. They finished their assignments and did them well so we—"

"I didn't mean it that way," Dax said, holding up a hand to stop her.

"Oh."

Smiles spread across Ivy's and Fern's faces. They hurried back to the mat, picked up the bracelet they'd made and brought it to him.

"This is for you." Ivy held it out, but little furrows formed on both of their foreheads.

"Will you actually wear it?" Fern asked.

Had he really become that serious and unapproachable? He held out his arm.

"You bet I will. Tie it on." They did and he held up his wrist and admired it. "You two do good work. I'm never taking this off. It's staying right where it is. Right next to my pulse." He glanced at Pippa, and her lips parted.

"You know about that?" Fern asked.

"You bet I do. Now, how about you help clean up out here? Wait a minute. What is that?" He stepped over to the blanket with the girls at his heels. Even Pippa looked back down at the beads in confusion.

"What?" she asked, scanning the blanket for something odd and not finding anything he'd be particularly intrigued by.

"That, right there. That's no glass bead," Dax said. They all leaned in. He snatched the last *mandazi* and ran out into the clearing, holding it high over his head between bites. Ivy and Fern chased after him, laughing. Laughter that sounded somehow different from ever before.

Because it'd come from his own joy.

PIPPA SHOOK HER head emphatically at the twins. The past few days had gone by without any issue, but taking them on a campout was more of a challenge than she cared to take on.

"Girls, you should spend your dad's day off with him."

"We would be with him. That's the point. If we're camping, he can't get distracted by his computer and work," Fern said.

"But I have things to do, as well. Like teaching at the villages."

"We've been going with you and you haven't missed any lessons yet, so how far behind could one day make you? We promise to help you catch up at all your next stops. If three of us are teaching, you'd finish in less time, and then you could fit in more stops in a day. Besides, what could be more important than having fun with the two of us?" Ivy said, waggling her brows.

"Spending time with you is priceless and at times an adventure in and of itself. You drive a hard bargain. However, I'm willing to bet your father is going to say no."

"What are you willing to bet?" Ivy said.

"It was an expression. I'm not teaching you to gamble."

"So does that mean yes?" Fern asked.

"You two are more persistent than Mosi."

"Who's Mosi?"

"A little monkey that lives at the Busara Elephant Research and Rescue camp where I live. He's always begging for food. Just like his father used to when I was younger than you are now."

"Wow. You live with monkeys and elephants? Can we visit sometime?"

"I'm sure that could be arranged," Pippa said, remembering her aunt's invitation.

"But for now we want to go camping."

"Don't you get scared?" Pippa asked. "There are noises that sound pretty menacing in the dark. Laughing hyenas. Lions roaring. The rustling of leaves as snakes slither by. Hungry eyes glowing in the moonlight—"

"You're not scaring us," Fern said. They both folded their arms and tapped their right foot on the ground.

"Well, then, maybe *I'm* the one who's too scared to camp with *you*," Pippa joked.

"Let's make a deal. That's not gambling, right? If we can convince Dad to let all four of us go camping tomorrow, then…" Ivy made eyes at her sister for help.

"…then we'll…wash all that dried mud off your jeep when we get back," Fern said.

"I don't wash my jeep in a drought. Water is too precious, even if it seems abundant at this lodge."

"Fine. Then we'll clean out an elephant stall so you don't have to."

"Smart. You're ensuring that you get to go camping *and* you get to visit Busara."

They looked so proud. What they didn't know was that Busara had plenty of staff and Pippa rarely, if ever, had to muck elephant poop.

"You convince your dad, and we have a deal."

DAX PUT ANOTHER log in the shallow fire pit he'd dug out and encircled with lava rocks. He watched Pippa walk back with the twins from collecting several more armfuls of wood and sticks to keep the fire burning through the night.

An old acacia tree sprawled out its canopy to their left and he could hear Pippa warning the twins about the thorns that covered the trunk and branches. Ivy carried her bundle of sticks and went over to the tree for a closer look. Fern stayed next to Pippa, who waiting patiently for Ivy to rejoin them. The closer they got, the better he could hear them. Pippa was really in nature-hike mode, giving them all sorts of information on what they were seeing in the surrounding environment. Even Dax was interested and listened as he continued to set up their fire pit.

They were only thirty minutes west of the lodge…close enough to head back if there was an emergency or someone got sick, but far enough for the twins to enjoy the experience. It didn't take much to be in the wild, considering Tabara Lodge was fairly remote to begin with.

Pippa had told them that Camp Busara was yet another thirty minutes to an hour west of here by the edge of the Maasai Mara and into Kenya's Serengeti ecosystem. The amount of time she'd been spending in daily commute said a lot about how much she wanted to build a school house. What did the fact that he commuted an hour north of Tabara say about him?

Ivy climbed onto a small, rocky outcropping to their right and jumped off without dropping a stick. Fern looked a little nervous, but went ahead and made the climb and jump, too, before running to catch up with Pippa.

"That's looking good," Pippa said, jerking her head toward his campfire. She set down her armful of wood and the twins followed suit.

"I've done my share of camping. Not surrounded by lions, but I can start a fire and pitch a tent."

The lodge had access to family-sized tents for tourists. Rather than rent two, they decided to share one, letting the girls sleep in the middle so that Dax and Pippa could be on opposite sides.

At first, Pippa had insisted she bring along a pup tent for herself, but the twins had been adamant about her sharing theirs. The said that they'd feel safer if she slept next to them. And Dax had to admit he felt it was safer for Pippa, too. He'd never forgive himself if something had happened to her in the pup tent. It wasn't a question of her being able to take care of herself. She lived here. It was a matter of conscience and doing what was right.

You can't pick and choose which right and wrongs to follow. Are you doing what's right with your job?

"Are any of you hungry?" Pippa asked. Not only had she brought along a cooler that her mother and aunt had presumably packed for them at Busara, but Alim had also shown up when they were loading the jeep and handed Dax a bag of pastries from the lodge's kitchen. All he'd said was, "For them. For breakfast," and then he'd hurried back to his restaurant duty. Curious old man.

"Not yet," the twins said simultaneously.

"There's too much to do before dark,"

Ivy added. "We want to hike down near the river."

"Not alone," Dax said, standing up.

"We're not stupid, Dad," Fern said.

"No, you're not," Dax said. "Just a little too daring for my comfort."

Dax and Pippa exchanged a look. He was pretty sure the same thought had crossed her mind. *Do we trust them not to disappear on us?*

"I tell you what. If we make sure the food is locked up and head out now for a short hike, we can be back with enough daylight left to get the fire going and eat dinner," Pippa said.

"Sounds like a plan to me," Dax said.

The girls eyed them, and he almost missed the nudge Fern gave Ivy. They were up to something.

"Sounds perfect," they said.

"No tricks out here, Ivy and Fern. I mean that. There are real dangers behind every tree," Dax warned.

"We'll stick within an inch of you, okay?" Ivy said.

Pippa laughed at the expression on his face.

"I might trip over you. Make it a couple of feet."

"Wow. A whole two feet. You're not as protective as we thought you were." Ivy smirked.

"Just wait until you try to bring boys home," he said.

"I'm so sorry for you both," Pippa told the twins. She curled her lips in to keep from laughing, then trotted over to the jeep and grabbed her camera.

"We can't let you return to the States without photos of you out here," she said. Why don't the three of you go stand in front of that acacia? It'll make a classic photo of you in Africa."

Dax followed the girls to the tree and put his arm around each one. Pippa snapped several shots, then lowered her camera.

"I'll make sure you get copies of these," she said.

"Would you trust me with your camera?" Dax asked. "I'd love to take one of you, Ivy and Fern."

The twins ran up to her and wrapped their arms around her waist. She hugged them back, then pulled her camera strap over her head.

"Of course. I'd love a photo with them."

The twins grinned at each other, then pulled her over to the shade of the tree.

Dax focused the lens. For a brief moment, he just looked at them through the lens and the idea that these were the women in his life…the three most important people in his life…hit him like a boulder. He blinked, then took a few shots. *The three most important people in my life.*

"We know you were upset with us when we took your battery, but if we promise to be careful, can you show us how to focus it?" Fern asked.

"You can be standing next to us," Ivy added. "I want to try taking a photo of that scene."

She pointed beyond the tree to where the slender blades of savanna grasses glistened like threads of gold in the late afternoon sun. Boulders and jagged outcroppings dotted the landscape like crumbs, leading their eyes to a dry creek bed. A herd of gazelle stopped briefly, then bounded away when no water was to be found.

"Did you see that?" Fern asked.

"Those poor things were thirsty," Ivy said. "Please, can we try the camera? What if more animals show up? I might get them in the photo."

Pippa looked pointedly at both of them.

"You remember what I told you about the camera, right? You'll respect it?"

Dax gave them yet another look.

"Of course we will," Fern said. "Besides, you're both standing right here."

"Okay, but if you fight over who goes first, no one gets to try it," she said.

"Here you go, then," Dax said, handing over the camera.

Pippa proceeded to show them how to focus and which button to push. She handed the camera to Fern first and took a step back. She wanted Fern to feel confident. She wanted her to go first for a change. Ivy didn't argue. She simply stood closer to Fern, looked over her shoulder, then whispered something in her ear.

"No funny play," Dax warned again.

"We're not. I was just telling her not to use up all the battery before I get a chance to take a photo." The two of them took a few steps forward and began taking aim.

Pippa went and stood by Dax.

"They'll be fine," she said to him. "This is good for them. Maybe they'll take photography up as a hobby. It's a lot better than boredom," she said.

"Thanks for all this. The camping. Letting them use your camera. All of it," he said.

"I want them to have good memories from their time here," she said.

The sound of Fern and Ivy giggling had them breaking eye contact and looking at the girls. Fern was pointing the camera at Pippa and Dax. She took another shot. Ivy grinned. Pippa blushed. She hadn't expected to take a picture with Dax any more than he had with her. He had a funny feeling the twins had planned it. In any case, he hoped it would be among the photos Pippa sent them.

"This photography thing is great," Ivy said.

"I wish you could come home with us," Fern said.

"Yeah. Me, too," Ivy said.

Dax stuffed his hands in his pockets and didn't comment. The twins had never said anything like that to their previous nannies. They were actually going to miss her. He understood why but it worried him.

He knew he would miss having her around, too. And not just because of the girls.

PIPPA TRIED NOT to look at Dax through the firelight as he told the captivated twins a story. Firelight was too dreamy. It masked reality almost as well as darkness could. But she had to admit, seeing him so relaxed was nice. Scary nice, because she liked this side of him—too much. But he had made it clear that anything between them was impossible.

She gazed at the embers popping and rising like startled fireflies. She hugged her knees close to her chest and listened as Dax described one particular week he'd been doing field research for his master's degree. He'd been working hard on his thesis paper, and rather than putting his things away and crawling into his tent, he fell asleep by his campfire. What he hadn't realized was that there was a farm nearby, and by morning, the fire was fizzled out and a goat was finishing off the last bite of his thesis for breakfast.

"So 'the dog ate my homework' excuse can really happen." Fern chuckled.

"Which is why we don't have one," Dax pointed out. "Knowing you two, that dog would be gnawing away at a couple of hundred dollars' worth of electronics."

"Pippa, did an animal ever eat your homework?" asked Ivy.

Pippa bit her lower lip and scrunched her face.

"Once, when I was ten, I took the shared laptop we had at Busara that I used for homeschooling and brought it over to one of our biggest elephant orphans. I slipped it as close to his foot as I could and got him to stand on it."

Ivy, Fern *and* Dax stared at her in disbelief.

"You did not," Ivy said, with clear admiration in her voice.

"I'm afraid I really did."

"What did your parents do?" Fern asked.

"That's what I want to know." Dax

grinned as he stoked the fire, but when he glanced up and their eyes met, something shifted in his face…something smoldering and daring.

His smile softened and his gaze lingered a few seconds too long. The embers popped like a dangerous shot in the dark, then a burning log fell to its side as the twigs beneath it cracked and crumbled, throwing sparks carelessly between them. They were playing with fire.

Pippa forced herself to look directly into the flames between them. Maybe the twins hadn't noticed and would think Pippa and Dax had been staring at the fire all along. She picked up a small pebble from the dirt next to the log she sat on and rubbed it between her palms.

"Don't you remember?" Ivy asked.

"What? Oh." She cleared her throat and gathered herself. "They made me clean out elephant poop from the pens for an entire week." Nothing like elephant poop to kill whatever she was sensing from Dax.

"A whole week?" Ivy asked.

"Yep. Not all of them, but enough of

them to teach me a lesson." It had been the last time she'd had to do that.

"Thank goodness we only have to do one, once." Fern made a face.

Dax stopped stoking.

"You're making them clean elephant poop?"

"Don't look at me." Boy, did that carry a double meaning at the moment. "It was their idea. I lived. They will, too."

Dax took a deep breath and added another log to the fire.

"I have to see this to believe it."

The fire hissed just as the rhythm of insect song was interrupted by grunts and howling. The girls tensed.

"Don't worry. They're far off," Pippa said. The girls seemed to relax. They all sat there in comfortable silence for a while, staring at the fire. She didn't dare glance over at Dax.

"I wish we had marshmallows," Fern said.

"You've had plenty of sugar." They'd convinced him to let them eat a couple of the pastries Alim had given them. Dax shuffled his boot against the dirt.

"It's so pretty," Ivy said, staring into the

flame. "I love the way the burnt pieces of wood at the bottom glow red-hot."

"Should I be worried?" Dax joked.

"No, Dad. It reminds me of the volcanoes in those documentaries we watched once. There was that one in Iceland people used to think was the door to hell. Mount Hek...something," Ivy said.

"Hades?" Fern tried. "No, Hecate?"

"Those names are from Greek mythology. The volcano is in Iceland. Sheesh," Ivy said. Fern's face turned red.

"Mount Hekla," Dax said, trying to break up any argument.

"I was just trying to remember the name that started with *H*," Fern defended. "I *know* those names are from Greek mythology, just like Erebus was the brother of Tartarus, Gaea, Nyx and Eros, who were the gods of the underworld, earth, night and *love*. Right, Dad? I'm not stupid."

Did she have to bring up Erebus? *Erebus. The flame. Wood burning. Coal. Fossil fuels.* Pippa tried reminding herself that he wasn't the man for her. That he'd lied about it all.

"You actually got them right," Ivy said. "Kind of interesting that, here we are, surrounded by earth…sitting around a fire that's kind of like the underworld…in the dark at night…with *love* in the—"

Dax coughed loudly, then pretended to wave away the smoke. Pippa's cheeks burned and it wasn't from the heat of the fire.

"I think it's time for bed," Dax said.

Ivy yanked Fern's arm and pulled her up.

"You're so right, Dad. We're going to bed," Ivy said. They both stretched and yawned a little too dramatically.

"Good night," Fern added. They ran into the tent faster than wildfire.

Neither one said anything for a few moments after the twins zipped up their tent.

"Sorry about that," Dax said, finally.

"I know you had nothing to do with it. I'm flattered that they like me enough to pull a stunt like that," Pippa said.

He pressed his lips together and nodded.

"I can stay out here and watch the fire. You go ahead and use the tent," he said, reading her mind. After what the twins just did, sharing the tent wasn't a good idea.

"I can stay here. I've tended plenty of fires," Pippa offered.

"No. I'm sure you have...and could... but so long as I'm here, you get the tent."

Pippa tossed her pebble down and stood.

"Thanks. I guess I'll see you in the morning, then."

"Pippa—"

He was going to say too much. She could almost hear his thoughts. It was the smoke and wilderness and darkness playing tricks with their hearts.

"Good night, Dax," she said, then she disappeared into the tent with the twins.

DAX DUMPED THEIR camping supplies just inside the door of the bungalow. None of them had spoken much that morning. They'd smothered the fire and taken down the tent, but everyone seemed exhausted. He hadn't slept a wink and he needed to go out to his research site to check on things today, even if for only a couple of hours.

Pippa followed the twins inside the room, helping them carry a few things. Dax wiped his palms against his jeans and waited for Ivy and Fern to pass by on their way to their room so he could speak to Pippa alone.

"Pippa, about last night. I don't want things to feel awkward. I don't want you uncomfortable. I can talk to the girls or—"

"Dax, it's okay. Kids do things like that. They have wild imaginations and don't always see the reality of situations. Just let it go," Pippa said.

Stress and fatigue were gnawing at his muscles and brain like parasites. He was too tired to think. She was brushing off what the girls had said, but was she also brushing off whatever had passed between her and him before that?

He was the one who told her it could never work out between them. He was the one who wanted to protect his daughters. He had no right to wonder if Pippa was also finding it impossible to ignore the pull between them. She was acting so...professional...it bothered him.

"Maybe the twins are getting their hopes up too much at this point. I'll look harder at getting someone new out here to help with them. Maybe it'll be best for all of us," he said.

"Oh, you're not doing that until we figure out what's happening at Erebus. We need to work together on this anyway. Plus, I have a school to build and scholarship to fund. You can't fire me now."

"Okay, then. I appreciate your staying, Pippa. Today and the near future."

She shrugged and started for the wash-basin.

"Just don't be late coming back. I have a schedule to stick to," She said.

Right. He'd had that one coming. And then some.

Two DAYS SHE'D been on schedule, and now Dax was running late. At least he'd called this time. Pippa simply couldn't risk hav-ing to stay the night with him and the twins again. Not after that night at the campfire and not since then, either. The twins were clearly determined to match-make. Pippa had even slipped in comments…little re-minders…about how they'd stay in touch after they returned to the United States but the message didn't seem to be sinking in. And now, she'd overheard them whisper-ing about how they liked the way Pippa was there whenever their dad got home. Like they were all a family. She definitely needed to limit the number of times she slept over, for their sake as much as her own.

The satellite phone sputtered static in her ear. She moved a few feet to see if she'd get better reception. She really needed to talk to him. Instead of her staying over, she had just suggested taking the twins with her to Busara. It would give them a chance to see the elephants, too, killing two birds with one stone. But his voice cut out before she got an answer.

"Can you hear me better now?" she asked.

"Yes, I've been hearing you. You can't hear me for some reason."

"I can now. Wherever you're standing, don't move. Listen, Dax, if you heard what I said about Busara, then you'd have to agree it would work out perfectly."

"I still don't think it's a good idea for them to go all the way there without me. That's a long drive. I'm not even sure there's enough daylight left."

"I've done it plenty of times and I know how to play it safe. If we leave now, we'll make it well before sunset. Look, the experience would be phenomenal for them.

They'd love it. The entire family is gathering tomorrow, so I can have my Uncle Mac pick you up at Tabara after work, or even at your site if that's easier for you. Then you can come to Busara yourself and see what a great place it is. You'll witness firsthand how much fun Ivy and Fern are having, and you'll get to meet my family."

It hit her as soon as the words left her mouth. She'd just invited him to meet her family. Surely, he wouldn't take it that way. It was clear the entire purpose was for him to join his daughters. Still, there was an uncomfortable pause on the other end of the line.

"I don't know. I definitely don't want to open Pandora's box with your uncle or the rest of the family regarding Erebus."

"Then we won't mention it. Mac can pick you up with his helicopter from here. Dax, do you trust me with Ivy and Fern?"

"Yeah. I do."

"Then it's settled. We'll see you tomorrow. In the meantime, be safe."

CHAPTER ELEVEN

BUSARA WAS A hive of activity when they arrived, and after singing with the girls in the jeep for the past hour, they'd all worked up an appetite. The aroma of Auntie Niara's cooking wafted to her from the kitchen, making Pippa's mouth water. She hopped out of the jeep, and the twins followed suit.

"Over there." Pippa pointed toward a row of pens built out of wooden poles and topped with thatched roofs. "That's where we keep the orphaned elephants. The part attached to it is the clinic where all the supplies are kept. We keep the emergency cases or surgical recoveries there, too. And off to the right, those older-looking framed tents are where I grew up, from the time I was born until I was about six years old."

"You lived in a tent. Permanently?" Fern asked.

"Yep. Not even a modern bathroom.

We took bucket showers out back. At the time, my mother was raising me on her own. My dad wasn't around back then. It was just my mom, her best friend, whom I call Auntie Niara, and her son Haki, who was a little older than I was. My mother's colleague, Kamau, worked here, too. He ended up marrying Niara and adopting Haki. You'll meet them along with Haki's younger brother, Huru. You'll also meet my younger brother, Noah."

"What about your dad? Why wasn't he around? Work? Our dad used to not be around a lot of the time because of his job," Ivy said.

Pippa put her arm around her. She didn't want to overload their minds with the fact that her dad hadn't even known about her until she was four.

"Oh, he was working in America, but he did end up moving here permanently, and that's when they built that house over there." She pointed to the left of the circular clearing in the center of the buildings. "That made life much easier. We even got a real bathroom."

"I want to see the baby elephants."

"Can we really touch them?"

"You can. I haven't forgotten about the stall-mucking deal, you know."

Their faces fell.

"Well, if we can pet a baby elephant, it'll be worth it." Fern said.

"Pippa! We've been waiting," her mother, Dr. Anna Bekker, called out from the clinic doorway.

"Hi, Mom." Pippa motioned for the girls to follow her. "Come on. My mother is queen of the elephants. In fact, her radio name ever since I can remember has been Mama Tembo, which means *elephant mother.* She's probably dying to introduce you to the babies."

"Oh gosh! Ivy, look!" Fern pointed toward a keeper who was walking one of their most recent rescues out into the courtyard area. He was leading the baby toward a nearby clearing where they took the elephants to be fed and exercised. Anna stopped him as Pippa approached with Ivy and Fern. She'd never seen such huge smiles on their faces.

"Mom, this is Ivy and Fern."

"Hi," Ivy said. She wasn't as bold as usual.

"Hi...Mama Tembo," Fern said. Pippa chuckled at the surprised look on her mom's face. Poor Fern's cheeks reddened. "I'm not sure what I'm supposed to call you."

"I was just telling them about the code name you earned," Pippa explained. "I should have told you girls that her real name is Dr. Anna Bekker."

"I thought your last name was Harper," Ivy said.

"It is. I have my dad's last name. Mom kept her maiden name for professional reasons."

"You can call me anything you like. I answer to all of it," Anna said with a welcoming smile. "And this little one is Amani. It means 'peace' in Swahili."

Amani raised her trunk and poked at Fern's belly, then Ivy's. The girls giggled and tentatively reached out to touch her trunk.

"What's she doing?"

"She probably thinks you're hiding her milk bottle in your pockets," Pippa said.

"She has hair on her head," Ivy noticed.

"The babies are quite fuzzy," Anna said. "Most people don't realize that."

"This is so cool." Fern looked like she was about to cry from the experience.

"Dad isn't going to believe we got to pet an elephant. This is so amazing." Ivy held out her palm and scrunched her nose when Amani tickled it.

"He'll be able to see for himself soon. I believe Mac is going to do rounds in his helicopter to pick everyone up," Anna said, as Amani was led away.

"Everyone?" Pippa assumed he was picking only Dax up.

"He's stopping at Camp Jamba-Walker to get Tessa. His wife," Anna explained to the girls. "And he's also picking Haki and Maddie up from the airstrip at Hodari Lodge."

"They're making it in from Nairobi?"

"That's the plan."

Pippa had seen them plenty of times since her return from abroad a year ago. Her trip had been more about needing to reevaluate her life and identity than about trying to avoid them. And things were okay now between them all, sort of. She still felt awkward around them, but things were civilized because they had to be. She wasn't sure how she felt about Dax's meeting Haki, though. She wasn't sure why. It just seemed strange, even if she and Dax weren't together.

"Well, then. You'll get to meet my cousin and friend, too, Ivy and Fern. Why don't you come in the house for some snacks and I'll introduce you to Noah and Huru. Oh, and no doubt Auntie Niara is cooking up a storm. She's an incredible cook. Sorry, Mom."

"Don't be. Everyone is safer when I work with wildlife, as opposed to food. Ivy, Fern, make sure Pippa brings you out here again to see the clinic and meet the other orphans. I need to get back to work."

"Thank you," the twins chimed, as Anna returned to the clinic.

"Now, only one rule out here," Pippa warned them. "You don't wander off. Got it?" The girls nodded. "I mean it. This isn't Tabara Lodge, not that you should wander off the grounds there, either. But this camp is pretty isolated, and the reason we have orphans in our care is because there are poachers out there. Evil people you don't want to encounter. And then there are wildlife dangers. I don't want you anywhere I can't see you. Promise?"

"We promise. For real."

Interesting qualifier on a promise.

"Okay, let's go inside. I'll show you my bedroom. All my stuff is still in it from when I was your age."

They headed up the steps to the front porch of the single-story home. Mosi, the vervet monkey who'd been hanging around Busara all of his life, just as his father, Ambosi, had before him, jumped out of the tree overhanging the porch and screeched at the twins. They both jolted and screeched right back, terrified. Both of them gripped onto Pippa's arms and stood slightly behind her.

"He won't hurt you. This is Mosi, the monkey I told you about. He's a self-appointed guard for the camp. Trust me, once he realizes you're not strangers, he'll start flirting or begging you for food instead of trying to scare you."

"I wasn't scared," Ivy said, slowly peeling herself off Pippa's side. Nope. Not scared at all.

"He just surprised me," Fern said.

"It's okay. You'll get used to him. Mosi, I don't have any food, and that's not a nice way to greet our guests."

The monkey cackled and scampered back up the tree.

Pippa held the screen door open for the twins.

"After you. I'm starving."

BETWEEN GOING THROUGH her books and photographs and visiting the elephants again, Pippa lost track of time. The twins had fallen asleep on her bed, poring over the photos of her, Haki and Maddie as kids.

Seeing those pictures used to make her throat close up and her chest cramp. Tonight, the twist in her stomach had been a little less harsh. Was it because she now had Dax and the girls around—temporarily?

She took one last look at the twins sleeping on her bed. They looked so harmless and innocent while sleeping. She'd heard people say that about little kids, but now she knew what they meant. She closed the door and went to the living room to sleep on the couch.

"Hey." Her mom was standing in the corner of the kitchen making a cup of tea. "Do you want a cup?"

"No, thanks. I'll end up falling asleep before it cools enough to drink."

She followed her to the couch, and they both curled their feet up.

"I like them. The twins," her mom said. "Good kids, despite the stories you've told me."

"I like them, too." Though it was more accurate to say she loved them. Her mom tipped her head to the side and gazed carefully at Pippa.

"Don't do that, Mom."

"Do what?"

"Try to read me or put pressure on me to speak without your saying a word."

"I don't do that."

Pippa gave her a look.

"Okay, but I'm a mother and something tells me your liking the girls isn't the whole story."

"There is no story."

"I guess I'll find out for myself tomorrow, when their father gets here."

"Mom."

"Pippa. I just don't want you hurt again. I'll know when I see the two of you together if something is going on."

"Nothing is going on. Nothing whatsoever."

"Just remember that he's already a father. If you grow too attached to his children, you could become an instant mother—twice over, in this case. Trust me, that's not easy. I was a single mother raising you out here, and we didn't even have this house. I know a thing or two about responsibility."

"And I don't? Mom, I'm not the same person I was two years ago. I know who I am and what I can handle."

Anna patted her on the knee.

"Personally, I think you're amazing, and any man you fall for had better be worth it. Don't get mad at me. I'm just saying my piece because I noticed the way the twins looked at you and vice versa. Get some sleep."

She got up and disappeared down the hall. Pippa put her head on the pillow and pulled the throw over her shoulder. An instant mother. Could she handle it? Did she want to? Dax was right. Anything between them was impossible anyway, so why waste time wondering? She had goals. A school to build. And he would be leaving. Their lives were too different. If they were meant to be, one of them would have to decide the other was worth dropping everything for. One of them would have to leave behind life as they knew it. There were too many uncertainties, but if there was one thing Pippa was sure of, it was that neither one of them would be willing to sacrifice it all.

THE WHIR OF Mac's helicopter approaching the following day caught Pippa off guard. She had become engrossed in showing the girls how to take photos, teaching them about lighting and composition. But at the sound of the helicopter, her stomach knotted. Had Haki and Dax gotten along on the trip over? What would Dax think of Busara? Why did she need to keep reminding herself that he was coming here only because she'd dragged his daughters over. This had nothing to do with seeing her or her family, although she'd been anticipating seeing him all day.

"Is Daddy on that?"

"Sure is. Come on." Pippa led them out toward the edge of the camp and they watched as Mac land his chopper in the clearing he always used just up the dirt road…far enough away not to churn up dust in the camp's courtyard area or disturb the baby elephants. She and the girls waited by where the Busara-marked vehicles were parked. Pippa watched as Haki helped Maddie out and they started over toward Pippa. Dax emerged next and held a hand out to help Tessa down. They waited for Mac to join them before catching up to Maddie and Haki.

"Hey, come give me a hug," Dax said when he approached the girls, holding out his arms. The twins ran to him, and Pippa managed to stop herself from following. She knew he was talking to his daughters, not her, but despite her mother's warning, she wished he was welcoming her with open arms, too. He kissed the girls on the tops of their heads, then made eye contact with Pippa. The corner of his mouth lifted. "Hi."

"Hi."

"Hey, Pip." Haki waved as he strolled right past Dax and stopped in front of the twins. Maddie was by his side. "These must be your daughters," he said, glancing back at Dax with a smile.

"Yes. Ivy and Fern," Dax said. Pippa could hear the pride in his voice.

"Nice to meet you, Ivy and Fern." Haki held out his hand to shake theirs.

"You're as pretty as your dad said you were on our flight over," Maddie said.

The twins blushed.

"Thank you," they said.

Pippa's stomach pinched like it always did whenever Haki and Maddie came around. She tried not to show it. She had her pride. They looked so happy together. Besides, if they hadn't followed their hearts, she would have ended up marrying before she was truly ready. She hadn't been, in retrospect, and now she was grateful that Haki had seen that. She'd been devastated at the time, but now she understood that everything had happened for a reason. She wouldn't have stopped Adia from being forced to marry. She wouldn't have accomplished so much with her teaching. She wouldn't have met Dax, Ivy and Fern. But maybe her mom was right. Maybe she still wasn't ready for a long-term commitment. At twenty-four, was she prepared to start one with a single dad? Instant motherhood had never been on her to-do list. She had plenty of kids out there who were relying on her as it was. But the twins relied on her, too, and she felt...like a mother to them.

She smiled at Haki and Maddie.

"Hey, guys. It's good to see you," Pippa said, giving them both hugs. "How's the PhD going? And the law practice?"

Haki had gone back to the city for a doctorate in veterinary science, and Maddie, who'd been practicing humanitarian law in the United States, now worked for the office branch in Nairobi. Eventually, the two planned to build their own place and clinic in a remote area not too far from Busara.

"Everything is great. Actually, better than great. We have some unexpected news, and we'd actually like you to be the first to hear it," Maddie said.

"Have you gotten the land you wanted to build a home and vet clinic on, yet?" Haki had had a location on a hill he'd been dreaming about building on for years now. As a vet, he wanted to provide medical care to the Maasai for their herds.

"No, that's not it," Haki said.

"You're going to be an aunt," Maddie blurted. "I'm eight weeks along."

"Oh my God! That's incredible!" Pippa hugged her and then Haki. "I'm going to be an auntie." *An aunt. Not a mother.*

She was truly overjoyed for them. But she had just barely begun learning to cope with the fact that they were married. Maddie was now carrying Haki's child.

Mac walked up with his wife, Tessa, on his arm. They looked at each other, and Tessa nodded.

"Well, then," Mac said. "Not to steal the moment, but if we're celebrating starting families, we might as well do it all at once."

Everyone's mouth opened in shock. Even Pippa's and Haki's parents had walked up to meet Dax and greet the rest but stopped in their tracks. Tessa had been battling early miscarriages since they'd gotten married around seventeen years ago. They'd given up. And now she was in her forties and pregnant?

"I know what you're all thinking," Tessa said. "I'm not pregnant. We decided to adopt. Actually, we started the process some time ago and weren't sure it was ever going to happen. But we just found out that by next week, we'll be the parents of a three-year-old boy."

There was a slurry of tears and congratulations to both Tessa and Maddie. Everyone also apologized to Dax and the twins for leaving them standing there, but they didn't seem to mind. Dax kept glancing over at her. Her mother and Niara kept glancing between the two of them. Pippa put all she had into keeping a neutral face. So much was happening. Why had she thought that bringing Dax and the girls here would be a good idea?

"I hope you're all hungry," Niara said. "The food is ready."

The entire group started for the house. They squeezed around the long, rough hewn wood table that sat in the open-concept dining room. They'd added a small extendable table to the end to accommodate everyone. Dax looked out of the large wall window that overlooked the valley and river beyond Busara.

"So, this is home for you. That's one amazing view," he said.

"Busara is a special place," Pippa said.

"We made a deal to do some poop scooping," Fern reminded Pippa.

"Good luck with that." Huru adjusted the cap on his head.

"Why would you remind them?" Noah asked.

"I think you and Noah should supervise," Pippa's father, Jack, said. "Take them to meet the keepers and make sure they have good technique."

"How much technique could be involved?" Ivy asked.

"It's all in the wrist," Jack said. Jack had sampled many a pile of dung as part of his genetic research.

"He's messing with you," Pippa said. "Stop it, Dad. Noah and Huru, please take them to the pens. I'm not holding you two to the cleaning, but go have some fun petting and maybe helping with bottle-feeding."

"We'll clean, too. But we're totally bottle-feeding," Fern said.

Huru and Noah took them over to the elephant stalls.

Pippa excused herself from the group and walked after them. She watched until the girls reached the stalls, then turned at the sound of the screen door opening and closing. Dax stood on the porch.

"They're going to be preoccupied for at least the next hour or two. I need some fresh air. I'm going for a ride. Coming?"

"You're taking off with everyone here?" Dax asked.

"I just want a break." She couldn't take any more all-eyes-on-her…especially from her parents. "Trust me, the twins couldn't be any safer with my family. If you don't want me to show you the area, you don't have to go," Pippa said, grabbing her camera. "I'm heading out for a while whether you come or not." She really needed some space.

Dax glanced back toward the girls and

then at the jeep. It wasn't leaving the girls here that worried him. It was being alone with Pippa. He didn't trust himself, or whatever it was about her that he couldn't get out of his system. And she clearly had been hurt before. Plus, his days here in Kenya were numbered. Getting any closer to Pippa wouldn't be fair to her. He'd only end up hurting her, too.

But something about her sudden desire to flee told Dax that she shouldn't be alone right now.

"Let's go, then," he said. "We'll be back before dark, right?" Camping under the stars with the twins was one thing. Being alone all night with Pippa would be an entirely different situation.

"Dax. We're not going that far, and we'll be home well before nightfall."

He followed her to her jeep and didn't say much as they headed past the landing area for Mac's chopper. She suddenly veered left off the dirt road, torturing whatever was left of her shock absorbers, then floored the jeep through a clearing, slowing down only when the tall grasses masked whatever lay ahead.

"Boy. Is that always how you vent?"

She pressed her lips together.

"I told you I needed air."

"I do want to make it back alive. The whole fatherhood thing. Remember?"

"You were perfectly safe," she said, pulling up a few meters from a giant granite outcropping and pulling to a stop. She slumped back and sighed. "I know that stretch and just about every pebble and blade of grass around here like the freckles on my nose."

His attention shifted to her nose, and her cheeks flushed.

"Um. Follow me. There's a great view up ahead."

She slung her camera over her shoulder, then opened a locked compartment at the back of the jeep and pulled out a rifle and left behind what looked like a tranquilizer gun and a case. She had guns? A part of him could understand why, but the other part felt uneasy.

"Have you used that thing around the twins?"

"No, I keep them locked up securely in here. I follow all safety precautions, and

I'm trained in their use. I don't want to kill anything. I carry them just in case I run into trouble. I'm out between places alone. I make the long drive between here and the lodge to watch the twins. We're surrounded by dangerous wildlife, if you haven't noticed. We also have even more dangerous poachers to contend with at times."

"I get it. I just wasn't expecting it."

"Because you tend to put blinders on. Focus too hard and you miss what's around you."

He knew she meant his daughters and life in general, not her, but he found his gaze lingering on her wild curls. She waved her hand to draw his attention away from her and pointed to a herd of gazelle grazing peacefully in the distance. A family of giraffes rose above them, moving gracefully through the grasses toward a grove of trees. Pippa leaned her rifle against a nearby boulder and took out her camera to capture the scene.

It was truly breathtaking. The sun hung low enough in the sky to singe it with burnt orange, crimson and fiery reds. A row of acacia trees stood like charcoal silhouettes framed by the outstretched necks of giraffes to either side. The juxtaposition of a beautiful woman, shooting her camera—capturing the wildlife—with a gun resting impotently in the background was more than perfect. The way the late sun lifted the red highlights and flecks of gold in her wild curls made him want to capture her, too. He wanted to hold her. Touch her hair.

She lowered her camera and looked at him as if she sensed his thoughts. She gave him a shy smile and scratched the bridge of her nose.

"There's another great view if we pass those trees. You'll see Mount Kilimanjaro in the distance."

"Great." Geologic landmarks were supposed to be his thing, but right now all he cared about was Pippa. He marched after her, trying to keep his head on straight. He really needed to get it together. He was playing with fire. Only he wasn't playing. He hadn't felt this intensely about anyone in years.

She slowed her pace so they were side by side. Maybe that meant she sensed it, too. He needed a sign from her. A signal.

Even a slap across the face, if that's how she felt about him.

They passed through the tree grove, ducking under one branch and avoiding the thorns of another.

"Don't walk under that one." Pippa grabbed his hand and urged him to the right. "Sausage tree. Kigelia. Those sausage-shaped fruits weigh as much as ten kilos. You don't want one dropping on your head."

Maybe it would knock some sense into him.

He looked up as they maneuvered around the tree. Some of those dangling fruits were over three feet long. He ran a quick calculation. Ten kilos was a little over twenty pounds. That would hurt.

She let go of him and adjusted the strap on her shoulder as they cleared the trees. The savanna beyond them was dappled with boulders and acacia trees. As promised, Mount Kilimanjaro rose in the far distance, its snowcap glistening with the same golden hues that shimmered across the dry grassland. She stopped to capture the scene with her camera.

"The lighting is so stunning." She spun

around and took several photos of him. He ducked his head and peered at her.

"I'm not a good subject."

"That's up to the photographer, isn't it?" She took another, and he shook his head and chuckled.

"No, really."

"Okay, fine. But trust me. You're photogenic. And you should have photos of yourself to give Ivy and Fern."

To give his daughters. In case he ever passed away, like their mother. He scratched the back of his neck. She didn't mean it that way. He knew that.

"I can even take a few more family portraits for you before...you leave," she added.

There. She'd said it. A good reminder for him. They'd eventually head back to the United States, and her life was here. Then why did the energy between them feel impossible to ignore?

"That's probably a good idea. Especially since I don't know if we'll ever get the chance to return here."

Was she planning to keep one of those

pictures she took of him? He didn't need one of her. He'd never forget her face.

She put the cap on her camera and headed for the nearest boulder.

"Speaking of work, Pippa, I meant to ask you yesterday, when we were walking near the lodge, did you feel the ground shake?"

She turned and grinned.

"Is that a seismology pickup line? Because that is so bad." She shook her head and took a few backward steps in the direction of the rock.

"What? No. I meant for real." A laugh—probably embarrassment—escaped him. He scratched his jaw and mustered up a little courage. "You want seismologist-to-geologist pickup lines?" he teased. Man, his face felt warm. "Pippa, you must be a ten on the Richter scale because you've rocked my world."

"Oh, that was even worse!" She laughed and pushed her hair back.

"I haven't said anything about it yet because I needed the courage to be a bit *boulder*."

"Stop *cracking* me up."

Now he couldn't stop laughing. She

smiled over her shoulder at him and almost stumbled on a small branch. He reached out to steady her.

"Don't *Krakatoa*," he said. She nearly burst. Only someone who knew their volcanoes would get that reference.

"This is terrible. You're killing me." She tried to catch her breath and hiccupped.

"I'm feeling something *shift* between us," he said as he stepped closer.

Her laugh mellowed into a softer chuckle. She leaned against the rock and looked into his eyes.

"Would you ever take me for *granite*?" she asked, trying to make light of whatever was happening between them. It was a good one, but neither of them was laughing anymore.

"The thing is, I really can't stop thinking about you, but I know none of it makes sense and it can't work, so I feel like I'm stuck between a *rock* and—"

"You."

"Me," he whispered as he rested his forehead against hers and pressed his hands against the cold rock to either side of her. He was all out of jokes.

"I'm going to kiss you," he said.

"I know." Her chest rose and fell rapidly. Her hair smelled of mangoes and coconut and jasmine.

"Tell me now if you don't want me to. Say no and I'll walk away."

She didn't say a word. He shifted closer and held her face in his hands. She put her palms against his chest, then slid them around his neck. They stared at each other, barely brushing their lips once, then twice.

His head swirled and everything around them—the scenery, the danger…time— it all disappeared. She met him halfway, drawing him in. She tasted like fresh berries and mint tea on a hot afternoon. She held him tighter, running her fingers through his hair. He put his hands behind her and pulled her around so his back would be against the hard rock. He didn't want her to be hurt. He wanted to give her control. He wanted more than he deserved. He wanted her to know that this was more than a kiss. He loved her. He tore his lips from hers.

He loved her.

It hit him out of nowhere. He stared at

her. They both struggled to catch their breath, and then they kissed again with both a desperation and a fear of it ending.

He finally pressed his head to hers, then kissed her hair and let her rest her cheek against his chest.

"We should probably get back," he said, running his fingers up and down her spine. It was getting dark. The girls would be worried. He could feel her nodding against his chest, but she rested there a few seconds longer before straightening. She kept her eyes on the ground. He lifted her chin with his fingers and made her look at him.

"Pippa. Whatever this was, it was real. Okay?"

She nodded again and licked her swollen lips.

"It was real for me, too."

They didn't say anything else after that. They simply wove their fingers together and walked back to the jeep as the last streak of light faded from the sky.

CHAPTER TWELVE

DAX HAD NOT felt a significant tremor since the last one he reported…only a minor one near the lodge. According to Ron Swale, the heads at Erebus didn't agree with his concerns and found no valid correlation between the small quake they'd experienced at the survey site and any of their fracking activities. Dax was taken aback by that message. Were these heads CEOs or actual scientists who knew how to interpret data? How could anyone deny the correlation?

He had stayed out here with his crew a few nights ago, wanting to be on-site and monitoring all the readouts himself. He needed proof they couldn't argue with.

Pippa's aunt had gotten back to her about the water samples and there had definitely been contamination. What they needed to do now was report it to the ministry in charge in Nairobi to start an investigation.

Dax's understanding was that groundwater tests from around the fracking wells would be compared to those taken at the villages to see if the contaminants matched. He was willing to bet they would.

If Erebus had been experiencing seismic activity like that last one, there was a chance the cement casing in their wells could have cracked. And if they injected the high-pressure water used in fracking into cracked wells, that slurry, loaded with metals, salts and chemicals, could get leaked into underground fresh water springs. Truth be told, even without the tremors, fracking carried a high risk of contamination. He was glad Pippa's aunt was contacting people she trusted in government to start an audit.

But until the right officials stalled any drilling, the field was still active. He was also expected to move forward with the mapping he'd been hired to do. He needed to keep his eyes and ears peeled.

Pippa wasn't happy with his absences. If finding worms in his shaving kit again was any indication, the twins weren't, either. But this was important. She knew that.

Dax wasn't making it back tonight. Darkness had already fallen and he was waiting for Alberto without chancing Steven or any of the Erebus people overhearing.

Lee and Syd were supposed to keep watch at camp while Dax and Alberto took a hike. Literally. Was spying illegal?

"Hey, I'm ready," Alberto said in a low voice. "You sure we won't be killed by something wild? Or worse, be killed and have our deaths blamed on some wild animal?"

"Be a warrior, man," Dax said, wishing he had borrowed a gun from Pippa, too. All he had on him was a large pocket knife.

Alberto rolled his eyes and followed Dax away from the camp. They didn't need to go far. Not between the binoculars Alberto carried and Pippa's high-zoom camera. Dax couldn't believe she'd entrusted him with it.

They walked along the shadows, getting as close to the oil field as they dared. The water disposal basins were located on the side of the field closest to their approach. Bright lights cast an artificial glow on the areas where workers continued their duties after dark.

Alberto scanned the area with his binoculars. Dax looked through his lens.

"Sheesh. Over there," Alberto said. "Look who's having a late-night party."

Dax aimed the camera and zoomed in on where Alberto was pointing.

"I'm not surprised Ron's standing there. But I can't believe what I'm seeing."

A small team of men were in the act of disposing of frack water in an unlined pit. It was definitely not a typical holding well for wastewater.

"So that's how they handle things when they think nobody is looking," Dax said.

"Sweeping it under the rug, so to speak," Alberto added.

"What do you want to bet Ron never passed our data on to the higher-ups?" Dax said, as he began shooting photos.

"Well, if we end up jobless, I'm guessing you could fall back on a private investigation business."

Dax lowered Pippa's camera.

"Very funny."

Something grunted and bushes rustled

about ten yards to their right. Animal? Human? Alberto gripped Dax's shoulder. Dax jerked his head in the direction of their trailer camp.

"Let's get out of here while we can."

PIPPA TRIED CALLING Dax's satellite phone again, but he didn't pick up. It was dark outside, and he hadn't come home. She knew he'd planned to stay with his crew last night, but now an entire day had passed and she still hadn't heard from him. His driver was familiar with the region, but that didn't mean an accident couldn't happen. She had been planning to share the water test results Hope had provided her with after he came home from work. The results had sadly been positive, and she was hoping they'd be able to compare data to find correlations. Anything statistically significant.

But he still wasn't home. Just what exactly was he really using her camera for? Did someone at Erebus find out he was on to them? What if something had happened to him at work? A wave of cold crashed through her.

"What if something bad happened to him?" Fern asked.

"I'm sure he's fine," Pippa said in as confident a tone as she could muster. "He's probably just working overtime. They have super bright lights that make a person forget night has fallen." Maybe that really was what happened. What if he was slipping back into his habit of hiding behind work? She was beginning to understand how Sandy felt, only Sandy had had babies on her hands.

"Why didn't he call to say he was working late?" Ivy asked.

Pippa tried to think of an answer, but she really was worried at this point. If it turned out he'd forgotten the time, she'd let herself get mad, but until then, she needed to do something. Her Uncle Mac had a helicopter, but he didn't take his chopper out after dark and he was too far away.

"Can I trust the two of you to stay here, or do I need to drag you to the front desk with me?" They were in pajamas.

"We'll stay here. It's dark out. But what are you going to do?" Ivy said.

"Alert the authorities. Maybe they can

find out whether your dad's jeep got stuck on the way here. I'll be right back."

She opened the front door and Dax stood there, his hand reaching for the knob.

"Dad? Are you okay?" Fern ran over with Ivy close behind. He hugged them.

"I'm fine."

"Fine? Do you have any idea how worried we were? I was about to go get a search party in motion. You can't just stay late and say you're fine. You didn't call even once today to check in."

"I'm two-flats-and-one-spare-tire fine." He closed the door behind him.

"Two flats."

"For real. We changed one out and patched the other."

Pippa threw her hands to her sides.

"No satellite phones?"

"I did try once and couldn't get through. Ivy and Fern, I'm here. I'm safe. If you want to go to bed, you can."

Pippa rubbed her arms. This must have been how her family—and Haki—had felt whenever she rode off in the jeep in search of the perfect camera shot and didn't answer her radio.

At least the girls seemed satisfied.

"Are you sleeping over again?" Ivy asked her. Did she have a choice?

"It seems that way, Ivy."

"Cool. We'll leave the bathroom light on for you." They gave her a hug and went off to bed.

"Dax, I can't keep staying over like this," she said, her voice hushed. "I'm all for looking into things… I even gave you my camera, so I'm being serious…but you may never get answers on your own. You can't forget the girls. You're starting to be obsessive again."

"It couldn't be helped."

"Look, I agree with what you're doing. It's just that you have to have some structure to it all. You were so adamant about the girls sticking to a schedule. What about you? You have to learn to leave work at work. For their sake. I'm not telling you to stop. We're working together on this. But look at my parents and family. They've dedicated their lives to fighting poaching. But they don't stay up at night. How effective would they be if they did? You have to try to make life better, yes, but you have to have your own life, too. Strike a balance, Dax. Let the authorities deal with this. That's all I'm saying."

They were on the same side, but she didn't want the quake and water safety concerns to drive him back to the way he'd described he'd been in his marriage—obsessing with work to the point of missing out on family.

"This isn't me burying myself in work. There was something I had to do. You were right about the water," he said, handing her the camera. "Only it wasn't cracks in wells from tremors. They're dumping fracking wastewater illegally. They're burying it."

"What?"

"Cutting corners. Dumping. It's no wonder the area's water wells are contaminated. I personally doubt the head of Erebus would take a risk like this. I think it's a rogue act. Ron Swale and a few of his guys." He wondered if Steven was involved or if he was naively answering to Ron. What if Ron had not put Steven out at the camp to spy? Maybe he needed him out of the way. But Ron had been standing there at the dump plain as daylight. But if he was actually answering to someone on this… Just wow. He couldn't wrap his head around it.

"Oh my God," Pippa said. "I need to let Aunt Hope know."

"What I witnessed was criminal activity, Pippa. It's all on your camera. My men are still up there. We need to go through the right channels. I'm not sure who to trust at Erebus, even if protocol lays out who to report to. I'm not taking chances."

"What do you mean? You can't confront Ron or anyone else there yourself. That would be dangerous."

"I'm not. I'll send the information to the company CEO, but I'm going to copy the Kenyan Ministry of Environment and Mineral Resources and anyone else who should know."

Pippa knew what that meant. He was going to be a whistleblower in the mind of other oil companies, too. Even if they did things by the books, they'd never hire him. He'd never get another contract. He was making a choice. A moral one.

"What's going to happen to your crew and the rest of the data analysis?" she asked.

"My guess is the head of Erebus will

decide. He'll probably fire me for ruining the company's reputation publicly. May even sue me. But I can't risk this getting covered up, no pun intended."

"Be safe, Dax. If you need legal help after all this blows up, talk to my cousin Maddie. She's a great lawyer. My family knows people who'd support you and watch your back for you. They'd even keep your team safe. My Uncle Ben was a marine and knows security well."

Dax held Pippa's face in his hands and gave her a light kiss. It felt…different…like a thank you. A possible goodbye. It scared her. This was it. He wouldn't be here for weeks or months more. He could potentially be out of a contract soon. If the government put a moratorium on Erebus until all the contamination was cleared, that would mean no work for Dax…and no work visa.

"Let's not imagine what could happen and might not happen," he said.

She nodded.

"Okay. It'll be okay."

Only she wasn't so sure.

CHAPTER THIRTEEN

DAX LOOKED ON as the last of their private equipment was carefully packaged and loaded for transport back to the United States.

"Don't worry about any of this," Syd said. "You did the right thing."

"Yeah. We're behind you one hundred percent," Lee added. "We'll be okay. You just take care of yourself and your daughters."

"Thanks, guys. I appreciate it," Dax said. "I'll make it up to you as soon as I'm back."

"Let us know if you need anything when you do get home. At a minimum, stay in touch. We can all meet for drinks, or something," Alberto said. "We can beef up the story of our adventure. Tell people we encountered a few *cheetahs* along the way." He said it as if he was saying *cheaters* with flair.

Dax chuckled and slapped him on the back. Leave it to Alberto to crack a joke at a time like this. Dax shook his head and smiled but he didn't really feel it. He still had to break the news to the twins. And he hadn't told Pippa just how soon they were leaving.

Kenya was home for her. He's seen Busara. He'd met her family. She couldn't leave any of it. He wouldn't let her. The work she was doing here was important. She was passionate about her teaching. And the Maasai children who were suffering from the water crisis? They'd need her more than ever now. She couldn't abandon them. He couldn't ask her to.

A truck and jeep sat waiting to give them rides—the truck for his crew and equipment and the jeep to get him back to Tabara. The guys headed for the truck.

"Have a safe trip back home," Dax said. They'd be catching a charter back to Nairobi and then start the main leg of their journey home to the States. They'd come all the way across the world for nothing.

He couldn't say the same for himself. It was meant to be. Had he not contracted with Erebus, or met Pippa, who knows how many families would have suffered from the water contamination. Who knows if Erebus would have ever been caught in the act.

He wasn't trying to take credit or glory. He didn't want any of that. He simply wasn't going to regret the time he had spent out here.

He'd done the right thing, though, and he'd do it again. He knew that. He wouldn't have been able to live with himself had he not made waves and started an official investigation into the impact of the company's drilling practices. At least he could respect himself now.

But this also meant he was leaving Kenya sooner than expected. The company wasn't sponsoring his visa and he'd been fired. Yes, Erebus's drilling was suspended and the head of the company had even thanked him for discovering what their chief manager had been doing. But he'd been fired on the grounds of conflict of interest. Funny how business worked.

He had enough savings to get them through a few months of rent on their place in the United States. He'd have to find a new job, though, something in research or academia. He'd need to get a grant again. So long as he could support the twins, it didn't matter. Just not anything in the petroleum industry. He was done with that.

THERE WAS A tap at the bungalow door, and Pippa walked in.

"Alim is playing cards with the kids in the lounge," she said. She walked up to him and wrapped her arms around his waist. "You don't have to go. We can do this. You said yourself that people can be happy on basics. There would be a transition period, permanent visas and such, but there are ways to make that happen faster," she hinted. She stood on her toes and kissed him. It was a promise of forever, and he held her face and kissed her back. Maybe it could happen. He could marry her. No. He had no job. Nothing to offer her. She'd tire of him, and history would repeat itself.

He broke his lips away from hers and let his hands slide away from her cheeks.

"I can't do this." He kept his hands on her shoulders, wanting to let her go but unwilling to. He rested his forehead against hers.

"What are you afraid of?" Pippa whispered. She curled her fingers against his shirt and held on.

"I'm afraid that I'll fall into the same habits that destroyed my marriage with Sandy. I'll rely on you to care for the girls while I bury myself in work. It doesn't matter if there aren't luxuries, I still have to provide food and shelter. Nothing is free. I can't do that to you. You have your own dreams. The school. Teaching. I did that to Sandy, and it drove her away from me. And…and sometimes I still wonder if the stress I put her through weakened her immune system and made her get sick."

"No. You can't think that. Life doesn't always work out as planned. Relationships don't work out as planned. Trust me. I know this. I've been through it, and I can't tell you how many times I beat myself up, wondering what I did or what was wrong with me. But I'm not the same person I was then. I know what I want now. And you're not the same person you were, either, Dax. You can't experience life and not change. You're an amazing father. Ivy and Fern are here because you didn't want to leave them behind. I can tell how much you love them."

Could she tell that he loved her, too? That he was falling for her hard and fast? He pulled away and raked back his hair.

"No amount of experience can dampen the need to protect your children and those you…care about."

"I'm not known for keeping quiet," Pippa said. "I'd say something if I thought you were too buried in work. I've warned you before." The corners of her lips lifted into a soft smile, and he desperately wanted to kiss her again. But he couldn't. It would make leaving that much harder, not just for him, but for her. She'd had her heart broken once already. He wasn't about to break it again. Or rather, breaking it now would be easier for her to get over, than if he let their relationship go on longer.

"I'm not known for always listening."

"I'd show you. Remind you."

She reached up and wrapped her arms loosely around his neck. Her scent teased him. The way she looked at him made him falter. Emotion weakened his resistance. Being around her made logic crumble into piles of rubble. He slipped his fingers through her curls and held her face close to his, battling the need to either bridge the gap between them or break free and save them both.

She kissed him.

Just once, but it was soft and tender and so full of promise. He didn't kiss her back. Her lids barely fluttered, but her eyes remained closed…waiting…hoping. She bit the corner of her lip, and lines formed between her brows as she let go of him and stepped away. He needed to be strong. The sooner he let her go, the less damage he'd leave in his wake. His chest ached and eyes stung.

"I'm sorry, Pippa."

"No, I'm sorry," she said. A small, self-deprecating laugh escaped her. "I should've realized. I've been through this before. Right? Lessons learned and all that."

She wiped her cheeks briskly and straightened her shoulders. He reached out, but she took another step back and shook her head.

"Pippa, I don't want to hurt you. I'm trying to do what's best for—"

"Don't say it. Just…don't. You're doing what's best for you. You're all into studying and predicting risk and danger, yet you're afraid to take any risks yourself. You can't predict everything, Dax. You can't protect everyone from what the future holds and keep them from embracing life in the process. You're not really living, Dax. You're surviving. You're letting life pass you by. How is that any better than death? You're overprotective of Ivy and Fern, but I'm not sure that even comes close to how protective you are of yourself."

"That's not true."

"Isn't it? I'm not sure if you'll ever let anyone in, or if it's just me you're pushing away, but I refuse to let a man mess with my emotions again. I don't want anyone tiptoeing around me, thinking that they're protecting me when they're not. That's what happened with Haki and Maddie. I've forgiven them, but I'm also a stronger woman now. I promised that I'd always let you know…that I'd call it as I see it. You want to protect yourself, fine. But don't protect me. Don't say that you're doing what's best for me. Only *I* can say what's best for me."

"Can you? Your roots are here, Pippa. You have family here. A dream of helping all those young Maasai girls gain an education and a future. I have daughters. I get how important that is…how critical it is. You can't walk away from all of that to become an instant mother to twins in the US."

She stood there, her nose red but lips pressed firmly together.

"You're right. I can't do that any more than you could quit your job or quit being a father. We're all wrong for each other."

She was agreeing with him. That was what he wanted, wasn't it? Then why did he feel like he'd taken a deadly blast to the chest? A dark wave washed through him, a tsunami that pulled him down and under. *How is that any better than death?* It wasn't. At least the dead couldn't feel pain.

"The twins. They'll be wondering what happened to you." Yet another mistake he'd made as a father. He'd let them grow attached to Pippa.

"I'll still watch them until you leave, if you're okay with that. I don't want to miss out on these last few days with them. They're…" She cleared her throat, but he'd already caught the hitch in her voice. "They're special, to me."

"I know. You're special to them, too. This is going to be hard on them. But I won't be working—at least not in the field—the next two days, and our flight's the day after. Maybe it's better if I just keep them with me. Like a transition period. I'll tell them you had to get back to teaching."

Those words hadn't come out right. He could hear them twist midair into "others need you more than we do." Pippa flinched, confirming that's what she'd read between the lines. She simply nodded and rubbed her palms against her shirt.

"Okay." She hesitated before turning to leave. "Um. I'm going home now. Hug them for me. And take care, Dax. I hope someday you'll find someone worth the risk."

With that, she rushed out to her jeep and sped away.

He stood there. Stuck in his spot. Stuck in his life. Haunted by the sinking feeling that he'd found *her*. The one worth the risk. The one who made his blood rush like a river in spring. But for all the life they gave, some rivers also ran deep enough to drag you under and never let you go.

CHAPTER FOURTEEN

PIPPA LAY CURLED up on the couch with her head resting in her mom's lap and tried to let her mother's soothing touch make her forget all about Dax and the girls. She missed them already, and the ache bore through her like one of those monstrous drills tearing effortlessly through solid earth, deeper and deeper, as if unsatisfied with the damage in its wake. She tried blinking away the dry grittiness in her eyes, but she had no tears left. No feeling left in her. She reached for another tissue and wiped her nose.

"I just don't get it, Mom. Why can't I seem to learn?"

"Falling in love happens. Where would we all be if it didn't? If there's one thing I *don't* want you to learn, it's how to lock up your heart. Pippa, sweetheart, your capacity to love life and love others is part of who you are. One of the very best parts. If you let this keep you from falling in love again, then from what you've told me, you'll be no better off than Dax."

"Maybe I'm not meant to fall in love. Maybe I'm not destined to ever marry or have my own children."

"Don't say that."

"No, really, Mom. There are so many kids out there who need me and whom I care about. Adia and the others. Maybe that's my destiny…my purpose in life. To make a difference in their lives. Maybe I wasn't meant to make a difference with Ivy or Fern."

"I think you already did. It's more than that, though, isn't it? You didn't only care for them or want to make a difference for them. It was more than that."

Pippa sat up and tucked her knees in. She tried to steady her breathing, but every exhale sent weak tremors through her chest.

"I really love those girls. I don't know why. I just do. Each one has something about her that reminds me of myself. I can't explain it. It's as if they're a part of me even if I never gave birth to them. And—" A sob

escaped her and she caught her breath "—
and now it's as if I've lost my children."
The tears came, and sobs shook her.

Anna wrapped her arms around Pippa
and pressed a kiss to her temple.

"My little girl is all grown up. It hurts
me to see you suffering. I wish I could
make it all go away."

She wished that, too. No, no. That
would mean changing the past so that
she would never have met Dax or Ivy or
Fern. It would mean never having known
them. Somehow, that felt like one more
loss she couldn't handle. As raw as this
hurt was, she didn't want to erase them
from her memory…from her life. However
she might have touched their lives, they'd
touched hers even more. They'd made a
difference to her. She lifted her head and
wiped her eyes.

"I don't want to forget."

Her mom tucked a coil of Pippa's hair
behind her ear, then she secured the lock
and took Pippa's hand.

"Okay."

That's all she had to say. She understood. Of course she did. She was a parent.

She'd witnessed the suffering that took place when a parent and child were separated among elephants. She'd told Pippa the story of how her father had found out about her and of how, for a while, Anna had been scared to death that Jack would take her little girl away, back to America. Luckily, they all ended up together at Busara. But still, Anna had experienced the fear and pain of Pippa's loss. As for happy endings, perhaps that had been it for Pippa and there wasn't another in store for her.

"Can I ask you something, Pippa? It's not meant to upset you."

Pippa nodded, and her mom took her chin and gently turned Pippa to face her.

"Once upon a time, before Haki and Maddie realized they were meant to be together, you were in love with him and wanted to marry him. How was that different from how you feel about Dax?"

Pippa covered her face with both hands and pressed her fingertips to her brows. Her head throbbed, and her thoughts were scattered. Was Dax just another misstep? Another false love? She remembered holing up in her room for days after her devas-

tating and unexpected breakup with Haki.
It had torn her apart and left her feeling
embarrassed, worthless and alone. At the
time, she hadn't known who she was without him. That hadn't been a good thing. It
would have eventually weakened their relationship. And traveling to Europe afterward and rediscovering herself was the best
thing that had come from that devastation.
Just as she'd witnessed time and again in
nature, the death of something always led
to the birth of something new…something
better or stronger. From a sunset to a sunrise. Or drought to the first blade of grass
sprouting after the rains. Or from the death
of her relationship with Haki…to Dax and
the twins entering her life.

She closed her eyes and tried to make
sense of it all. But losing Dax felt different. It was deeper. More raw and primal.
More spiritual. It wasn't just that she'd lost
herself. It felt like her very soul had been
abandoned. *Soul mates.* The term filled her
head and seemed to push all her scattered
thoughts into place. She frowned and let
the idea sink in. Her soul mate. She blinked

away her tears and met her mother's worried gaze.

"It was different because with Haki, we'd grown up around each other for so many years that I couldn't define myself outside of 'us.' I didn't know who I was as an individual. Not really. That's not how it is—was—with Dax. I did love Haki, Mom. I still do. But as a dear friend. And I realize now that I always loved him that way. I wasn't *in* love with him. I had no idea what being in love was like. I didn't have anything to compare it to." She paused and nipped at her bottom lip. "I do now."

"Are you sure?"

"Mom, with Haki, I didn't want to leave Busara. He wanted to chase new dreams and build a new sanctuary kilometers from here. I held him back because something inside me was holding *me* back, too. But with Dax, I even offered to leave Kenya to be with him and the girls. I meant it, too. Not because I don't think my own dreams are important, but because I love him and the girls enough to find a way, so long as we're together. But he wouldn't let me. He obviously didn't care enough or feel the same way."

That made no sense. Weren't soul mates a two-way thing? If he was her soul mate, wasn't she his?

"Maybe he cared too much," Anna said.

"Maybe he didn't care enough," Pippa countered.

"Sweetheart, love can be scary, and he's been through a lot."

"Well, I can't give him that courage. I can't make him want me enough. And I can't spend the rest of my life waiting for him to realize what we had was worth taking a chance on."

For the first time, she truly understood the inexplicably powerful connection that Haki and Maddie hadn't been able to fight. She'd forgiven them for what they had done to her, but now that forgiveness seemed more genuine…deeper. She could empathize with what they'd gone through. It wouldn't bring Dax, Ivy or Fern back into her life, but not everyone was blessed enough to meet their soul mate during their lifetime. At least she had.

"Just promise me you'll give yourself

another chance at love. Someone is out there for you. You'll meet the right person at the right time," Anna said.

The right person at the right time? Dax was the right person at the wrong place and time. The only other option was settling for the wrong person at the right time.

"No. He was the one. The only thing I can promise is that I'm never falling in love again."

DAX HADN'T SEEN this degree of melancholy on Ivy's and Fern's faces since Sandy had passed away. Sure, they'd been younger and it had been a different kind of sadness, but they undoubtedly had the look of someone who'd lost a loved one. Disappointment, confusion and shock all rolled in one. It gutted him.

"Girls, she spent a lot of time helping us out. But she had to get back to teaching less privileged kids and giving them the kind of chance you two have. An education. Goals. The world at your merc—fingertips." He'd caught himself and almost chuckled at the image of the world being at the mercy of Ivy and Fern Calder. Heaven help him.

"But she didn't say bye to us," Fern lamented.

"She did. She asked me to tell you that she wished you well and to give you both hugs."

"That's not the same. That's a copout. Besides, I don't believe it. Miss Pippa wouldn't do that to us," Ivy said.

"Yeah, she wouldn't. She was nice. She never even left the *enkangs* without saying bye to everyone," Fern said.

Man, they'd even picked up some Swahili from Pippa. She had been more than good for them. She had been great for them. Great for him, too, but that was a thing of the past, now.

"Well, she did and that's that. I guess she had too much on her hands."

"We didn't put anything in her bag or jeep, we swear it. No spiders or anything," Fern said. Her eyes glistened, and he tugged her closer and gave her a hug.

"That's from Pippa, okay?"

"She wouldn't have been scared off even if we did pull a prank. She liked us too much to be chased off by a prank,"

Ivy insisted, shrugging him away when he tried to hug her, too.

"You're right. She did like you. She loved you both. She told me so. But sometimes grown-ups have to work. We have responsibilities. Life's not always simple."

"It can be if you want it to be. I think you two had a fight. *You* scared her off." Ivy folded her arms and glared at him.

"What are you talking about?" He understood full well what they meant, but he had no idea they'd noticed anything happening between him and Pippa. They really were growing up and starting to pay attention to things he wasn't ready for. Relationships. Not his, nor theirs. The idea of them dating in a few years jolted him. He couldn't handle his own love life, let alone the twins' ups and downs and heartbreaks. He rubbed the back of his neck.

"You know what Ivy means," Fern said. "You *liked* her and she *liked* you. It was obvious you two were all lovey-dovey and romantic. We want you to be happy. You've been acting different with her around. A good different."

"Yeah. Like she said." Ivy pursed her

lips. "But, apparently, you ruined everything."

"Okay, that's enough. You two are out of line. I don't want to hear another word about Pippa's not being here. We leave in two days. She wouldn't have wanted to come with us. As your nanny, I mean," he quickly added when the twins each raised an eyebrow. Both on the right side. He cranked his stiffening neck to the side, but it didn't help. "You two go do your work or read or something."

They just stood there.

"Go. Now. Please."

"Fine." Ivy looped her arm in her sister's, and they stalked off to their room, slamming the door behind them.

Dax let out a breath and lowered his head. He was doing the right thing. What he had to do. Then why did this feel like he was running away?

Pippa parked around the back of Tabara Lodge, as out of sight as she could be. Anyone lounging at the pool or dining near one of the panoramic windows wouldn't be able to see her here. She'd assured Dax that she'd disappear from his life, and she intended to keep that promise. But she'd received word from Alim, doing double duty at the front desk today, that two guests who were retired professors from the University of Nairobi had heard about her efforts from a colleague, someone she'd known when she was studying there, and they were donating books and writing supplies along with money to her school and scholarships. It was more than she ever could have hoped for. She'd asked him to leave the boxes around back, just inside the doors leading to the kitchen and storage area.

She slipped inside, spotted the boxes and hoisted one up, bracing it against her chest. These supplies were precious. The Maasai children desperately needed them. That's why she was here at the risk of running into Dax or the twins again. Wasn't it? Or did a part of her hope to run into them by accident? A fated meeting, one that was completely out of her hands. One that would prove they were meant to be together, even if they'd sworn to stay apart.

The coast was clear. She placed the box in the back of her jeep, moving her emergency blanket, pup tent and water container to the floor behind the front seats to make room for the other boxes. She hurried back inside the main lodge to get the next box, and then the next, securing them all with a rainproof tarp so that nothing would fall out if she hit a rut in the road.

The lodge grounds seemed quieter than usual. Deserted even. She popped back inside to leave Alim a thank you note, then she climbed behind the wheel. There was nothing deserted about the place, other than the fact that she was hiding around back. Everything around her seemed empty today because Dax, Ivy and Fern would be leaving, never to return. In reality, the only place that was truly deserted was her heart. But she'd fill it. She'd fill it until the hollow ache subsided. She'd fill it with children from every village she could reach and with the love of everyone at Busara, including the orphaned baby elephants.

She'd bury herself in work.

Just like Dax had done.

She closed her eyes against the blazing sunlight and took in a breath. She couldn't really blame him, could she? Here she was ready to hide behind something that sounded so right and legitimate and logical. She was doing it all in the name of love, just as he was for his daughters. Just as he'd started out doing for his parents and his friend who drowned in that tsunami and everyone else he wanted to protect, including his late wife. He'd been tortured by the people and relationships torn apart by disaster, and he'd wanted to stop it all from happening, yet he had driven everyone away in the process. First Sandy. Then her.

And now, as she'd told her mom, she'd never let herself fall in love again, either, because it was easier not to. Safer. And because she'd been second best before—settled for—and she couldn't do that to someone else.

I'd rather live my truth in pain, than a lie in vain.

Voices of guests laughing and talking carried through the air, none of them the voices she longed to hear. She started the ignition and headed onto the road, forcing herself not to look in the rearview mirror at the lodge disappearing in the distance, along with her heart.

A voice in her head urged her to turn around and go back. To knock some sense into him. To take the girls in her arms and refuse to let them go. To wrap herself around Dax and kiss him again. One more time. What if one more kiss would have made the difference? One more embrace. One more plea.

No. Pippa Harper did not beg. She had her pride. She deserved more. Just like she tried to teach the young Maasai girls she taught—and the twins—they were worth it. They had gifts and strength. So did she. She could stand on her own. She didn't need the support or approval of a man.

But she did want the kind of love only two people could share. The kind that filled and fueled a person like an underground spring pouring endlessly into a river.

Maybe she simply couldn't have it all.

The *enkang* came into view and she slowed her approach, coming to a full stop several yards from the thorny gate. The dust settled around her. She hadn't brought Ivy or Fern to this one, yet. Maybe that's why she'd decided to come here today. This place didn't carry memories of the twins. She swiped away a tear. Who was she kidding? She'd always remember them, no matter where she was.

She waved to the eldest son who was herding goats out the fence to graze in the grass. A young mother came around the corner, carrying a bundle of sticks into the *enkang*. Children peered outside the gate, giggling and smiling sheepishly at her. She'd seen this scene a million times, yet today it was different. She was different. Every child, every smile and every wide-eyed hopeful—or mischievous—look would remind her of two girls who felt like her own. She swallowed back the lump in her throat and jumped down, then began unhooking the tarp.

She yelped, jumping back and slapping her hand against her chest. She stared at the two sweaty faces that popped up from underneath the blanket in the back seat.

"Oh my God. You scared me to death! Ivy. Fern. What are you doing here? What have you done? Your dad is going to be worried sick. He's going to flip out."

"We decided to take that chance. Don't worry. We left him a note, as usual." Fern climbed out and gave Pippa a big hug. She sounded confident and proud of their escape. Pippa glanced at the fading tattoo on her wrist, just to make sure she wasn't Ivy.

"We did. The note says that we're sorry but we couldn't leave without seeing you first and that you'd bring us back. And that we've already decided on our punishments and plan to pay for any extra charges if we miss our flight." Ivy came over and hugged her, too. A ring of red ivy circled her wrist.

"You two. I know I should be scolding you for stowing away, but the truth is, I'm so happy to see you."

"We're happy, too. But why would you leave us without saying goodbye?"

How was she supposed to answer that without lying or putting the blame on their father?

"The truth is, deep down, I didn't want to say goodbye."

"So, you avoided us instead. Just like you're avoiding Dad, and he's avoiding you."

"Fern, you are one observant girl." Pippa

leaned against the bumper of the jeep and drew the girls to her sides, putting her arms around their shoulders. "It was wrong of me not to say goodbye. I admit it. Sometimes grown-ups take the easy way out. That's wrong, too."

"Does that mean you and Dad are going to hook up when we get back?" Ivy asked. Pippa's cheeks heated up, and it had nothing to do with the sun.

"That's, um, not exactly the right way to put it. Will I be brave and give the two of you and him a proper goodbye? Yes. But, girls, things don't always work out the way we'd like. And they don't work out for many, many reasons."

"But the only reason that matters is that you like each other," Fern insisted. "We saw you kissing."

"And we've seen the way he looks at you," Ivy added.

"Yeah, it's weird and goofy. Like he's daydreaming or lost."

"He spaces out and can't hear us. That's the funny part. We could ask for his credit card and he'd just say yes."

"And later say that he never did," Fern said.

"Yep."

"Plus, he's been more relaxed, even when you weren't there. He sat around and played cards and even went swimming with us. Until yesterday. Yesterday, he was his old self again. Not one smile," Fern said.

"You told us we could do anything we set our minds to, and that we should always follow our instincts—"

"And our hearts—"

"So, we've set our minds on bringing you back together. That's why we're here," Ivy said.

"It's part of the plan." Fern's eyes gleamed as she smiled.

"Wait a minute," Pippa said, standing up and facing them. "That's not what I meant when I said you could accomplish anything. You can't control people. Besides, what plan?"

"For Dad to marry you so he can be happy and you can be our mom. That's what we want more than anything," Ivy said. Ivy—the rebel who didn't want anyone looking out for her other than Dax. She wanted Pippa to be their mother?

Pippa's bottom lip quivered, and her nose stung. She pressed her hand against her mouth to stop the sobs escaping, but tears stung the corners of her eyes.

"That would be the greatest honor in the world, but it's not my call. It's not yours, either. You can't force love. You can't control it. It happens when you least expect it, and sometimes it simply can't be."

"Like with you and Dad?"

"Yeah," Pippa said, realizing what she'd admitted to only when Ivy's and Fern's faces lit up. They glanced at each other and shook hands.

"Step one accomplished," Fern said.

"What—"

"You admitted that you love him," Ivy explained. "We didn't force it out of you. You said it yourself."

"You tricked it out of me."

"Fair and square," Fern said. "Now, step two is to get Dad to admit it."

"We have to get him to crack. Push him to his limit so he blurts it out."

"Like the time we collected a bowl of

earthworms and put it on the table at breakfast instead of cereal. He freaked out and
yelled never to bring them near him again."
Both girls laughed uncontrollably, then
Fern caught her breath. "We suspected he
was scared of them, but he wouldn't admit
it."

"He's fine with snakes. But earthworms
totally creep him out. He always blurts the
truth when he's scared. That's why we ran
away with you today." Ivy smirked and
winked. Oh boy.

"This is so wrong," Pippa said. "You
have to tell him what you're up to. You
can't do it this way. Look, let me radio the
lodge and ask them to give him the message that you're okay. Then I'll let you help
me unload these supplies and teach the kids
this one last time. But after that, we return to Tabara and you both confess what
you've been up to. If you don't tell him,
I'll have to."

"But—"

"No *buts* about it."

"Fine."

"Okay, then. Give me a second to radio
in. You each finish removing the tarp and

grab a box." Pippa wished the satellite phones hadn't belonged to Erebus. Surely he'd get the message…especially if Alim picked up.

The twins complied with sullen faces. But once they started passing out note-books, pencils and storybooks to excited and grateful children, the smiles were back on Ivy's and Fern's faces. Their hearts were in the right place. She knew that. But how did one explain how complicated grown-up relationships were to eleven-year-old girls?

And why did relationships have to be so complicated? Why couldn't life always be as simple as it was through a child's eyes? The way it had seemed to be for Pippa when she was their age.

She led the twins and the other children to wooden stools and benches set up inside the cool shade of a mud-and-plaster struc-ture that stood outside of the *enkang* itself. From what she knew, it had been abandoned decades ago, after a group of missionaries in the area had left. It was a slightly larger space than *inkajijiks* each family lived in. She'd been using it for her classes at this village. It was how she'd gotten the idea to build a more centrally located school. Pippa smiled as she watched the kids scrambling to find a spot to sit.

"Do you want to help the older kids with writing, or teach these little ones the alphabet?" she asked the twins.

A little six-year-old girl named Mina, with striking brown eyes rimmed with dark lashes, tugged at Ivy's cargo pants. She let go and clasped her hands together when Ivy glanced down. Her beaded bracelets, which matched her crimson wrap dress, clinked together, almost in harmony with her tiny giggles.

"I want to sing with you," she said.

Ivy grinned back and looked at Pippa. She shone with the pride of being chosen… of being looked up to.

"Okay, I guess I'm doing ABCs," Ivy said, as she set her water bottle down next to Fern's on a corner table and pulled up a stool. Pippa ushered the five youngest boys and girls over to where Ivy sat. Three girls between the ages of nine and eleven congregated next to Fern, who smiled as wide as a schoolteacher on the first day of class. She began doling out paper and pencils.

Pippa pulled two third-grade-level reading texts out of one of the boxes and called over the two remaining twelve-year-old girls. Their names were Namunyak and Namelok, which meant "the lucky one" and "the sweet one" in Maa. They were both lucky.

The sound of the little ones reciting their alphabet filled the tent with joy. Pippa dared to let herself live in the moment and relish every last minute spent with Ivy and Fern. Life was too short to waste perfect moments like this one.

Perfect, except for the fact that they'd be leaving today. It didn't matter what the twins had intended to do, Dax was obligated to return to the United States. He wanted a scheduled, financially stable and predictable life. He needed to provide for the girls. He was bound by an oath to their mother. A promise to keep. Pippa understood that with every breath she had. Children had to come first. They were a priority. She wouldn't expect any less of him or have it any other way. She only wished he had the will to try to make things work between them. The courage to

love again and to not fear the unexpected…
and to let her in.

She listened to Namelok as the teen
read a story about a girl who climbed a
mountain in order to reach the stars. Pippa
listened, but she was so tired. All the crying she'd done over the past few days had
drained her. She closed her eyes just for a
second and listened to the comforting buzz
of children reading and reciting.

This was her place, her purpose. This felt
right. Yet Dax kept entering her mind. His
kind face, the way his eyes softened when
he looked at her, the way he ruffled up his
hair when he got excited over data he was
analyzing. Her chest squeezed around her
heart, and she felt like she'd lost her balance.

No. She was fine. It was stress and exhaustion. Maybe dehydration, but she was
usually careful about drinking enough
water. She opened her eyes. Everyone was
reading. She didn't feel dizzy. She looked
around the room. It took a millisecond to
register. Less than that for her to stand up.
The water in Ivy's and Fern's bottles. The
bottles stood upright, but the water level

was at an angle. It defied physics. The strings of beads covering the entry swayed back and forth, but there wasn't so much as a breeze. Her instincts screamed.

"Children let's go outside now. Everyone. Quickly."

She felt it again. The ground moved. Someone outside in the village yelled. Fern's arms shot out to her sides, and her eyes widened. Ivy grabbed Mina's hand.

"Namelok and Namunyak, help get the little ones outside. Now!"

They ran, grabbing hands and rushing for the exit. Two of the children began to cry. Ivy and Fern were near the back of the room trying to pick them up.

"Hurry, leave. I'll get them," Pippa called out. She tried to get to the kids, but the earth rippled, sending her careening sideways. Ivy screamed and held on to Mina as the desk slid down and hit her in the side.

It happened too quickly. The shaking, the screams, the stools falling and sliding. The walls crumbled like dry bread, and the air filling with dust. She couldn't see them. The twins and Mina and Adu, one of the little boys.

"Pippa!"

That was Fern. Adrenaline surged through her. She had to get to them. She scrambled up, but the ground rumbled and shook like a maniacal beast, then undulated, lunging her forward. Wooden poles framing the roof fell like matches from an opened box and pain engulfed her.

Then everything went dark and still.

DAX CROUCHED OVER the young boy he'd pulled away from the pool when the tremors began. The kid had been standing too close to falling debris and too far from his parents. He was okay, though. Dax quickly scanned the area as the shaking subsided, took the boy to his parents and reluctantly accepted the frantic mother's embrace and father's gratitude.

He needed to find the twins and Pippa. Panic twisted and burned at his core and sent his pulse scattering. He needed to get to them now.

He didn't have to check his equipment to know this wasn't the epicenter. There wasn't much damage here. His guess was maybe a four or five at the lodge. God he wished the twins hadn't pulled a stunt and run off. He wished all three of them—Ivy, Fern and Pippa—were right here with him and not out there where— He had to stop thinking like that…expecting the worst… but the twins weren't the only ones with intuitive connections. Parents had them, too.

So did soul mates.

Something shifted in him. *Dax*. The thought…his name…came as unexpectedly as the quake. *Pippa*. He knew something was wrong. *Fern. Ivy.* His gut screamed.

He ran toward Alim, who, along with other lodge staff, was trying to calm and reassure the guests. He was the one who'd given Dax Pippa's message about the girls stowing away in her jeep. He'd have an idea of how to find the village they'd gone to. Those *enkangs* would turn to rubble after anything stronger than a five. Their structures wouldn't hold. Or what if they had been in the jeep and it had overturned? He swiped his forehead.

"Can you radio her?" he asked, gripping Alim's arm. No explanation was needed.

"I did, Mr. Calder. No response. Her family radioed in to check on her because they could not reach her, either. She isn't answering."

"How far is this place? Can you get me to them?"

He no longer had the company-assigned driver. He didn't even have a vehicle. He and the twins were supposed to have already left by now. On a plane. In the air, where they wouldn't have felt the quake. But Pippa wouldn't have been with them. And he wanted her safe, too. He *wanted* her, period. In their lives. A part of their family. He'd let the earth swallow him whole if it meant Pippa and the twins would all be okay.

"An hour, but I can make it in less. Follow me," Alim said, running to where a lodge-marked SUV was parked, unscathed.

Alim floored the gas pedal and headed west. *West.* Deeper into the Great Rift Valley. Closer to where the risk of plates sliding beneath the earth's crust would be greater.

They sped along a fissure that he knew had nothing to do with the drought. The fissure was only a few inches wide, but stretched far ahead. Alim crossed over it and tore through the expanse of savanna grasses to their left.

Dax covered his face with his hands, then ran them through his hair.

They had to be okay. They had to be. This was why he had studied earthquakes. Not to work for oil conglomerates, telling them where to drill and destroy and ravage the earth. The very idea made him sick.

What if he'd never abandoned his research? Could he have predicted this quake? Or even others by now? Could he have stopped the unexpected? He'd never know.

He hadn't predicted falling in love with Pippa.

God, he loved her. He'd had every guard up, every sensor and warning system on alert, determined never to fall in love again, yet he'd never seen it coming.

Pippa.

Meeting her was the most wonderful, unexpected thing that had ever happened to him. And now he had no idea if she was dead or alive or badly injured.

The twins were his life and Pippa had been right. He'd taken the girls for granted.

Just because they were nearby didn't mean he was being present for them. And all the hours he'd spent away from them in the name of protecting them had been wasted. He'd had every system and plan and rule in place, yet none of it had worked, and the more he tried, the more they had rebelled. If they weren't okay right now...

"We'll find them. They are going to be okay," Alim insisted. Dax nodded but couldn't speak. They hit another rut, and he was nearly thrown from his seat.

"We need to get to them, Alim, but we can't risk a flat." They'd never find Pippa and the girls if he and Alim got stranded out here themselves. He glanced at his watch. They'd been driving only thirty minutes. It felt like hours.

This was all his fault. He'd pushed Pippa away. And in doing so, he'd inadvertently pushed the girls to run away. He'd devoted his life to fighting disasters that tore families apart, and all along, he had been fracturing his own. Isolating himself. Protecting himself, albeit emotionally, instead of loved ones.

You did this, Dax. If they're hurt, it's your fault.

He squeezed the bridge of his nose, and when he opened his eyes, he saw it. Pippa's jeep was in the distance. Most of the village huts looked crumbled and the fence around the *enkang* was no longer circular in shape. Even over the engine noise, he could hear the wails of terrified children and the cries of the herds scattered nearby. Men and women, in their bright garbs, were easy to spot, scurrying about, surveying the loss. At a glance, the damage was much more severe here than at the lodge. Dax swallowed hard. All these people…all these children…and no shelters. No homes. And it wasn't over. There would be aftershocks. Possibly, almost as damaging.

But what gnawed at him most was that he couldn't see the ones he loved. Pippa, Ivy and Fern. He couldn't see them anywhere. A group of Maasai were clearing debris, lifting poles and moving them from a pile. The rubble didn't match that of the Maasai huts. Plaster. A small plaster and possibly even concrete or stone building.

Panic waved through his chest. They were buried. Dear God, they were under there.

He opened the jeep door and was ready to jump out before Alim skidded to a full stop. He ran with Alim at his heels and began moving debris at a frantic pace with the villagers.

"Are there people under here?" he asked as he grabbed a heavy chunk of dried mud and straw. "The women? Pippa and two girls. The girls look the same." He didn't know who spoke English and who didn't, but he figured they'd recognize Pippa's name.

"Yes! Yes! She was teaching here. And two girls helping." The middle-aged man spoke with a heavy lilt, but Dax was relieved his English was good. The lines on his face looked taut and determined. He didn't seem fazed by the bleeding gashes on his sandaled feet and upper arm.

"Is anyone else missing?"

"Two more children. Little ones. The other children Pippa was teaching said they were with her," another one of the men clearing the rubble said. The way they tackled the debris…all Dax could think was that these men were truly warriors.

Dax heard a whimper, and his soul seemed to coil and catch in his throat. He moved another pole and beneath it was a hand, scratching at the rubble. Around the dust-covered wrist, he could make out a faint, delicate pattern.

"Ivy! It's Dad! Talk to me, sweetheart."

"Daddy!" She broke into sobs.

"Honey, can you move at all?"

A slew of possible injuries flashed in his head. Broken bones. Injured spine…

"I can't move. Miss Pippa's on top of me."

On top of her? She'd protected his little girl with her body. Why couldn't Pippa move? He tried to ignore the fear of death that stretched its bony fingers around his heart. More soft crying rose through the pile. He lifted another mass of caked mud and straw and some thatching and he found her lying there, hunched over. She wasn't moving.

"Pippa!" If her back or neck were injured, he'd make it worse by picking her up. But he had no choice. The aftershocks could hit at any moment. They had to rescue the children. All of them. He positioned himself to lift her while supporting her spine. The others followed suit, ready to help. She twitched. At first it was such a small motion, he almost thought he'd imagined it. But then she gasped and arched slightly, trying to raise her body.

"I've got you. Pippa, I'm here. I've got you. We're getting you out. Go slow."

He slipped a hand under her and across her chest, and she reached up and grabbed his shoulder.

"Dax. The kids. Pain." She winced as she straightened too quickly. He started to lift her out by her waist. She pushed at his arm and struggled. "No. I have to help the children."

"Shh. We'll get them out. Hang on to me." The men helped lift her out safely and Dax carried her a few meters away and set her down. Her leg was swelling just above the ankle. He untied the laces of her boot and carefully slipped it off. She was very pale.

"I'll be right back." Several women crowded around her, checking on her. He wanted to hold her and comfort her. He couldn't. Not yet.

He hurried back for Ivy, who was already getting rescued by the others. She made eye contact with Dax, and her face quivered like she was going to burst into tears. He took her in his arms and held her tight.

"It's going to be okay. You're okay."

Alim helped lift another little girl out, and one of the women cried out and rushed to hold her.

"Mina!" No doubt the woman was the little girl's mother. A horrifying experience for any parent. The one Dax had nightmares about. And now he was living through it.

"Ivy saved her. She was curled over her," Alim said, his face wrought with emotion. Dax knew this had to be hitting him hard, too. Alim…a man who'd lost his children… was helping others save theirs. And Dax also knew that it had taken a lot for the guy to open his heart up to Ivy and Fern. He had been worried to death, too.

Dax kissed the top of Ivy's head. His Ivy. Responsible and brave. She'd used her body to save a younger child and Pippa had used hers to protect them both. He felt pride, but he was only partially relieved. Fern was still missing.

"Thank you," he told Alim. "You hear that, Ivy? You did good. I need you to come sit next to Pippa. She's injured. Her ankle, but I think she may have a concussion, too. Stay with her. I need to help get Fern and the other child out."

Ivy nodded, but her knees wobbled and almost gave out under her. He helped her to the ground next to Pippa and watched as they wrapped their arms around each other. Pippa rocked Ivy against her chest and looked up at Dax.

"I'm so sorry. I tried to get them all out. And when I couldn't, I tried to protect them. But Fern was farther away." Tears brimmed along her lashes, and she shook her head. "I'm so sorry."

All Dax could do was step closer and kneel down. His eyes locked on hers, then he kissed her forehead. Then he held her cheeks and kissed her lips. It was light and swift, but it said more than any words ever could. He hoped she understood. It had to be enough for now.

He left her there with Ivy. Comforted that his daughter was with her. Scared like no man's business that Fern might not be okay.

He started moving debris with the others. Someone was crying. It wasn't Fern's voice. It had to be the other little kid. But crying meant the little one was alive. Crying was good. He wished Fern would cry or call out.

Then he heard it. The singing. Soft and shaky...and haunting. He knew he'd hear it in his dreams for the rest of his life. The crying subsided, and everyone turned toward the sound of Fern's voice. She and the younger child were singing the alphabet. His Fern, calming the other child. His amazing girls and the one amazing woman who'd set an example for them.

"Fern. We're gonna get you out of there."

Dax moved faster. He could see her hair now. A leg. Her voice was barely a whisper. But she'd spoken. She was going to be okay. His eyes and nose stung, and he curled his lips. They'd get through this. Everything would be okay.

"I see you, Fern. You're both almost out."

The singing stopped as they moved one last load. Fern sat cocooned around a little boy in what Dax guessed would have been the corner of the room. A small table was perched at an angle over them, giving them just enough protection from falling debris.

"Daddy." Her voice cracked, but her face was dry and lips pressed in a line that said she was ready to do whatever was needed. His shy Fern, holding down the fort. Showing strength under pressure. Heaven help him, she was showing more inner strength in this moment than he had had in years. She moved to help lift the boy over to Dax and the child's father.

"Is he all right?" Dax asked the father as he pressed his son to his chest.

"Yes. Yes."

Dax reached back in, pulled Fern into his arms and held on tight.

"Tell me you're okay."

"I… I'm okay." She looked over and saw her sister and Pippa, then rushed over to hug them. Dax followed her and crouched down beside them.

"Pippa, do you feel faint? Any idea how long she was out, Ivy?"

"I'm sure it wasn't long," Pippa said. "It was the pain shooting up my leg. It made me feel light-headed, and I couldn't move."

"We need to get you to a doctor," he said. He tore off his shirt and used it, along with a couple of flat pieces of wood scattered near them, to form a makeshift splint. "I wish we had ice or a cold pack."

"I'll be okay until help arrives. Sitting here feels better than being buried alive."

"Okay. I've got to go help Alim and the others make sure no one else is missing. Sit tight. Don't panic if there's more shaking. I'll be right back."

He hurried over to a group of women tending to an elderly man with a cut on his leg. Dax took the swath of material one of the women tore from the bottom of her wrap and bandaged the wound.

"Help will be here soon," he assured them. The guy was going to need antibiotics on a wound like that. But all he could do now was stop the bleeding.

Alim ran to their jeep and got on his radio. He gave Dax a nod. Help was on the way. Everyone was out in the open. No one else was missing or badly injured. Even the village's goats, albeit agitated and loud, were gathered in an open pen. He jogged back to where Pippa and the twins sat huddled together.

"You scared me to death. All three of you," Dax said, crouching down.

"We shouldn't have taken off without your knowing," Ivy said.

"Sorry," Fern added. "You always said dangerous things can happen at any time. You were right. We should have stayed at the lodge."

Dax shook his head.

"No. Someone else is a lot wiser than me, and a lot smarter than I've been in a long time." Pippa cocked her head when he looked at her. "And that very special person was right. Danger is out there, but we can't let it rule us. If you girls hadn't been here, those other two kids and all the other children might not have made it out okay. You were here at the right time. Maybe you were meant to be here. Who can say? Life's about the unexpected and taking chances."

"Like taking a chance on love?" Fern

asked, as she elbowed Ivy. Dax smiled and threaded his fingers through Pippa's. Her eyes fluttered shut, and a tear escaped from the corner. He wiped it away with his thumb.

"Like taking a chance on love."

"You should kiss her, Dad," Ivy whispered.

"I should, should I?"

Pippa kept her eyes closed, but her mouth curved into a smile.

"Yeah," she said. "You should. I think you owe me one. And it might dull some of the pain." She opened one eye and peered at him. Dax chuckled.

"I doubt one will be enough. Just don't disappear on me and I'll give you as many kisses as you want."

"I for one am not going anywhere with this ankle," Pippa said.

"I'm not—we're not—going anywhere, either."

It took a second for it to register on all their faces.

"Yes!" Ivy and Fern exclaimed simultaneously and hugged each other again.

Pippa narrowed her eyes at him.

"Do you mean what I think you mean? Don't mess with me, Dax Calder."

"I mean exactly what I said. I don't want to leave you ever again. I want us to stay here. Live here. With you."

"But what about all the danger and the risk of getting eaten by lions or swept away in a river during flood season or getting trampled by elephants or falling—"

He silenced her with a kiss, and this time it was slow and firm and everything wonderful.

"—in love?" she asked, breathless.

He rested his forehead against hers and held her hands to his heart.

"I'd die a million deaths if I could live each life with you." He kissed her again. "Ivy, Fern. Would either of you have any objection to my asking Pippa to marry me...to marry us? Or to us living here, in Kenya, as a family, forever?"

The twins shook their heads emphatically.

"No objections! Do it. Do it. Do it..." He had to laugh at their chanting. It also drew the attention of their Maasai friends. Several of the women came over and clapped for Pippa.

"I do."

They stopped at Pippa's words. Two words. Two small words that had the power to change all four of their lives.

"I didn't actually ask yet, but—"

She swatted his arm, and he laughed.

"Pippa Rose Harper. I love you more than life itself. From the moment I saw you, I knew life would never be the same again. You made it crazier, wilder and infinitely better. Would you marry us and face the future head-on with us, forever after?"

"Absolutely. I love you, Dax. I love all of you and never want to be without you," she added, reaching out her hand and linking it with Ivy's and Fern's.

They all glanced up at the sound of a helicopter approaching.

"That's my Uncle Mac's chopper," Pippa said. "I think I see my father in it, too."

"Just in time. We need to get you to a doctor, but also so I can ask him for your hand."

"Do guys really still do that?" Ivy asked. "I mean, you already asked Pippa, and she said yes."

"Any guys who plan to marry my daughters better pass inspection and ask for my blessing. I owe Pippa's father that same respect."

"Don't worry, Ivy and Fern. I'll be there to keep him from scaring your future boyfriends too badly," Pippa said with a grin.

"This is turning out to be the best day ever. Near-death experience and all," Fern said.

The helicopter landed a safe distance away, and a second one appeared over a copse of trees. The villagers waved and called out that help had arrived. Ivy and Fern ran toward Mac and Jack, no doubt anxious to update them.

Dax scooped Pippa up into his arms. She flinched from the pain in her ankle, but then she wrapped her arms around his neck and pressed her face to his shoulder.

"You need something for the pain."

"Your holding me is all I need."

"Then I'll be holding you forever. But there is one thing. You were unconscious for a few minutes back there, so what if you don't really know what you're saying? Tomorrow you could change your mind about marrying me. Or you might be suffering amnesia and have forgotten my many faults and how I pushed you away. I might have to ask you again, just to be sure."

"Dax, nothing could make me forget you. Not a blow to the head, not time, not death or even the loss of all my senses, be they of mind or body, because even then, my soul would recognize you."

"I knew, Pip. That first time we met. You turned around, and I couldn't speak. For a moment, I couldn't move. It was as if deep down, my soul knew it was you. That— as irrational and impossible as it all may seem—you were the one. And that the very next second would be the first step on our journey to forever."

"Forever sounds good to me," Pippa said.

She smiled up at him, a tender look in her green eyes. Her wild and dusty curls were matted with bits of straw, splinters and stuff he was a little scared to identify. Man, she was a beautiful mess. Life with her would be the best kind of adventure. He dipped his head and kissed her long and hard.

"Forever sounds good to me, too."

EPILOGUE

Sixty years later

"TELL US THE story again, Baba Dax."

Dax's weathered hand shook as he patted Nivia, the youngest of his five great-grandkids, on the shoulder.

She was the spitting image of her great-grandmother. Mama Pip, as everyone called Pippa. He could still remember the day Nivia was born. From day one, she had more hair on her head than he'd ever seen on a newborn, and within a month, there was no question she'd inherited Pippa's corkscrew curls, as well. Those auburn curls must have skipped a few generations, because their daughter, Sienna, had jet-black hair as straight as the blades of elephant grass that swayed gracefully when the winds caressed the savanna, and her eyes were as blue as the sky over the Serengeti. And her kids looked just like her.

But Pippa was still in Sienna. She was in all of them…from her wild spirit, to her wide-open heart, to that gleam in her eyes when she'd taken it upon herself to infuse life with a little mischievous fun.

"Which was your favorite part?" he asked all of them—Nivia, as well as her cousins, Ivy's and Fern's teenage grandkids.

His mind wanted to tell it all, but his body ached and his breath was tired and slow. Sitting with his grandchildren was the best part of his days now, but he needed to sleep, just for a little while.

Just long enough to see her again in his dreams. Just long enough to taste the sweetness of her kisses, smell her rain-fresh scent after hiking in a storm, hear her scold him for eating all the cookies she baked…and touch her soft skin. Even in her last days, her face had been rich and beautiful with lines that ran like deep rivers, filled with life and secrets. Every wrinkle told the story of her life…and his. He wanted to live it again. Or start the next

one with her. A new adventure. But every
night, she instructed him to wait. To be patient. She wasn't going anywhere. She'd be
waiting for him when the time was right.

For now, she wanted him to enrich the
life of their children and grandchildren and
great-grandchildren. That was Pippa. Always looking out for others. And he would
stay a while longer, because he loved them
and he still loved her and wanted to grant
her wish.

"He's sleeping again," Malia whispered.

He stretched one eye open and looked
at Fern's thirteen-year-old granddaughter.

"No, I wasn't," he grumbled. "I was just
resting my eyes."

"We can leave if you're tired."

"Nonsense." Dax tried to sit a little
straighter. He cleared his throat and coughed
twice. He hated the dust. It was everywhere.

"So which part did you want me to tell
again?" Dax asked.

"The part when you kissed and proposed
after the earthquake," Malia said with a
wistful look in her eyes.

"Yeah, that part." Reed, one of Ivy's
grandsons, frowned at his brother's smirk.

Reed was ever the romantic. A heart-breaker.

"I want to hear more about Great Aunt Fern and Grandma Ivy's antics," Raven, Reed's twin, said with a grin.

"Ah, those two. Never lost their sense of humor," he said with a wistful smile.

"What about all the children who were sick and the contaminated water wells?" Malia asked.

"There are good people in the world. I like to think most are. They responded... came in to help. The owners of lodges, including Tabara, helped supply clean water to the villages within reach. Maddie's contacts in humanitarian organizations stepped up and not only raised funds and awareness of the crisis, but also aided in supplies and water. Hope and other medical teams helped those who were sick, and eventually the children recovered. The few who had permanent problems, like with learning, well, your Mama Pippa kept them under her wing. Even took extra time with them when she finally had her school built."

"Did you ever find out what caused the big earthquake? Like if it just happened be-

cause of the fault line or if it had anything
to do with the fracking?"

Ah, Rose. Named after her Mama Pip's
middle name. Their budding scientist.

"Well, we never did find out for sure.
I knew what I thought, but there was evidence and defense thrown both ways.
Things were different back then. Not just
because of what we couldn't yet do, the
kind of data we couldn't yet gather. It was a
time when not everyone believed that what
they did would have a lasting effect. Money
spoke. Convenience was a priority. Not everyone looked to the future…to the way life
would be for our grandchildren and great-
grandchildren."

"Guess they know now."

"Yes. They now know that the fracking
and so many other things they were doing
to the environment at the time, shouldn't
have happened. Hindsight is a great teacher.
Your Mama Pip was a great teacher, too.
Nothing—not even an earthquake—could
stop her from making a difference in as
many lives as she could, including mine
and your grandmothers'. She liked to shake
things up and empower the young. She

spread the gift of reading and knowledge and an open mind."

Fatigue washed over him again. He turned and gazed outside the window as the sun set behind an old acacia tree.

"I miss her."

Sometimes he wondered if the universe had shaken the earth that day in Kenya just to bring him to her. It wasn't the way an old researcher was supposed to think about things, but then again Pippa had taught him to see the world through a kaleidoscope. To dream. To love completely and without reservation. To think beyond rules and expectations. So, perhaps science and logic weren't alone on that day. Perhaps the ground had indeed shaken to bring them together in a kind of cosmic or angelic nudge…or maybe it was their paths crossing that had shaken the earth.

* * * * *

YES! Please send me the **Home on the Ranch Collection** in Larger Print. This collection begins with 3 FREE books and 2 FREE gifts in the first shipment. Along with my 3 free books, I'll also get the next 4 books from the Home on the Ranch Collection, in LARGER PRINT, which I may either return and owe nothing, or keep for the low price of $5.24 U.S./ $5.89 CDN each plus $2.99 for shipping and handling per shipment*. If I decide to continue, about once a month for 8 months I will get 6 or 7 more books, but will only need to pay for 4. That means 2 or 3 books in every shipment will be FREE! If I decide to keep the entire collection, I'll have paid for only 32 books because 19 books are FREE! I understand that accepting the 3 free books and gifts places me under no obligation to buy anything. I can always return a shipment and cancel at any time. My free books and gifts are mine to keep no matter what I decide.

268 HCN 3760 468 HCN 3760

Name	(PLEASE PRINT)	
Address		Apt. #
City	State/Prov.	Zip/Postal Code
Signature (if under 18, a parent or guardian must sign)		

Mail to the **Reader Service:**

IN U.S.A.: P.O. Box 1867, Buffalo, NY. 14240-1867
IN CANADA: P.O. Box 609, Fort Erie, Ontario L2A 5X3

Get 4 FREE REWARDS!

We'll send you 2 FREE Books plus 2 FREE Mystery Gifts.

FREE
Value Over
$20

Both the **Romance** and **Suspense** collections feature compelling novels written by many of today's best-selling authors.

YES! Please send me 2 FREE novels from the Essential Romance or Essential Suspense Collection and my 2 FREE gifts (gifts are worth about $10 retail). After receiving them, if I don't wish to receive any more books, I can return the shipping statement marked "cancel." If I don't cancel, I will receive 4 brand-new novels every month and be billed just $6.74 each in the U.S. or $7.24 each in Canada. That's a savings of at least 16% off the cover price. It's quite a bargain! Shipping and handling is just 50¢ per book in the U.S. and 75¢ per book in Canada*. I understand that accepting the 2 free books and gifts places me under no obligation to buy anything. I can always return a shipment and cancel at any time. The free books and gifts are mine to keep no matter what I decide.

Choose one:　☐ **Essential Romance**　　☐ **Essential Suspense**
　　　　　　　　　(194/394 MDN GMY7)　　　(191/391 MDN GMY7)

Name (please print)

Address　　　　　　　　　　　　　　　　　　　　　　　　Apt. #

City　　　　　　　　　　　State/Province　　　　　　　　Zip/Postal Code

> ### Mail to the **Reader Service:**
> **IN U.S.A.:** P.O. Box 1341, Buffalo, NY 14240-8531
> **IN CANADA:** P.O. Box 603, Fort Erie, Ontario L2A 5X3

Want to try two free books from another series? Call 1-800-873-8635 or visit www.ReaderService.com.

---

*Terms and prices subject to change without notice. Prices do not include applicable taxes. Sales tax applicable in NY. Canadian residents will be charged applicable taxes. Offer not valid in Quebec. This offer is limited to one order per household. Books received may not be as shown. Not valid for current subscribers to the Essential Romance or Essential Suspense Collection. All orders subject to approval. Credit or debit balances in a customer's account(s) may be offset by any other outstanding balance owed by or to the customer. Please allow 4 to 6 weeks for delivery. Offer available while quantities last.

Your Privacy—The Reader Service is committed to protecting your privacy. Our Privacy Policy is available online at www.ReaderService.com or upon request from the Reader Service. We make a portion of our mailing list available to reputable third parties that offer products we believe may interest you. If you prefer that we not exchange your name with third parties, or if you wish to clarify or modify your communication preferences, please visit us at www.ReaderService.com/consumerschoice or write to us at Reader Service Preference Service, P.O. Box 9062, Buffalo, NY 14240-9062. Include your complete name and address.

STRS18